The Apex Hunt

A High-Stakes Race Across the World

Alejandro Alexander

ISBN — eBook: 978-1-956146-78-3

ISBN — Paperback: 978-1-956146-79-0

ISBN — Hardcover: 978-1-956146-80-6

Disclaimer

This is a work of fiction. Names, characters, businesses, places, events, locales, and incidents are either the products of the author's imagination or used in a fictitious manner. Any resemblance to actual persons, living or dead, or actual events is purely coincidental.

Table of Contents

Chapter 1: The Sky Above Arizona 5

Chapter 2: The Echo of the Drop 23

Chapter 3: The Silent Hangar 31

Chapter 4: Campsite 37

Chapter 5: Desert Road 45

Chapter 6: Carlisle Industries 49

Chapter 7: Coin and Current 61

Chapter 8: The Paper That Breaks It 71

Chapter 9: The Chase Begins 77

Chapter 10: The Presidio Cipher 87

Chapter 11: The Island and the Theft 93

Chapter 12: The Shadow of the Golden Gate 103

Chapter 13: Market Street Scramble 109

Chapter 14: Beneath the Lanterns 115

Chapter 15: Airborne Anchors 127

Chapter 16: The Parisian Shadow 135

Chapter 17: Passage 139

Chapter 18: The Bone Cathedral 147

Chapter 19: Across the Lagoon 153

Chapter 20: Murano Glass Dead-drop 157

Chapter 21: The Edge of the Water 163

Chapter 22: The Darwin Layover 175

Chapter 23: Under the Rock 183

Chapter 24: The Alice Springs Intercept 195

Chapter 25: The Hidden Frequency 201

Chapter 26: Uneasy Alliances 207
Chapter 27: The Signal Fire 213
Chapter 28: The Long Way Down 219
Chapter 29: Runway 19 225
Chapter 30: The Silver Sky Cipher 231
Chapter 31: The Desert's Truth 237
Chapter 32: The Wind's Command 243
Chapter 33: The Night Before the Blue 249
Chapter 34: The Silver Sky Flight 255

Chapter 1: The Sky Above Arizona

Three weeks before the semester started—before contracts, before departures, before the house began to come apart—they packed as if leaving were temporary. With a sharp rasp that tore through the morning quiet, Angela pulled the last strip of packing tape across the box. She sealed the edge, smoothing it with her palm. The CLOSED sign rested atop a stack of folded sweaters. It was a simple piece of plastic, the red letters stark on white, but it carried more weight than the suitcase waiting at the foot of the bed, marking something already decided.

Boxes lined the walls, some sealed, others left open as though she had stopped midway and never returned. The closet door hung open, a few hangers still in place. As she stood, her weight shifted and denim pressed into her skin—she had slept in them. A sharp, rhythmic twitch started in her right index finger, the tendon straining at a phantom resistance. She leaned slightly to the left, her internal compass already compensating for a crosswind that hadn't yet reached the curtains. Back then, the sailplane banked into the thermal at her lightest touch. At altitude, the air grew thin and cold, the scent of ozone biting the back of her throat. The instrument panel rattled in its housing, the high-frequency pitch that made the horizon lock in her vision. It had been the only place where things made sense, even with nothing to hold onto.

Now, the room was caught between states, no longer hers but not fully left behind. She crossed to the window. The blinds resisted for a moment before giving way, letting the morning rush in. Light filled the room, flattening the shadows. The sky was wide and empty, nothing like the one she remembered before the crash. A single bird circled high above the rooftops, riding a current that never reached the ground. It trusted the air. Trust didn't come easily anymore.

The bird adjusted its path, dipping as it caught a current—the same way the silver-gray hawk had drifted closer that day, matching her altitude with unblinking focus. Then the impact had come, driving the breath from her lungs. The fuselage bucked, the main spar giving way with a sharp crack. The horizon had twisted, the ground surging upward until the iron-veined face of the mountain filled the windshield. The world broke apart into sound—loud, directionless, impossible to track. The frame's last, violent shudder—a resonance that shook her teeth in their sockets before the silence took hold.

The silence always gave way to the memory of the cardiac monitor's needle and the sterile bite of antiseptic. Mike Santiago stood in the trauma room with his coat half-off, he watched her chest rise and fall, matching his breathing to it without realizing. He stood with his frame locked, his shoulders hunched as if the ceiling were descending. When he reached for her hand, his fingers had been ice-cold.

The ghost of his terrified stillness tightened her throat when the door burst open.

"You're ready!"

Sam's voice hit the room before his footsteps did, bright and immediate, cutting cleanly through everything she had just managed to build.

A slight flinch, but enough. She didn't turn right away.

"Told you I would be."

She glanced back over her shoulder, pulling a small smile into place.

Sam stood in the doorway, already moving, his energy outpacing the morning. At twelve, he carried a restless awareness; little slipped past him, and once a detail took hold, he didn't always let it go.

His eyes narrowed.

"Did you sleep in your clothes?" he asked, stepping inside.

A shrug, then she turned back toward the window.

"Yeah. So?"

He didn't answer immediately.

His silence measured the space between what she said and what was actually there, letting the silence sit long enough to matter.

"You look awful," he said. "Still having nightmares?"

Angela's hand tightened on the frame before she let it fall.

"No. Just tired."

She answered too quickly. Sam noticed. The words sat in the air, hollow and discordant; Sam's eyes narrowed.

Silence stretched, giving him time to decide what to do with it. Usually, he would push. This time, he didn't. He shifted instead, glancing toward the boxes.

"You're not even packed," he said. "We're supposed to leave today."

"I am packed."

He pointed. "That's not packed. You're just... stalling. Like you're trim-locked and fighting the yoke. If you don't find some airspeed soon, we're going to get left behind."

Angela almost smiled. "It's organized chaos."

"That's not a thing."

"It is if you understand it."

"I don't think you do."

Angela's fingers went still, pressing white to the window frame. Outside, the bird dipped again, caught another current, and rose. Angela stepped away from the window.

"Go get your stuff," she said. "We're not late yet."

"Yet," he repeated, as if filing it away. Then he turned and disappeared down the hall.

Angela stayed where she was a moment longer, listening as the house went quiet again, but it didn't feel settled. When she finally moved, her boots sounded too loud on the hardwood. She passed the guest room and the den, both of them stripped of their familiar clutter and reduced to hollowed-out boxes of light. In the living room, the rectangular shadows of removed paintings marked the walls like scars. She followed the draft from the hallway toward the kitchen.

The kitchen still carried the residue of yesterday: coffee gone cold, toast left too long, something forgotten. The smell lingered without settling into anything specific. Angela poured cereal into a bowl she didn't want to eat. The milk hit the bottom with a soft splash, contained and predictable.

Across from her, Sam turned his spoon between his fingers, his eyes on her.

"Aren't we a little old for hide-and-seek?" he asked.

Angela reached for the cereal box again. "Hey—don't eat that."

She paused. "Why not?"

"That's the zombie corn. It basically turns a bug's stomach into a tiny grenade."

The box hovered for a second before she poured the milk anyway and took a bite. "So?"

Sam leaned forward. "So it's bad for you."

"You read that somewhere?"

"I watched a two-hour video about it."

"Two hours," she repeated.

"From this guy on a forum who wears a lab coat in all his thumbnails. He's basically a genius."

Angela labored over each bite, then shrugged. "I like to live dangerously. This is me taking risks."

The edge in her voice slipped through before she could smooth it out. Sam didn't smile.

"I'm serious," he said. "You never think anything through."

Angela raised an eyebrow. "You say that like you're not twelve."

"I'm just saying," he pressed, leaning forward, "I'll probably be the one who finds the treasure anyway. You just rush into things. I actually have a plan."

"It's the Apex Hunt," Angela said. "And don't forget your inhaler, Mr. Planner."

He leaned back slightly. "It's still treasure."

"We are not pirates."

"It's still kind of like—"

"Don't go teaching your brother about treasure like that."

Their father's voice cut in as he stepped into the kitchen. Mike hadn't slept. His glasses sat slightly off-center, his hair uncombed; he moved with a leaden, mechanical rhythm, his shoulder clipping the doorframe unaware of the room's boundaries.

Angela forced a smile. "Morning."

"Dad," Sam said, "I already know about treasure."

"I'm sure you do." Mike gave him a quick pat on the head, but his attention had already shifted. He turned toward Angela. "Did you sleep okay?"

"Yeah. Fine." Her focus stayed on the bowl.

Sam nudged her foot under the table. "Like a baby."

Mike nodded, but the gesture didn't settle. "Good. That's good."

He poured the remaining coffee. It had gone cold, but he didn't react. He just drank it. "You both ready?" he asked.

"Yeah," Angela said.

"Obviously," Sam added.

Mike hesitated, turning back to Angela. "You sure about this?"

The question was casual in phrasing alone. It wasn't. Angela met his eyes briefly, then looked away. "We already talked about it."

"That's not what I asked."

Sam looked between them, alert. Angela set her spoon down and stared at the floor for a moment before answering. "I'm sure."

Mike held her there a second longer, weighing whether to push. Then he nodded. "Okay."

The word hung there longer than it should have. It wasn't an agreement or approval, but the slow, heavy exhale of a man who had finally run out of arguments. The quiet that followed wasn't tense, but it wasn't comfortable either.

Then Sam reached across the table, grabbed the cereal box, and dropped it into the trash. Angela stared at him. "Seriously?"

Mike blinked. "What was that for?"

"It's the bug-killer corn," Sam said.

Mike considered that longer than expected. "Right." Mike's gaze stayed fixed on the cooling coffee. "Okay."

He set the mug down. "Let's get going."

Angela pushed her chair back, crossed the kitchen, and retrieved the cereal box with a small shake of her head. She brushed it off and set it back on the counter. When she turned, Sam's expression remained unreadable, his presence impossible to ignore. He wasn't smug or apologetic, but focused, still working something out. She held his gaze for a second longer than necessary, then looked away. They moved out of the house as a unit, their footsteps echoing through the stripped-down shell of the hallway. The front door groaned on its hinges, letting in a rush of dry desert air as they crossed the threshold for the last time. Outside, the Jeep waited in the driveway, its metal body already radiating the first real heat of the day.

The Latitude Run was a stark interface, now a smear of dust and fingerprints. Sam wiped it with his sleeve as he climbed into the back seat. The Jeep shifted under his weight with a tired creak in the suspension. He didn't look back at the house. He studied the coordinates, though the device was as worn as everything around them.

Nearby, saguaro cacti lifted their long arms toward the sky, holding their positions in slow, deliberate stillness. The morning air was already warming, drawing out the scent of dry vegetation until it settled into the space around the vehicle.

Years of exposure had dulled the Jeep's once-bright paint. The Tucson Parks and Recreation emblem on the driver's door had faded until it was barely visible. A fine grit of pulverized caliche settled into the creases of Angela's boots, the parched scent of creosote rising from the earth as though the ground itself were exhaling. Angela remained outside. The passenger door stood open beside her, but she didn't step in. Instead, she rested her hand along the frame, her fingers tracing the edge without thinking as she turned back toward the house.

The front porch sat empty in the early light. The windows reflected the sky instead of revealing anything inside, offering no sign that anyone had been there at all. From this distance, the house was smaller than it had been the night before, more contained, as if it had already begun to close in on itself the moment she stepped away.

"It might be a while," she said, her voice low.

"I have faith," Sam replied from the back seat without looking up. "Five minutes. Tops."

Angela didn't answer. Her gaze stayed on the house, searching without settling. The front door. The kitchen window. The section of wall where the light shifted in the afternoon. Everything was ordinary, yet the air remained heavy and unsettled. Nothing moved.

For several seconds, the space held still. It felt occupied, as if something inside hadn't settled yet—or hadn't decided to let them go. Then the front door opened. Mike stepped outside with his keys in hand.

"There he is," Sam said, glancing up before returning to the GPS. Mike pulled the door closed behind him and reached for the lock. The faint metallic jingle of the keys carried across the yard with more clarity than it should have in the still air. His hand hovered for a moment, the keys hanging from his fingers.

The silence between them thickened, a sudden, heavy stillness that neither of them could find a way to break. Mike stood there longer than necessary, staring beyond the door he had just closed, as though the space behind it still held him. Then he turned back. He unlocked the door and went inside. The door closed behind him with a soft click that carried farther than it should have.

A trapped breath escaped her chest. Her grip tightened on the edge of the door before she forced her hand to relax. "He forgot something," Sam said, though his tone carried doubt.

"Maybe," Angela replied.

Sam glanced toward the house again, then back at her. "Or maybe he didn't want to leave yet."

"Those aren't different things," Angela said.

Sam leaned back, settling into the seat as he turned that over. "You think he's coming back out?"

"He will. He just needs a minute."

"For what?"

Angela didn't answer right away. "To decide something," she said, as a hawk cut across the pale sky. He fell silent, the answer enough for now. They waited. .

As the sun climbed higher, the metal of the Jeep warmed until it began to radiate a faint heat. Somewhere down the road, a car passed, the sound rising briefly before fading again. A breeze moved through the yard just long enough to stir the mesquite branches, then disappeared.

Angela shifted her weight but didn't move away from the door. Part of her wanted to get in, shut it, and leave before anything else could interrupt the moment—before the pause stretched into something harder to step away from. But she stayed. When Mike came out again, he carried a backpack. This time, he didn't hesitate.

Sam leaned forward. "That looks like more than keys."

Mike didn't respond. Angela stepped into the passenger seat and pulled the door closed behind her. The vinyl was already warm, sticking to the back of her legs as she adjusted and reached for the seatbelt. Sam took a quick, practiced puff from his inhaler, the soft hiss cutting briefly through the quiet. Mike approached the driver's side with a measured pace, as if he hadn't fully settled into the moment yet. Up close, fatigue weighed on his face—the heaviness around his eyes, the strain that hadn't lifted.

"Dad," Sam said, leaning forward between the seats, "we still have to pick up the compass."

Mike paused with his hand on the door handle. "Isn't the GPS enough?"

"It's not reliable," Sam said. "Not if we're actually going to use it."

"We are going to use it," Angela said.

Mike opened the door but didn't sit right away. "And what exactly are we doing?"

Angela met his eyes. "We follow the coordinates. We find the Great Meridian. We see where it leads."

"And after that?"

She held his gaze. "We keep going."

For a moment, he said nothing. Then he climbed into the driver's seat and shut the door. "Let's just wing it," he said, settling his hands on the wheel.

Sam made a small sound that landed somewhere between disbelief and protest. "That's not a plan."

"It's worked before."

"No, it hasn't," Sam said. "You just think it has."

Angela almost smiled, though it didn't quite reach the surface. Sam lifted the GPS. "This thing barely works. The signal drifts if you even stand near a tree."

Angela glanced back at him. "What does that mean?"

"It means we're basically invisible to the sky," Sam said, his voice sharpening. "The signal hits the walls and gets confused. It's like a faulty gyro—you think you're in a level glide, but the horizon is already banked."

Angela turned forward again, but the phrasing lingered. Sam shifted, letting the explanation fall away.

"I'll buy a new one," Mike said, his eyes fixed ahead.

Angela leaned toward the center console, her voice quieter. "We can use Mom's."

The air in the car shifted. Mike's hands tightened on the wheel, the movement small but immediate. "I'm not going to the hangar," he said. His voice held level. Closed.

"You haven't been there in months," Angela said.

"That's not the point."

"Then what is?"

Mike let out a slow breath. "The point is we're not going there."

Angela leaned back, turning toward the window. "Fine," she said. The word carried distance.

From the back seat, Sam muttered, "Nothing's open this early anyway."

No one answered. Mike turned the key. The ignition caught with a familiar rumble, a weightless float in her stomach. He shifted into gear, and the Jeep rolled forward, the tires crunching over gravel before finding the road.

They drove without speaking. The neighborhood slipped past—familiar houses, driveways, mailboxes—each an unremarked blur. Soon, even that gave way to open land. The road stretched ahead in a long, uninterrupted line, cutting through the desert. Heat shimmered along its surface, bending the distance just enough to make it waver.

Inside the Jeep, the silence settled in, shaped as much by what had been said as by everything left unsaid. Mike kept his eyes on the road, his posture fixed, leaving little room for anything else. The landscape scrolled past the window, her reflection faint in the glass. Behind them, Sam sat back with the GPS resting in his hands, turning it once before letting it settle.

The road unspooled beneath them, an unbroken line through the dust. None of them said anything. The distance closed anyway, the desert highway eventually yielding to the cracked, sun-bleached asphalt of the airfield. The Jeep slowed as it approached the perimeter fence, its tires kicking up a fine spray of grit. Ahead, the familiar, hunched silhouette of the hangar emerged from the heat haze, a solitary island of corrugated metal standing guard over the empty runway.

A single sailplane wing leaned against the far wall of the hangar, stripped down to its frame. Without its fabric, it stood exposed, its ribs curving inward in an ordered skeleton, precise and measured but unfinished without the surface that once held them together. Filtered light slipped through the seams of the closed doors, casting a delicate shadow across the concrete floor—an outline of something that had once moved through air and now stood still. The hangar doors were locked. A weathered sign hung slightly crooked at eye level, its edges warped by years of sun and wind. Most of the paint had faded into a pale wash, but one word remained clear enough to read without effort. CLOSED.

The Jeep rolled to a stop in front of the building, gravel shifting beneath the tires in an uneven crunch before the engine cut. The sound lingered after the movement ended, then faded into the surrounding stillness, leaving the space unnaturally vast. For several seconds, no one moved. The engine cooled with a series of metallic pings that echoed in the dry heat. Heat pressed at the windows. Beyond the windshield, the hangar remained unchanged by their arrival.

Mike broke the silence first. He stepped out of the Jeep without looking at either of them and crossed the yard toward the office, his pace measured, as if stopping might force him to reconsider. His shadow stretched behind him across the parched ground. The seatbelt unlatched with a click louder than intended in the stillness. She rested her hand briefly on the door before turning toward the back seat. "You coming?" she asked.

Sam shook his head, his fingers gripping the seat. "No. I don't think I'm ready."

The hangar stood in front of them, its weathered frame bleached by the heat. Up close, the building felt smaller than she remembered, its presence diminished as the motion and voices thinned, leaving only the structure behind. "It looks like she's been gone forever." Angela's voice caught, thin as the hangar's shadow.

Sam swallowed, staring at the building. "Is he really going to sell it?"

Angela didn't answer right away. "I hope not," she said finally. The words were thin as soon as they left her.

"That's not the same as no," Sam said.

Angela glanced at him, then back at the hangar. "I know."

"Would you even want it?" he asked. "All of it?"

She hesitated. The answer came too quickly—too clean to say without consequence. "Yes."

Sam's gaze lingered on her as he leaned back, absorbing it.

Inside the office, the air was heavy and undisturbed. Heat lingered in the walls, and a fine layer of dust softened every surface, dulling edges until the room felt quieter than it had been. A row of silver flight trophies lined the mantle. Their shapes remained elegant, but their shine had dulled. Where they once reflected light, they now seemed to hold it. The engraved names were still there, faded into the silver.

Near the window, Maria's desk sat exactly as it had been left. Nothing had been moved. Nothing had been cleared. A fine mineral shroud coated the surface, carrying the dry scent of parched paper and old grease as it settled deep into the grain of the wood. Papers remained stacked in careful order, though their corners had curled with time. A pen lay where it had last been set down, angled toward the center.

Mike trudged toward the desk, the urgency that had carried him across the yard fading with each step and giving way to something heavier that required intention rather than momentum. The room pressed in around him, filled with the weight of things that had never been spoken aloud. He reached for the top drawer and pulled it open, his hand slipping inside without hesitation, guided by familiarity rather than sight. The compass was exactly where he expected it to be, and his fingers closed around it before its meaning could take hold. The metal was cool on his skin, a grounding contrast to the warmth lingering in the room. He lifted it, turning it until the needle shifted, steadied, and found its bearing. For a moment, he stood there with the drawer open, the compass resting in his palm.

You always check it twice.

The thought came without warning, less a full memory than the shape of her voice carried in its rhythm. It was audible, though not clear enough to repeat—only enough to recognize.

His grip tightened before he reached into the drawer again, his fingers brushing something else—a folded slip of paper. He paused, then pulled it free. A set of coordinates, written in Maria's handwriting.

Mike stared at it longer than he intended. At first, the numbers meant nothing, just a sequence to be read and dismissed. Then they meant too much. Recognition settled in all at once. The muscles along his jaw bunched into hard knots.

For a moment, he considered putting it back. Instead, he folded it once more and slipped it into his pocket, then closed the drawer with a quiet finality.

Outside, Angela had drifted toward the hangar. She ran her fingers along the lock, brushing away the thin layer of dust clinging to the metal. The surface was already warm, heat mounting as the morning advanced. She tested it without thinking. It didn't give. Behind her, the Jeep remained where they had left it. Sam hadn't moved, yet her small, quiet actions—gestures that mattered little until the moment they did—played out in the quiet between them. The office door opened, and Mike stepped out, whatever had surfaced inside already contained again, folded back into something controlled.

"We've got to go before it gets too hot," he said. Angela turned toward him. "Can I have a key?" He didn't answer. "Come on," he said instead. "Let's go."

"Dad." She stepped closer, her voice hardening now, the hesitation gone. "Can I have a key? I want to come back. Just look around."

"You don't need to do that."

"But I want to." Mike shook his head, turning away. "What would be the point?"

A sharp pressure clamped beneath her ribs, making her next breath hitch. "You know I could run this place," she said, the conviction in her tone sharpening as the idea took hold. "Just for a year. I could get it going again." The hangar doors would swing open, planes restored and voices returning, movement replacing the long stillness.

"It's not happening," Mike said. "You're not throwing away your education for this."

"It's not throwing it away," Angela said. "It's continuing it. It's using it." She stopped, searching for something that would reach him. "It's all we have left of her." The words settled between them. A muscle ticked in Mike's jaw, a ripple beneath the hard mask of his exhaustion. Angela held his gaze. "Why are you so ready to let it go?"

He met her eyes, the skin pulling taut over his cheekbones as he braced himself under her gaze. "If I don't," he said, his voice dropping to a low rasp, "then I have to keep standing in it." Angela didn't respond. She hadn't expected that. Mike looked away first. "Please just get in the car," he said. "I'm not up for this today."

The attempt at normalcy didn't bridge the distance between them. If anything, it made the distance clearer. Angela stood there for a moment longer, then turned and walked back to the Jeep, opening the door and shutting it harder than she intended. The sound carried across the yard before settling again.

They drove in silence. The Jeep rolled back onto the road, the tires singing on the asphalt in a high, thin frequency as the desert opened around them. Heat rose from the ground in faint, wavering lines, bending the horizon just enough to unsettle the distance. Mike's hands remained fixed on the steering wheel, his grip locked. Warm glass pressed to her temple as she leaned her head against the window.

Outside, the landscape unspooled in a blur of brittle mesquite and ochre ridges, the silence in the cab underscored by the occasional sharp ping of cooling metal.

In the back seat, Sam shifted, the GPS resting loosely in his hands as he adjusted something on the screen, then again, the device tapping, breaking the silence with practiced familiarity. After a while, he spoke. "This looks right." Sam tilted the screen toward the light. "Do you want to check it, Ang?"

The paper map unfolded across her lap, smoothed by one hand as she took the device from him. A yellowed sticky note clung to the edge, its corners curled, the adhesive barely holding. "We're close," she said, tracing a point with her finger. Sam leaned forward. "That's a pretty big area."

Angela glanced out at the desert, then back at the map. "That's how it works," she said. Her fingers tightened on the paper, anchoring herself in the map and the certainty of its lines. "They don't just hand it to you." She folded the map just enough to still it, her focus narrowing as she settled into something she could follow. "You have to search."

The Latitude Run was tracking ghosts again. Sam scowled at the screen, his voice cutting through the static thrum of the engine pulling at the skin of her palms before the ignition died. He held the device toward the windshield, tapping at the signal bars that refused to climb. "The canyon is basically a signal-eating monster," he said. "Exactly like the guys on the forum said it would be."

Angela stepped out and rolled her shoulders. The creek, swollen by recent storms, rushed dark and fast below, the churning slurry of uprooted sage and iron-darkened runoff scouring the canyon walls. Damp earth and rising heat saturated the air, heavy and immediate. Layered plateaus rose around them, their edges clean in the open sky. Light caught along the ridgelines in hard, bright bands, leaving the lower spaces in shadow and making distance difficult to judge.

Ordinarily, the openness would have anchored her. Out here, it didn't. There was nowhere to disappear into, nowhere for the rigid set of their shoulders to soften or the silence to break. The land offered no softness, no cover. Everything was visible. Only the creek moved with any urgency, its pull drawing her toward it almost immediately.

Sam climbed out behind her, adjusting the strap of his bag as he scanned the narrowing stretch of sky. His thumb traced a restless circle over the plastic casing of the GPS, his jaw locked tight enough to ache as he checked the GPS again. "If this thing drops signal one more time, I'm throwing it into the creek," he muttered. "We're just wandering in circles while the map refuses to load."

A light nudge of her shoulder as she passed kept the gesture easy, even though the rigid set of their shoulders still held the memory of the silent miles behind them. "Try being positive for once, okay?"

Sam's frown deepened, but he didn't argue, the closest he came to agreement. She squeezed his shoulder briefly. "We're going to be fine." The words thinned in the open air, but she let them stand.

Behind them, Mike was already unloading gear from the Jeep, his movements sharp and frantic, as though he were still trying to scrub a phantom stain from the kitchen floor. He checked the seals on the water jugs twice, then a third time, his fingers fumbling with the plastic threads. He worked with a staccato rhythm, his hands moving before his eyes could follow, as if any pause would allow the silence of the canyon to catch up to him. "We have to set up camp," he said, his voice brittle. "We keep the site clean. We keep it organized. We stay focused on the tasks."

The plan was simple, almost too simple. A flicker of resistance rose at it. Nothing had been simple in a long time, and naming the day that way didn't make it true. Still, she said nothing and moved to help. They fell into the motions of assembling the tent, but the old synchrony was gone, replaced by a jagged, uneven rhythm. Mike fumbled with the tension lines, his hands stiff and uncooperative as he fought the canvas. He checked the poles with a frantic, repetitive touch, his world narrowed until Angela vanished from his view. In her pocket, the laminated corner of a playing card pressed against her thigh, a vintage Daphne Blake, a relic from the years Mike had spent calling her "Danger-Prone." He had given it to her as a joke, a talisman for the girl who always had to find the edge of the map.

Under other circumstances, the quiet coordination might have been comforting. Today, it carried weight. The sun climbed while they worked, heat gathering at the back of her neck and along her shoulders, dampening the collar of her shirt and making each movement slightly heavier than the one before it. Nearby, Sam hovered, looking from the GPS to the sky. "Feel like pitching in?" Angela asked, wiping her forehead before taking a drink from her water bottle. Sam didn't answer right away. Instead, he pointed upward. "Look."

A hot air balloon drifted across the sky above the canyon, moving, drifting above the heat below. It hovered rather than traveled, a distant speck in the blue. "It's a good day for being up there," Sam said. Mike didn't look up. "No."

Sam lowered his hand. "Why not?"

Mike drove a tent stake into the ground, the hammer glancing off the metal with a jolt that tightened the skin across his knuckles. He didn't reset his stance; he simply struck again, his jaw clamped, holding back a tremor, his eyes wide and fixed on the red dirt as if the desert were a threat he could only keep at bay with noise. "Because I said so." The answer shut the conversation down.

Angela straightened. "Nothing's going to happen. You know that."

Mike didn't look at her. "Drop it."

She didn't. "Are you ever going to let us go up again?" The hammer stopped mid-motion. For a moment, he stood there with it in his hand, his grip tightening and easing again. "I don't know," he said. The words settled heavily.

Angela stepped back, brushing dust from her hands more forcefully than necessary. "It's already too hot," she said, turning away. Sam had wandered a few paces off, kicking at loose stones, his shoulders rounded. She headed toward the creek. The rocks near the water rose sharply, uneven and jagged, but Angela climbed them easily. Her boots found holds without hesitation, her body moving with the quiet confidence of long practice.

"Be careful," Sam called. Mike's head snapped up. "Angela, get down from there."

"It's too hot," she called back. "I just need to cool off."

"You don't know how deep it is," Mike said. "It was one storm."

"It rained. It's fine."

She didn't answer. Instead, she stepped to the edge and looked down at the water rushing below, dark and fast, pulling in different directions at once. For a moment, she hesitated. Not fear—something sharper, more deliberate. Once she jumped, the momentum would no longer be hers.

The thought passed, and she jumped.

The drop was short but abrupt. The rush of air filled her ears before the water closed over her, the cold hitting instantly, sharp enough to lock every muscle and steal the breath from her chest. Above, Mike moved to the edge but stopped short. Sam stepped up beside him. "Do you think it was deep enough?"

"I don't know."

The seconds stretched before Angela broke the surface, pulling in air that turned quickly into a startled laugh. "Wow," she said, pushing her wet hair back. "That's freezing, but it's great." She waded toward the edge, the cold cutting cleanly through the heaviness that had settled in her chest. When she climbed out, water streamed from her clothes, darkening the dust beneath her boots. Mike didn't move, just stood at the bank with his hands clenched tight, his breath leaving him in a long, uneven exhale.

"You had your brother worried," he said. Angela turned to Sam, her expression softening. "I'm okay. You don't have to worry so much." Sam didn't answer. His gaze dropped.

"Your leg." A thin line of blood traced down her shin. She crouched and touched it. "I must've scraped it. It's nothing."

Sam picked up the GPS and turned away, the shift immediate.

"Sam—" He kept walking. She followed, her wet jeans clinging to her legs, each step a reminder of the jump. When she caught up, she wrapped her arms around him from behind and held him there long enough to matter. "I'm sorry." He didn't pull away, but he didn't lean into her either. "Why do you have to do stuff like that?" he asked.

Angela hesitated. "I can't just sit there and be afraid," she said. Sam stared at the ground. "Do you have to do stunts? You're not exactly on a GoPro."

"It wasn't extreme." Her voice was little more than a murmur. "At least not until I saw your face."

He glanced back at her, uncertain.

"I thought I was cooling off," she added. "You looked like I'd disappeared."

Sam looked down again. "For a second, I thought maybe you had."

The words lingered between them, quiet but present.

She stepped around so she could face him. "I'm here," she said. "Next time, I'll tell you before I do something dumb."

"Something dumb," he repeated. "So we agree it was dumb."

She let out a small breath of laughter. “A little.”

The tension in his jaw eased, his mouth softening at the edges.

At the time, none of them understood how quickly everything would fracture once they returned.

Chapter 2: The Echo of the Drop

The hospital had been a landscape of white light and artificial cycles, a place where everything was filtered and the monitors pulsed in steady rhythm. Returning to the house was a different kind of impact. It was a secondary crash, slower and quieter than the first, but no less absolute. Inside the Santiago home, dust had settled into the rooms, undisturbed since the emergency locator transmitter sent its final, frantic pulse in the mountains. Angela stood in the entryway, her boots still carrying the red silt of the airfield, and the ceiling seemed to lower over her.

Angela's right hand twitched, her thumb ghosting over a trim switch that wasn't there. In the sky, the world was a matter of energy and fluid dynamics, a series of problems that could be solved with a light touch on the stick or a subtle adjustment in the rudder. On the ground, gravity wasn't something she could negotiate; it pulled straight through her joints. She crossed the living room, where the curtains were drawn, muting the Arizona sun and casting the furniture into long, solitary silhouettes. Every surface carried the echo of the impact. The velvet sofa, the stack of unread magazines on the coffee table, the framed photograph of Maria laughing on the tarmac at Marana, her flight suit unzipped to the waist, a smudge of grease on her cheek—each of them marked the distance between then and now.

Angela walked into the kitchen. The scent of her mother was faintest here, buried under the smell of pine cleaner and the sharp, metallic tang of the copper pots hanging above the island. Her mother's chair sat empty at the head of the table. It was a persistent ache in the room, a hollow space that distorted the geometry of the house. Angela didn't sit down. She couldn't. To sit would be to acknowledge the permanence of the grounding.

Mike was there, hunched over the laminate counters. His knuckles were white on a blue sponge, moving in tight, frantic circles. He didn't look up when she entered. He focused on a microscopic stain near the sink, a phantom mark he pursued with the intensity of a man trying to erase the last year of his life. The hiss of the sponge filled the space between them.

"Sam's in his room." Mike kept his back to her, the sponge dragging over the laminate. "He's supposed to be finishing his history module."

"He's probably hacking a satellite, Dad." Angela leaned in the doorframe, her hands shoved deep into her pockets. "You know he doesn't do modules."

Mike didn't laugh. The sound continued, a relentless rasp in the quiet. "He needs the structure, Ang. We all do. We can't just keep losing our direction."

The word hit her like a downdraft. Drifting. It was what Mike called anything that didn't have a clear, terrestrial purpose. To him, the soaring school was drifting. The flight hours were drifting. Even the way she stood now, suspended between the memory of the thermal and the reality of the floor, was a form of drift that he couldn't quantify or control.

Angela left him to his cleaning. She needed a phone charger, something to tether her back to the digital world, and Sam had pilfered hers for some experiment. She walked toward the small room at the back of the house that Mike used as an office. It was a space defined by the Forest Service, filled with topographical maps, fire safety manuals with cracked spines, and a collection of heavy-duty flashlights, all missing their batteries. It was supposed to be a place of order, but as Angela rummaged through the top drawer of the desk, the order dissolved.

She found the charger, but it was buried under a stack of envelopes that hadn't been opened. They were tucked beneath a heavy manual on trail maintenance, hidden as if they were a secret that Mike wasn't ready to tell himself. Angela pulled them out. The paper was heavy and expensive, the kind that carried bad news with a certain corporate dignity. The words jumped out at her in bold, unforgiving strokes. FINAL NOTICE. ARREARS. FORECLOSURE

PROCEEDINGS. The bank's logo was a small, stylized mountain, a thin imitation of the jagged peaks she flew over.

She fanned the papers out on the desk. It wasn't just one month or two. It was an unrelenting, accumulating ruin. The medical bills from the first month after the crash were a secondary layer, a blizzard of white paper that threatened to bury the house. The sale of the hangar wasn't a choice for Mike. It wasn't just about his fear of the sky or his desire to keep her safe. It was a mathematical necessity. He had been keeping the depth of the debt from them, building a wall of silence that was now starting to crumble under its own weight.

The house had taken on a different kind of stillness. On the porch, a cactus wren broke it with a dry, clicking call, while inside the walls seemed to lean inward, the strain coming less from grief than from the hard edges of the ledger. Angela's collar tightened, her chest catching as the space seemed to thin around her, and the need to move rose quickly, to get up and away from the dust and the debt, from the abrasive scour of the sponge on the laminate, toward some way out that did not end in the liquidation of her mother's life.

She went back to the kitchen, the notices clutched in her hand like a weapon she didn't know how to use. Mike was still at the sink. He had moved on to the stovetop now, his hand tracing an obsessive, repetitive orbit across the metal. He was smaller than he had been that morning, his ranger shirt hanging loose on his shoulders, his face a mask of fatigue that the hospital light had only hinted at.

"How much, Dad?" The question was a stone dropped into a deep well.

Mike stopped. He didn't turn around, but his shoulders slumped, the tension leaving him all at once. He dropped the sponge into the sink. It hit with a heavy, sodden thud. "It's handled, Angela. I'm handling it."

"By selling the hangar? By tagging Mom's glider for an auction?" Angela slapped the notices onto the laminate. "You told me we were fine. You told me the insurance covered the recovery."

"The insurance covered the machine." Mike turned to face her. His eyes were red-rimmed and hollow. "It didn't cover the life, Ang. It didn't cover the six months I spent sitting in that waiting room instead of being on the trails. It didn't cover the fact that the school hasn't had a student since the accident. Nobody wants to learn to fly from the man whose wife didn't come back."

He stepped toward her, his hand lifting as if to take the papers, but he stopped short of touching her. "I'm protecting what's left. If we sell the equipment, we keep the house. Sam stays in school. We get a fresh start."

"It's not a start." Angela's grip tightened on the notices. "It's a burial. You're burying her twice."

Mike's face hardened. The ranger's mask snapped back into place. "We aren't talking about this anymore. The auction is set for next month. Until then, you stay grounded. No more solo flights. No more chasing thermals while the house is falling down."

Angela turned and walked out. She didn't head for her room; she headed for the garage, the only place where the air still smelled of something other than pine cleaner.

Sam was there, sitting on the workbench surrounded by the guts of an old GPS unit and a tangle of black electrical tape. He didn't look up when she slammed the door. He adjusted the plastic inhaler in his pocket and kept soldering.

"He told you."

Sam didn't look up. "He didn't have to."

"He didn't tell me." Angela fanned the notices across the workbench. "I found them."

Sam set the soldering iron aside. The tip hissed faintly as it cooled. "Look at this."

He wiped his hands on a rag and reached into the drawer beneath the bench. When he pulled his hand back out, he was holding a short, matte-black cylinder, about the length of his palm. It wasn't sleek or futuristic—just dense and industrial, with a seam running around its middle and a narrow band of glass set into one side.

"It came to the hangar yesterday," he said. "Addressed to Mom. No return label."

Angela frowned. "And you brought it here?"

"Dad would've tossed it."

He set it on the workbench between them. It gave off a faint, steady vibration—not quite a hum, more like the quiet insistence of something powered and waiting.

Angela hesitated. "What is it?"

"I don't know," Sam said. "But watch."

He reached past her and flicked off the overhead light. The garage dimmed, the only illumination now the thin strip of daylight slipping beneath the door.

Then he tapped the glass band.

A soft glow spread outward—not into the air, but across the surface of the workbench. Lines sharpened, resolving into a topographical map etched in pale blue light against the worn wood.

Angela leaned in despite herself.

The Arizona basin unfolded beneath her hands—contours, elevation lines, dry riverbeds. It shifted subtly, recalibrating with the angle of the surface and the position of her body.

"It's a projector," Sam said. "Short-throw. Probably micro-laser. It's using the surface."

Angela didn't answer. Her attention had already narrowed.

The map wasn't random. Pressure lines threaded across it in faint gradients—patterns she recognized before she could name them.

Thermals.

Her fingers hovered, then lowered, following the curve of one of the lines—not touching, just tracking. The way she would in the air. The way she had learned to read lift before she ever understood the math behind it.

The pattern tightened as she moved.

"It's reacting to you," Sam said.

"No," Angela said quietly. "It's not."

She adjusted her hand—less direct, more angled—mirroring the way you approach a column of rising air without breaking it.

The map shifted again. Subtle. Precise.

Recognition clicked.

"It's waiting."

"For what?"

"For the right input."

She traced the curve again, slower now, letting instinct guide her. The lines converged.

A single point brightened.

A soft tone sounded—clean, deliberate.

The wider map faded, collapsing until only a set of coordinates remained, fixed in pale light on the wood.

Sam exhaled. "Okay. So it's keyed. Pattern recognition, maybe. Motion tracking." He looked at her. "Not just anyone can trigger it."

Angela didn't move. "What is this?"

Sam pulled out his phone, tapped the screen, and turned it toward her.

An article. A name.

"St. James. The Apex Hunt."

Angela's gaze stayed on the coordinates.

"It's not just a game," Sam said. "It's closed circuit. You don't get in unless you have one of these. And the first gate—just getting there—it pays."

"How much?"

"Five grand."

The number landed hard.

Angela glanced at the notices, red ink catching the blue light.

"And the big prize…" Sam pushed through the hesitation. "It wipes everything. The bank. The notices. All of it. We keep the hangar. We keep the planes."

"Mike will never let us go."

Sam picked up his inhaler, turning it once in his hand. "He doesn't have to. He's already quit. He's just going to keep scrubbing that sink until the bank locks the door." He looked at her. "We're not staying for the auction, Ang."

Angela looked at him—at the certainty in his face.

The house was a cage of paper and debt. The air inside it was too heavy to breathe. Outside, the desert stretched wide, the sky waiting. The memory of the flight that morning—the hawk, the thermal, the clean, silent lift—cut through the noise like a line thrown to her.

"Get the bags." She reached for her flight jacket. "I'll get the keys."

The shift from ground to sky was no longer about hours or maintenance logs. It was about survival.

She didn't look back as she headed for the garage door—not at the kitchen, not at the man scrubbing ghosts into the sink. She looked toward the horizon, where red desert met open blue.

The echo of the drop was still there, a low thrum in her bones.

But for the first time since the crash, she wasn't falling.

She was ready to fly.

Chapter 3: The Silent Hangar

The hangar didn't breathe anymore. For years, the corrugated metal structure had been a living thing, expanding and contracting with the Arizona heat, vibrating with the low frequency of wind passing over wing-tips. The hangar was silent. The smell of dust and hydraulic fluid hung in the air, a scent that had once promised the start of a Saturday cross-country but now served as a sharp reproach. Angela walked the aisles of the racking system, her boots echoing against the concrete with a hollow, lonely percussion.

She stopped beside the Schleicher K-21. The fiberglass was cool and slick, no longer vibrating with the lift of a thermal. A thin layer of grit had gathered on the canopy, blurring the cockpit where she had spent a thousand hours learning the grammar of the sky. She reached out to wipe a smudge from the plexiglass, but her hand stopped an inch away. A new fragility clung to the aircraft, born less from its design than from the way the silence settled along its wings like frost. It no longer felt like a vessel, only an asset.

Across the floor, her father was a silhouette of industry. Mike stood by the workbench, a clipboard in his hand and a row of yellow tags hanging from his belt. He didn't look up as she approached. He was counting the spare instruments, his pen moving in a steady rhythm that made Angela's chest tighten. He moved with a detached efficiency, the kind of focus a man uses when he is trying to dismantle a bomb or a life. Every item he marked was a piece of her mother's legacy being prepared for the auction block.

"The variometers are still in good shape," Mike said, his voice flat and drained of its usual resonance. "We can bundle them with the oxygen regulators. It'll make the lot more attractive to the school in Nevada."

Angela leaned on the workbench, the wood scarred by years of spilled oil and dropped wrenches. "We aren't a lot, Dad. We're a soaring school. We have three students waiting for their check-rides."

Mike finally looked at her, but his eyes stayed focused on a point just past her shoulder. He looked older than he had a month ago, the skin around his eyes pulled tight by a fatigue that sleep couldn't touch. "The insurance won't cover the liability anymore, Angela. I've already told them we're winding down. It's safer this way."

Angela's gaze drifted to the main doors, where heavy chains now looped through the handles. On the concrete sill nearby, a sparrow lay coated in dust, its wings stiff and gray. She didn't answer.

Mike's jaw tightened, a small, involuntary movement that was the only sign he had heard her. He turned back to the shelf, his pen scratching across the paper with a sound like dry leaves. He didn't answer. He had replaced conversation with inventory, as if by labeling everything they owned, he could find a way to contain the grief leaking out of the corners of the house. He was grounding them all, one yellow tag at a time.

Angela turned away, the frustration rising in her. She needed to act, to touch something that hadn't been categorized for sale. She made her way toward the back of the hangar, where the older maintenance tools were kept in steel chests. She pulled open the drawer of her mother's personal toolbox, expecting to find the usual assortment of safety wire and torque wrenches. Instead, she found a false bottom, a piece of thin plywood that didn't quite sit flush with the metal.

She pried it up with a screwdriver. Tucked beneath were three weathered flight logs, their leather covers worn smooth by years of handling. These weren't the official school records. They were smaller, filled with Maria's cramped, precise handwriting. Angela opened the first one, her heart skipping a beat as she recognized the date—ten years ago, during a summer her mother was supposed to be at a competition in France.

Beyond mere data points, the entries read as an application of that sensory intuition. Angela traced the Silver Sky frequency scribbled near the sketches of the golden insect. She had spent nights trying to reconcile these coordinates with the school's aging charts, and finally, the pattern had emerged. It wasn't just a secret history; it was a flight plan that bypassed the grounded reality her father was trying to enforce.

A shadow fell over the page. Angela snapped the book shut, her thumb catching on the edge of the leather. Sam was standing behind her, his glasses sliding down his nose, his eyes fixed on the toolbox with a look of intense, quiet curiosity. At twelve, he was already a master of the unspoken, a boy who lived in the gaps between his sister's temper and his father's silence.

"You're tracing the frequency again," Sam whispered. He didn't look at her face; he looked at the way she was holding the log, as if he could sense the momentum building behind her eyes. "Did you find the start point?"

"I found the bridge," Angela said, tucking the logs into her jacket. "The vibration in the teeth, the shift in the marrow—it's the only way into the Apex Hunt. It's how she kept us in the air for so long."

Sam reached out, his fingers brushing the worn leather. He looked winded, his breathing shallow and careful, as if the house itself were beginning to crowd out the oxygen. He spent his days buried in textbooks about structural engineering and atmospheric physics, trying to find a mathematical reason for why their world had suddenly stopped making sense. To Sam, the logs weren't just books; they were data points in a mystery he was desperate to solve.

"Dad's calling for dinner," Sam said, his voice dropping an octave. "He's making the sound with the plates again."

Dinner was a strained affair. The ancient air conditioner provided a rhythmic rattle, punctuated by the infrequent clink of silverware on ceramic. Mike sat at the head of the table, his posture rigid, staring at his chicken as if it were another item to be inventoried. He didn't ask about their day. He didn't ask about the hangar. He simply existed there, his presence so fixed it seemed to drain the heat from the room, leaving any trace of warmth pressed flat to the floor.

Angela watched him, the flight logs a heavy weight in the pocket of her jacket. She thought about the yellow tags in the hangar, the way they looked like autumn leaves on a dead tree. She thought about her mother's handwriting, the secret coordinates, and the golden bug. The impulsiveness that her father feared began to clarify into a sharp, cold resolve. She realized then that Mike wasn't going to change his mind. He was paralyzed by a fear he mistook for protection, and if she stayed here, she would be buried alongside the school.

"I'm going to San Francisco," Angela said. The statement, though quiet, cut through the mechanical hum of the room like a blade. "I'm entering the Apex Hunt."

The clatter of Mike's fork hitting his plate was the loudest sound in the room. He looked up, his eyes finally meeting hers, and for a second, she saw the man he used to be—the pilot who could read a storm from fifty miles away. Then the fear returned, a gray veil that clouded his expression. He looked at her as if she were a malfunction he didn't know how to fix.

"You're going nowhere," Mike said, his voice low and dangerous. "That competition is a billionaire's playground. It's reckless. It's exactly the kind of thing that gets people killed when they stop paying attention to the ground."

"Mom was part of it," Angela said, the weight of the logs in her pocket lending her a borrowed strength. "I've decoded her logs, Dad. I know about the shift in the marrow and the frequency she used to reach the Apex. She wasn't just flying circles over the desert."

Mike stood up, his chair scraping harshly across the linoleum. He kept his eyes off the logs. He didn't want to see them. To him, anything that reminded him of Maria's spirit was a threat to the fragile safety he was trying to build. "Those books belong in the trash. This family is grounded, Angela. We are selling the equipment, and you are going to finish your certification at the academy. That is the end of it."

He walked out of the room, his footsteps heavy on the hallway floor. The silence shifted, the air turning thick and metallic, smelling of ozone and humming with the static charge of a wire pulled too tight. It was the same hollow pressure that fills a cockpit seconds before a structural failure. Sam looked at her, his eyes wide behind his glasses, his chest heaving as he struggled to catch a breath that wasn't there. He reached for his inhaler, the plastic click a small, desperate sound in the quiet kitchen.

"Are you really going?" Sam asked, his voice shaking. "Without him?"

Angela reached across the table and took his hand. His palm was cold, a mirror of her own. She thought of the hangar, the gliders waiting in the dark, and the secret map hidden in her pocket. She wasn't just leaving a house; she was chasing a ghost that might be the only thing capable of leading them home. The rebellion wasn't a choice anymore; it was a necessity of flight. To save the school, she had to stop being a daughter and start being a pilot again.

"We're both going," she said, her voice steadying as the plan took root. "Pack your bag, Sam. We aren't waiting for the auction."

She looked toward the window, where the desert moon was beginning to rise over the silhouette of the hangar. The vast, indifferent theater of the sky offered neither promise nor safety. It was exactly what she needed. She would find the Hunt, she would win the prize, and she would bring the hangar back to life. She wouldn't wait for her father to give her the controls. She would take them.

The desert wind picked up outside, rattling the kitchen window in its frame. It was a familiar sound, a call to movement that her father had forgotten how to hear. Angela stood up, her mind already navigating the thousands of miles between this table and the first coordinate. The silence of the hangar was behind her now. The only thing that mattered was the momentum.

The sky was waiting, even if it didn't have a voice yet.

Chapter 4: Campsite

The fire burned low and steady, its glow pushing back the darkness just enough to hold night at bay without ever fully overcoming it. The flames shifted in small, deliberate movements, folding inward and rising again as the wood settled deeper into the bed of coals. Every so often, a thin ribbon of sparks lifted and disappeared, swallowed by the blackness beyond the circle of light.

Past the reach of the fire, the desert stretched outward unseen, and that made its vastness feel larger rather than smaller. In daylight, the land had been all angles and distance, every ridge and canyon laid open beneath the sun. At night, those shapes were gone, leaving only space—unmeasured, unmarked, impossible to define. Heat still lingered in the ground, seeping through the soles of their shoes, though the air above had begun to cool, creating that strange desert balance where warmth and coming cold could exist at the same time.

Now and then, a breeze moved through camp and stirred the flames, carrying with it the scent of dust, brush, and the sharp tang of mineral, as though the land itself had spent the entire day storing heat and was only now beginning to release it.

Angela sat cross-legged near the fire, turning the geocache coin over in her hands. It caught the firelight with each turn, flashing gold and then dimming as it came to rest in her palm. She flipped it once more, letting the repetition anchor her. The coin was small, solid, and real in a way that kept the day from drifting too far into something unreal.

Across from her, Mike sat with his elbows resting on his knees, staring into the flames as though the answer to something might reveal itself there if he looked long enough. Firelight glinted in his glasses, shifting with every change in the coals, but his attention seemed fixed somewhere deeper than that, somewhere neither of them could easily follow.

Sam hovered close to Angela, angled toward her without seeming to realize he was doing it. He had always done that, positioned himself just within reach, as if proximity alone could keep things from shifting too far away.

For a while, no one spoke. The sound of the creek had faded with distance, replaced now by the quieter noises of camp: wood settling, fabric rustling in the breeze, the occasional scrape of someone shifting their weight in the dirt. The silence stretched into the dark until it was lost among the ridges. It came from a weariness that made pretense impossible.

Angela turned the coin again, firelight rippling across its surface.

"Thanks for doing this."

Her voice came out softer than it had been all day, worn down in a way that made it more honest.

Mike didn't look up.

Angela let the coin rest in her palm. "I'm going to miss you guys."

The words landed with more weight than she intended. Saying them aloud made the truth feel closer, more immediate, as though time had accelerated while she wasn't paying attention. She had been thinking about leaving in abstract ways for weeks—boxes, schedules, orientation packets, the shape of a dorm room she hadn't seen yet—but this felt different.

This felt like the edge of something.

She turned the coin once more, watching the light slide across it as though the small movement might distract her from what she had just admitted.

"I could just commute." She leaned toward the fire, the words coming in a rush now that they'd started. "It's only ten minutes to campus. I don't have to stay there."

Mike's posture didn't change. His gaze remained on the fire.

"I think it'll be good for you. Campus life. Getting out there."

Angela looked at him, waiting for something more. For him to hear what she had actually meant instead of the easier version of it. For him to meet her halfway and admit that leaving would change things for all of them, not just for her.

But nothing followed.

The space between what he said and what he chose not to say lingered just long enough to make the omission obvious.

Before she could push further, Sam spoke.

"I saw the trunk in the hallway," he said.

Something in his voice made Angela turn toward him. The tightness in it was impossible to miss.

"The one with the St. Mary's crest," he continued. "It's already halfway packed, isn't it?"

The fire snapped between them, one small sharp sound in the middle of the pause that followed.

Mike shifted his gaze, though he still didn't look at either of them.

"With your sister starting college," he said, "there won't be anyone around to help out with you."

Sam blinked, thrown off by the direction of the answer. "I'm twelve," he said. "I wipe myself. No diaper change needed."

The line was so immediate, so Sam, that Angela laughed before she could stop herself. The sound escaped, bright and brief, and for a second she thought Mike might let it stand.

Instead, his mouth tightened.

"Don't be crass," he said.

The silence that followed was heavier now, weighted by the spoken words and the truths still circling them without landing.

Somewhere beyond the campfire, out in the dark where the land dropped away toward the wider desert, a long, low howl drifted across the night.

Sam stiffened. His eyes flicked toward the edge of the firelight, and he shifted closer to Angela, silent. He reached for a piece of wood beside him and tossed it onto the fire with more force than necessary, as though reinforcing the boundary between them and whatever moved outside it.

Angela nudged his shoulder, pretending her attention was elsewhere, offering reassurance without calling him out.

"The hangar's going to be so quiet." Angela turned her attention back toward Mike. "It feels like we're just… clearing the runway for someone else."

The image settled with a weight she hadn't expected. She hadn't planned to say it that way, but once the words were out, they felt right. Too right.

Another howl came, closer this time, carrying across the open land.

Sam's shoulders tightened.

Angela brushed a twig along his back, her focus remaining on the flames.

He scrambled to his feet, his skewer nearly tipping into the coals. "What was that?"

She laughed. "Relax. It's a stick."

Sam shot her a glance, offense lingering even as some of the tension eased.

"Not funny."

"It was a little funny."

"To you."

"To me, yes."

The corner of his mouth shifted despite himself, and Angela took the small victory without pushing it.

Mike didn't react to any of it.

"The bank doesn't deal in history, Angela," he said, his voice even and distant in a way that made it clear this was an argument he had already been having with himself. "They see a liability. I'm not risking the house for something that hasn't made money since the accident."

The word settled into the air and stayed there.

Accident.

It carried more weight than the rest of the sentence combined.

Sam frowned. "It was an accident," he said. "They said it wasn't her fault. People know flying's risky."

Mike didn't answer.

For a moment, Angela thought he might. Something in his face changed, or almost changed, as if a response had risen far enough to be seen before he pushed it back down again.

"You say that like she did something wrong," Angela said.

Mike's gaze sharpened with strain. "I didn't say that."

"You didn't have to."

"Angela."

"No, because that's what it sounds like." Her voice stayed quieter than it felt. "Every time you say it like that, it sounds like you think the whole place is contaminated now. Like if we keep it, we're clinging to the worst day of our lives instead of everything that came before it."

Mike let out a slow breath through his nose, and when he looked back at the fire it was with the expression of someone already regretting being drawn into a conversation he had hoped to avoid.

"The place was already struggling," he said. "Before she died. I'm not rewriting numbers because you miss her."

The words hit harder than he intended.

Angela sat motionless.

"I'm not asking you to rewrite numbers," she said. "I'm asking you not to act like numbers are the whole story."

Mike stood.

He walked away from the fire toward the Jeep with his usual contained movement, a man finished with a conversation long before the others were. His retreat was so familiar it barely registered as surprising anymore. Conversations didn't end with him. They simply stopped, left unfinished at the point where they became too difficult to continue.

He crouched beside the front tire and pressed his hand to it, then went to the next, checking and adjusting with steady precision, giving himself something practical to do.

"The wind's picking up from the north. Clouds are building over the ridge. If the pressure drops, we'll sleep in the car."

Angela lowered her gaze to the coin in her hands, her thumb tracing the outer edge.

"The logbooks are still in her desk," she said, raising her voice just enough to reach him. "All those hours. You're just going to let someone else fly her planes?"

Mike stood, but he didn't turn around right away.

"The overhead's too high," he said. "The numbers don't work."

He came back to the fire, picked up another stick, and tossed it into the flames. A scatter of sparks lifted and disappeared into the dark before they had gone far.

Then, to Angela's surprise, he stayed.

He stood for a moment longer, looking past her toward the shadows beyond the fire.

"You think I don't know what it meant to her?"

Angela looked up.

"You think I don't know what it meant to all of us?" His voice remained controlled, but the control sounded costly now. "I do. That's exactly why I'm not going to stand there and watch it finish sinking everything else."

No one answered.

Mike looked away first.

"I'm turning in," he said.

The tent flap rustled closed behind him a few seconds later, cutting off what little connection had remained.

For a while, neither Angela nor Sam said anything.

The fire burned lower. Wood collapsed inward with soft cracks, the circle of light narrowing as darkness closed in. Angela stared into the coals, but her thoughts had moved elsewhere—to the hangar, to the planes lined up in shadow, to the cold, metallic stillness that would soon take hold there like a seized engine.

Beside her, Sam's breathing changed.

It was subtle, but the pattern was too familiar to miss. The slight tightening first, then the careful control. The extra effort it took him not to let it become something more obvious.

Then came the quiet sniff.

He turned his head, as if that alone might hide it.

Angela ignored the change in his breathing in the most obvious way possible. She reached for the marshmallow bag, pulled out two, and slid them onto a long metal skewer before handing it to him without looking directly at him.

He took it.

They leaned toward the fire together, the heat brushing their faces as the marshmallows browned and blistered at the edges. The smell turned sweet and faintly burnt, familiar enough to soften the edges of the moment.

After a while, Angela said, "I'll talk to him."

Sam kept his eyes on the marshmallow. "About what?"

"About the school. About St. Mary's. About all of it." She paused, then added, "It might not be as bad as it sounds."

She didn't fully believe it, at least not in any steady way, but it was something she could offer, and right now that mattered more than whether it was true.

Sam didn't answer. He watched the flames, his metal skewer steady.

When he finally looked up, his eyes caught the firelight in a way that made them look brighter than they were.

"I'm just going to be another blue blazer," he said. "In a line of blue blazers. I won't even look like myself."

Her chest tightened. The fear beneath the words was so clear it didn't need to be named.

"Dad thinks it'll be good for you," she said, then winced. "That came out badly."

"A little."

She nodded. "Okay. More than a little."

Sam looked back at the marshmallow. "Everybody there is going to already know how to do everything. How to talk, how to dress, how to walk around like they belong there."

"You walk around like you belong everywhere," Angela said.

"That is absolutely not true."

"It kind of is," she said. "You correct adults in public."

"That's because adults are wrong a lot."

Angela laughed, a short, quiet sound.

But when she looked at him again, the humor gave way to something softer.

"You're not going to disappear in a blazer," she said. "You're still going to be annoying, intense, smarter than everybody, and weird in exactly the same way."

Sam turned toward her. "That was mean for the first half."

"It got better."

He thought about that, then nodded. "A little."

Angela leaned her shoulder lightly to his.

"You'll still be you," she said. "Even if they make you dress like a penguin."

This time the laugh that came out of him was real. It wasn't much, but the tension eased.

After a moment, Sam dipped into the marshmallow bag again and held it out for her. "You want one?"

She took it. "Only if you toast it for me."

"You're dripping with competence all day, and suddenly you can't roast your own marshmallow?"

"I'm delegating."

"That's not leadership."

"It absolutely is."

Sam gave her a glance but obliged, turning the skewer with painstaking focus as the firelight reflected in Angela's eyes.

Above them, the sky stretched outward in a field of stars that felt remote and diamond-sharp at the same time. The desert, which had seemed so empty in the dark, now felt full of things they couldn't see.

Angela looked down at the coin again.

Its surface caught what little light remained, and she realized that what had felt exciting only hours earlier now carried a different kind of weight. The coin no longer felt like a simple discovery. It had become a marker at the edge of a change already underway.

She turned it once more in her hand and listened to the fire settle.

Chapter 5: Desert Road

By the time the sun had crested the horizon, the desert already heated, the brittle clarity of the dawn fading into something sharper and more insistent. Light stretched across the clearing in long, pale bands, drawing everything into definition as the day took hold. Color seeped back into the landscape—the oxidized crust of the caliche, the faded green of the scrub, the washed gold of dried grasses—as though the world had to be rebuilt each morning from outline into substance.

At the far edge of the campsite, another team had gathered around the saguaro cactus where Angela had left her card. Even from a distance, they moved with a confidence that set them apart from the stillness. They moved with a swift, practiced economy. Nothing about them was improvised. Behind them, their truck gave a sharp, rhythmic ping as the metal cooled in the rising heat. Whatever this was to them, it wasn't a novelty.

Quinn Monroe stood at the center, broad-shouldered and solid, his focus fixed on the opening in the cactus. Beside him, Tom shifted his weight with restless impatience, scanning the surrounding area for interruption, competition, or opportunity. Closest to the hollow stood Suzette Saunders, her posture composed and exact, every movement controlled, urgency disciplined into usefulness.

She reached inside without hesitation, and when her hand emerged, it held only a single object—a playing card.

Suzette studied it for a moment, her thumb tracing the card's edge with a hint of begrudging respect—the look of one artisan recognizing another's craft—

before her expression hardened once more. She handed it to Quinn.

"It's gone," he said, turning the card once between his fingers before passing it back. His tone remained measured, but something in it had tightened.

Tom let out a low laugh and pulled a gold coin from his pocket, angling it toward the sun so it flashed in the growing light. "Good thing we didn't rely on this one," he said. "Tombstone paid off."

Quinn gave a small nod, though he lingered on the card a moment longer than necessary, searching for meaning beyond the visible surface.

"That makes this the last coin in the first phase," he said, his gaze lifting out across the open desert, mapping the next stage. "We're still in it."

Suzette paused. Her fingers constricted around the edge of the card, her eyes already moving beyond the cactus and into whatever came next.

"We can't afford to be second," she said at last, her voice dropping to a register of quiet, desperate precision. "My father doesn't believe in near-misses; he believes in dividends. If I go back without this win, I'm not a daughter—I'm just a bad investment. I won't be the one who lets him close the books."

Tom's expression shifted, not quite sympathy, but something more attentive. "We're not out," he said. "We've still got ours."

Quinn tracked the coin in Tom's hand, then shifted back to Suzette. "And now we know at least one team's ahead of us. That helps."

Suzette folded the card once and handed it back to him, though the tension in her posture didn't ease. "Then we'd better find out who they are."

Tom glanced down the road where the fine, white grit of departing tires had long since settled. "Won't be that hard," he said. "Not out here."

Quinn tucked the card into his pocket. "Then let's move."

For one brief second longer, Suzette stared into the hollow in the cactus. The emptiness gave it a new significance. Then she turned away.

A short distance off, Angela and her family were already breaking down camp.

The tent collapsed, each movement familiar enough that none of them needed to speak. Stakes came free from the ground with small, dry resistances, poles collapsed inward, and the fabric folded into tight, practiced shapes, destined to be made again. Gear disappeared into bags, and bags were stacked into the back of the Jeep in a practiced rhythm that left little room for distraction.

Within minutes, no trace of them remained. The campsite returned to the same stripped-down neutrality it had held before they arrived, as though their brief occupation had altered nothing. Only the resinous, medicinal scent of creosote remained to mark the disturbance of the earth.

Angela glanced once toward the cactus before closing the rear hatch. The distance blurred the details, but the hollow's new contents stayed sharp.

The others climbed into the Jeep. Doors shut one after another, and the engine turned over with a low, familiar hum that resonated in the hollow morning air. Gravel shifted beneath the tires as they pulled away from the clearing and back onto the road, where dirt gave way to pavement and the desert opened around them in long, uninterrupted lines.

For a while, no one spoke.

The tires droned along the highway, and the landscape beyond the windows stretched outward in muted layers of scorched sienna and ash, softened by distance.

Up ahead, another vehicle stood parked off to the side of the road. The same team from the campsite walked back toward it. Their movements were efficient and purposeful; they were already focused beyond the place they were leaving.

"Look at that," Mike said, gesturing toward the vehicle. "We're not the only ones out here chasing nothing."

He gave a brief nod as they passed, more acknowledgment than investment.

Angela turned her head toward the glass.

For one brief moment, she met Suzette's eyes.

Recognition flared. It went beyond familiarity, pulling up memory: chlorine in the air, the ache in her shoulders after long sets, the silence before a race when everyone stood behind the blocks, feigning indifference toward the others ready to win. There was the face, the shape of the focus in it—the focus of a competitor who had already measured the field.

The moment passed as quickly as the Jeep moved beyond them, but the tension lingered.

Suzette's expression held, caught somewhere between surprise and something sharper, more deliberate. The recognition lingered between them, unwanted and mutual.

Angela turned forward again, letting her face settle back into neutrality.

"Hey," Sam said from the back seat, leaning slightly between them. "Why does that girl look familiar?"

Angela kept her eyes on the road ahead. "I don't know."

But she did.

Chapter 6: Carlisle Industries

Rex St. James took the corner too fast, leaning hard into the turn as the back tire of his bike skidded before catching again. Rubber shrieked on the pavement, the sound bouncing off glass storefronts just as a taxi horn split the morning in irritated protest somewhere behind him. He corrected instinctively, redistributing his balance and adjusting without slowing, missing the yellow fender by inches—the near-miss now behind him.

San Francisco was only beginning to wake.

Fog clung low to the streets, softening the edges of buildings and swallowing distance before it could fully take shape. Overhead, trolley cables hummed faintly with the first movement of the morning, and the metallic scent of the bay drifted through the damp air, mixing with exhaust, old concrete, and the faint sweetness of something baking somewhere he passed too quickly to identify.

He went too fast to take the city in as anything more than motion and resistance.

The bike jolted when it hit the trolley tracks, the impact rattling through his hands and up into his shoulders, but the shock barely registered. Adrenaline flattened everything else—the cold on his skin, the drag of the morning air in his lungs, the noise of the city organizing itself around him. What remained strongest was the pressure still sitting in his chest after last night's call with his father.

The conversation had followed its familiar pattern. His father called the hunt unserious, and Rex called it the future. Somewhere between those two positions, the call had hardened into silence.

By the time he skidded to a stop in front of Carlisle Industries, his lungs burned and his legs trembled from the effort he had spent trying to outride that feeling. The building rose in front of him in clean, reflective planes of steel and glass, untouched by the messier rhythms of the street. Its surface held the city at a distance, as if nothing disordered could remain once it crossed the threshold.

He pushed through the lobby doors, dragging the bike in behind him. The rubber tires squeaked wetly on the polished stone, a shrill, rhythmic violation of the stillness that usually held the room in place.

Inside, the environment changed immediately.

The air was cooler, stiller, meticulously controlled. Sound softened, and movement slowed without anyone consciously deciding to act differently. Even the lighting was measured, balanced to flatter the stone and metal surfaces without ever becoming warm. It was the kind of space designed to erase unpredictability —where everything had a place and remained where it belonged.

Rex wheeled the bike into a nearby empty office, propping it on the edge of a lacquered desk without checking if it held. He stood there for a moment before stepping back out, leaving the door slightly ajar—a small, jagged gap in the corridor's perfect line. His reflection flickered in the glass as he turned.

His hair was windblown, his face flushed, his breathing uneven and ragged. He was more alive like this than he ever was in a suit—a frantic, salt-streaked shape the room hadn't yet figured out how to claim.

For a second, he stayed where he was, then ran a hand through his hair, forced his breathing to even out, and stepped back into the lobby.

Carrie sat behind the reception desk as though she belonged to the space and had been refined by it. Her posture was straight without stiffness, her makeup precise without drawing attention, her expression warm but never careless. Nothing she did was accidental. Even when she appeared relaxed, there was intention behind it.

Her smile widened as he approached.

"Good morning, Rex. Biking to work again? I'm so jealous."

He leaned on the marble counter, the cool surface grounding him more effectively than the ride had. "You know," he said, grinning, "you can come with me anytime. Early mornings, empty streets—San Francisco actually makes sense before everyone wakes up."

Carrie looked up at him, and for a moment something less polished surfaced in her expression. "I'd love to," she said, her sincerity cutting through the polish.

"Then let's do it," he said. "Tomorrow."

Her eyebrows lifted, caught between interest and reality. "I'd love to, but tomorrow I intend to arrive at work looking like a competent adult."

Rex placed a hand over his chest. "You're implying I don't."

"I would never say that out loud."

He laughed. "Coward."

The interruption arrived with a white pastry box and the unmistakable scent of sugar.

Morgan approached from the side corridor carrying a dozen donuts already opened to the morning air, their glaze catching the lobby lights. He moved with the ease of someone who had spent years in corporate environments without letting them flatten him entirely. Even in the same suits as everyone else, he wore them for convenience rather than allegiance.

"What?" he said, setting the box down. "I brought your favorite."

Carrie laughed and lifted a hand, already refusing. "Oh, no. Not today. Just take them to the break room."

Rex straightened slightly as the moment shifted. "Are you a bad influence on sweet Carrie here?" he asked. "She's supposed to come riding with me tomorrow."

Morgan froze mid-motion and looked between them. "Don't do it, Carrie," he said. "We can't lose you too."

Carrie blinked. "Lose me?"

"You know tofu guy, Dan?" Morgan said, turning to Rex.

Rex shrugged. "Yeah."

"He used to be drinkin' Dan," Morgan said, shaking his head. "Best happy hour guy I ever knew. One hike with you—one—and suddenly he's meal prepping and talking about plant protein. Life hasn't been the same."

Carrie laughed, the sound loosening the careful stillness of the lobby just a little.

Morgan lifted a donut like it represented a serious moral decision. "Please, Carrie. Not you too."

She hesitated, then smiled and took one. "Sorry, Rex. Maybe next time."

She took a bite and closed her eyes briefly in approval. Rex laughed and grabbed one himself, glaze sticking lightly to his fingers.

"Even extreme adventurers need fuel."

Morgan gave him a sidelong look. "Extreme adventurers also need to stop terrorizing traffic before eight in the morning."

"That taxi was overreacting."

"The taxi was alive. That feels like a fair response."

Carrie covered a smile.

The ease of the moment didn't last.

Because despite the lobby's meticulous control, the boardroom still waited.

"You look like you're about to go to war," Morgan said more quietly once Carrie turned back to her screen.

"Board meeting," Rex replied. "Same thing."

Morgan studied him. "That bad?"

Rex wiped glaze from his thumb. "He thinks the hunt is a funeral I refuse to leave."

Morgan nodded. "And you want to be anywhere else."

"I want to be where the thing is actually happening."

Morgan gave a short breath of agreement. "That would be a yes."

"That would be a very strong yes."

Morgan closed the pastry box. "Well, when your father starts talking like civilization depends on quarterly discipline, just remember I'm nearby with contraband sugar."

"That may be the most helpful thing anyone's said to me this morning."

"I know," Morgan said. "Try to deserve it."

By the time Rex stepped through the boardroom doors, the morning outside receded into something distant.

The suit didn't help. The fabric pulled lightly across his shoulders, the tie sitting too close to his neck. He adjusted it once out of habit, already knowing it wouldn't fix the real problem.

It wasn't about the clothes—it was about what they required.

The boardroom filled gradually. Executives took their seats with quiet efficiency. Chairs slid into place, papers aligned, tablets lit up in subdued sequence. Even the low hum of conversation stayed contained.

Rex sat at the head of the long table, his laptop open.

The numbers were strong. Engagement climbing. Sponsorship revenue accelerating. The kind of data that should have ended the argument.

His fingers moved lightly across the keys, a quiet effort to resist the stillness.

"Your dad's on the warpath," Morgan murmured.

Rex angled the screen slightly. "The numbers are good. What more does he want?"

Morgan nodded, but cautiously. "It's solid. But he still thinks geocaching is a fad."

Rex leaned back slightly, jaw tightening.

Of course he did.

"He wants you here," Morgan added. "In the office."

"Not happening."

The calm didn't hide the edge beneath it.

"The tie-ins with this hunt are bigger than anything else we're doing," Rex said. "This isn't a side project anymore. It's where everything's headed."

Morgan crossed his arms. "So what's your next move?"

Rex reached into his pocket and set a coin on the table.

"The domestic circuit is closed," Rex said, sliding a silver coin across the glass. "I'm increasing the friction. If they want the next step, they'll have to look at the sky the way she did."

Morgan frowned. "International? How are you tracking that?"

Rex tapped the coin. "Embedded tracking."

Morgan looked at him. "And by 'we,' you mean you."

"I'm going to be the obstacle," Rex said. "I want to see who actually has the stomach to solve it when the map runs out."

"In your dad's jet."

Rex didn't hesitate. "Yeah."

Morgan exhaled slowly. "That's risky."

"I know."

"You could get fired."

Rex held his gaze. "If this doesn't work, being his son won't matter anyway."

That settled between them.

The door opened.

Arthur St. James entered, and the room shifted around him with quiet precision. At sixty, he carried authority without effort. Everything about him was exact.

Morgan leaned slightly. "I think he'd rather have me climbing a rock than sitting in here."

Rex exhaled a quiet laugh. "You should come."

"I'm too scared of your tofu lifestyle."

"Fine. No tofu."

Morgan sat as Arthur gave Rex a brief nod—acknowledgment without warmth.

Rex returned it.

Then he stood.

"The hunt is moving to Europe," he said. "The U.S. phase is complete. We're going global."

Arthur set his pen down.

"No, Rex. We are ending the charade."

The disappointment in his voice cut deeper than criticism.

"The Board doesn't trade in nostalgia, Rex. They trade in certainty. This hunt is a variable we can no longer afford. You are turning your mother's legacy into a riddle for the bored and the desperate, having grown men chase a ghost that isn't there."

"The riddle is the point," Rex said, his voice level. "She never believed in straight lines, and neither do I. If they want the prize, they have to earn the perspective."

"It is a distraction," Arthur replied. "You are trading dignity for spectacle."

"I am turning us into a destination," Rex said. "If we don't move forward, we lose the only momentum we have."

Arthur's eyes narrowed. "Leadership requires presence, Rex."

"I'm chasing the future," Rex said. "You're trying to keep the furniture from moving."

The meeting continued.

The disagreement didn't resolve. Rex knew he was right.

The slice was a mistake the second Sam picked it up.

Cheese stretched in long, uneven strands, grease catching the dim light as it gathered along the edge and threatened to slide. He adjusted his grip carefully, pinching the crust tighter and angling the slice upward, but the tip still sagged, bending under its own weight with slow inevitability.

He wasn't worried about the table, only his shirt.

The white fabric of his Catholic school uniform had become the only thing that mattered. The crease down the front was still sharp, pressed so cleanly it felt less like clothing and more like a statement. The collar sat straight. The buttons aligned. The sleeves were smooth. Everything about it suggested structure, control, belonging.

That mattered more than he wanted anyone to admit.

Around him, Enrico's pulsed with noise and warmth. College students crowded into booths, leaning across tables as laughter bounced off the walls. Voices overlapped in a constant hum, and the smell of tomato sauce, garlic, and melted cheese settled into everything. A red-checkered tablecloth stretched beneath his forearms, and framed photos of Sophia Loren watched from the walls with quiet, enduring confidence.

None of it mattered. Only the shirt did.

Across from him, Angela leaned back in the booth, her posture loose in a way that made his effort look almost theatrical.

"Why are you wearing the uniform?" she asked. "School doesn't even start until tomorrow."

Sam kept his eyes on the slice. "Just making sure the crease is sharp. I'd hate to look like I didn't belong in the place you're sending me."

Angela's expression shifted, something softer passing through before she could cover it.

It might have become something more if their father hadn't arrived at that moment.

Mike dropped into the seat beside them with a tired exhale. "Sorry I'm late. Still wildfire season. We're basically babysitting every extreme-sports yahoo in the county."

Angela straightened slightly. "Why? What are they doing?"

"Camping wherever they feel like. Leaving fires, trash. Half the time we're just cleaning up after them."

Angela lowered her gaze. "Dad, we're not all like that."

Mike didn't answer. His attention had already shifted to Sam, to the uniform, to what it represented.

"What's this about?" he asked.

Sam shrugged. "Just a dry run. Figured you'd want to see where the scholarship money went."

Mike rolled his eyes. "Just don't get pizza on it. We can't afford another one."

Sam paused.

Then, slowly, he loosened his grip.

The slice folded inward. Sauce and cheese slid forward, landing squarely on the front of his shirt, spreading across the white fabric in a bright, uneven stain.

For a second, he just looked at it.

"Whoops."

Angela's eyes snapped to their father.

Mike's expression hardened. "If you want to be the kid with the stained uniform, so be it. I'm not buying you a new one."

Sam didn't react outwardly, but his fingers curled slightly on the table.

Angela stepped in quickly. "Why don't you see if they have club soda?"

Sam nodded once and slid out of the booth.

Angela waited until he was gone.

"Does he really have to go to that school?" she asked quietly.

Mike was already guarded. "You know he has a scholarship."

"So it's a reward? He's smart enough to get sent away so the house can stay quiet?"

"That's not what this is."

"Then what is it? Because it looks like we're cutting things off one piece at a time and calling it a plan."

"It's an opportunity for him."

"At what cost?"

Neither of them answered.

Sam returned before the argument could deepen. The stain remained, darker now, impossible to ignore.

Angela leaned back, letting the moment settle instead of pushing it further. The coin turned in her hand, catching the dim light as it moved.

"So," Sam said, nodding toward it, "did you figure out if that's a clue?"

"Not yet," Angela said. "I don't want to be disappointed."

Mike leaned forward. "Who are you talking about?"

"The guy from the article. What if it really is a clue? We could use the money."

She hesitated, then added more quietly, "And the adventure."

Mike leaned back again. "College will be enough of an adventure."

Angela didn't argue.

But the coin kept turning.

The dorm was chaos.

Voices echoed down the hallway, doors slammed, and furniture scraped across tile floors as students and families moved in waves, carrying the pieces of lives that had to be rearranged to fit somewhere new. Fullness pressed at the building's walls, but nothing had taken hold. Everything remained in motion, including the people.

Mike pushed through the doorway carrying a box and dropped it onto the growing pile.

"Last one," he said.

Angela sat on the edge of her new bed, her hands resting lightly on the mattress; the furniture hadn't yet accepted her. The fabric was stiff and unfamiliar

—too clean, too impersonal, a witness waiting for a claimant it hadn't yet recognized.

Sam sat beside her in a faded T-shirt with a cracked graphic on the chest. The uniform was gone, abandoned in a rest-stop trash can somewhere between the pizza parlor and the dorm.

He draped an arm around her shoulders.

"He's going to notice the shirt's absence," Angela said.

"That was the plan."

"You really left it in the trash?"

"Stain-side up."

"That's bold."

"It's symbolic."

"Of what?"

"Of expectations being unrealistic."

Angela let out a small laugh.

The door opened, and Sally entered with a plate of cookies, the warm scent cutting through the sharper smells of the room.

"Look what I brought."

Sam grabbed two immediately.

Sally laughed, then caught Mike's eye and gestured at Sam's change of clothes. Mike gave a small, weary shake of his head.

"You have all my numbers, right?" Mike asked.

"I'll keep an eye on her," Sally said.

Angela had gone to the window.

The campus sprawled below, but her attention extended past the visible horizon. Students moved below, carrying boxes, saying goodbyes, beginning something new that she didn't yet feel part of.

Sally joined her. "Are you excited?"

"I'd rather be anywhere else."

"We covered that."

Angela crossed to the desk and picked up the framed photo.

Her mother stood beside a small airplane, sunlight catching her face.

"What do you think she would have said?"

Mike hesitated. "I don't know."

Sally stepped in gently. "But what about being on your own? It could be fun."

Mike frowned. "She needs to focus."

Sally waved it off. "We had a great time here."

Angela let out a short laugh. "Ask Dad. He's been checking the rearview mirror since the state line."

Mike lifted his head. "That's not fair."

"Isn't it?"

"That's not what this is."

"Then what is it? Because it looks like everything that reminded you of her is getting packed up or sent away."

"Mija—" Sally began.

But Angela didn't stop.

"The hangar. Sam leaving. Me being here. What's left?"

"What's left is us trying to move forward."

"Without her."

"Yes."

The word came out sharper than he intended.

A catch in her throat made her next breath shallow, her hand gripping the edge of the desk.

Sally squeezed her hands. "Recuerde a su mamá."

Angela pulled away, wiping at her face as anger rose quickly enough to cover the break.

"You're the only one who still carries her name like it matters," she said. "For him, she's just something he's finished packing away."

Mike turned and walked out without answering.

Sam hesitated, caught between them for a moment, then followed.

The door closed behind them, leaving the room abruptly quieter.

Angela sank back onto the bed as the tension drained out of her all at once, leaving her hollow in its wake. The effort it had taken to hold herself together gave way, and the sobs came before she could stop them.

Sally sat beside her and smoothed her hair, her touch steady and familiar.

"Your dad does miss her," Sally said softly. "I know he does."

Angela didn't answer.

The need to believe that throbbed in her chest.

That was what hurt the most.

Chapter 7: Coin and Current

Rex hit the turn too fast, gravel snapping beneath his tires as he leaned hard into the curve and the frame shuddered beneath him as the trail dropped sharply along the canyon wall. The edge of the path ran closer than it should have, a narrow margin between control and consequence, but he didn't slow. He had entered the descent with too much speed for caution to be possible, and some part of him had stopped wanting caution several turns ago anyway.

The voices from the boardroom still pulsed in the back of his mind with a sharp, ringing clarity that made his temples throb, deliberate, critical, controlled in that polished way that gave every dismissal the weight of reason. His father's restraint, the questions from the executives, the flicker of skepticism they were too practiced to name, hidden beneath every carefully worded concern had stayed with him long after the meeting ended. Only speed pushed the world far enough away for him to breathe without being cornered.

Wind tore past his ears as his focus narrowed to the line ahead. He adjusted by instinct now, firing corrections with precision, stripping the world away until the thrum of the frame vibrated through his teeth and only the instinct of reaction remained. That was the thing no one in the boardroom understood. Out here, nothing lied to him. A surface either held or it didn't. A turn either opened or closed. Risk declared itself honestly.

Then the front wheel caught, a thin, buried root invisible until the last possible second, and jerked the handlebars sideways, tearing control from his grip. The bike snapped off-line, the frame twisting beneath him before he had time to recover it. For a fraction of a second, weight vanished, the ground dropping away as sky and earth traded places in a blur of ocher, shadow, and hard afternoon light.

The impact followed before he had time to brace for it.

His shoulder hit first, then his hip, and then the side of his helmet struck stone with a crack that flashed white behind his eyes. The bike skidded away in a spray of dust and gravel, metal scraping on rock as it spun off the trail and lodged itself in a scrubby outcropping several yards below. Rex rolled once, twice, then slammed into the packed earth, winded and stunned.

For a moment, everything went still.

He didn't shift. Part of it was uncertainty, since he wasn't sure yet if he could, and the canyon's stillness held around him, indifferent to the violence of what had just happened. Somewhere nearby, a pebble loosened and clicked down the slope.

He drew in one breath, then another, waiting for the rest to come.

Pain came in sections, a flare in his shoulder, a hot scrape along his forearm, a deeper ache blooming along his side that promised a bruise before the day was out. Nothing was broken. He let out a shallow, jagged breath, his lungs finally expanding as the frantic pressure behind his ribs eased, though the sudden lightness felt like a stolen thing, leaving a bitter hollow in his gut.

He pushed himself up slowly and sat there for a moment, dust coating his clothes, his pulse beating hard.

His father was going to love this, not because the crash had broken him, but because it hadn't broken him badly enough to teach him a lesson.

Rex's teeth ground together, his jaw locking until the muscles in his neck pulled taut, the heat of the thought finally forcing him back to his feet. He stood carefully, tested his balance, and climbed down to retrieve the bike. The front wheel remained mostly true, though it tracked slightly wide, and one brake lever had curled inward toward the bar.

He stared at it for a moment, breathing hard, then let out a short breath of laughter, more to keep from swearing at the canyon than from any real humor.

The handlebars resisted at first, then shifted under his grip. When they were as straight as he could manage, he paused and looked back up toward the trail.

He should have gone home.

Instead, the bike came up with him as he started pushing it uphill.

By the time he made it to the top, sweat had dried in a gritty film on his skin, and the ache in his side had deepened into something more persistent. The trail stretched out ahead in a line of dust and rock—less escape than evidence. The boardroom version of this story already echoed: reckless judgment, unnecessary exposure, precisely the sort of behavior his father had meant when he asked how much of the hunt depended on Rex himself.

Too much, apparently.

Rex stopped beside a stand of scrub and rested both hands on the handlebars, breathing through the pulse of pain in his ribs. The absurdity of it threatened to turn into laughter again. He had spent all morning defending adventure as disciplined vision, then launched himself down a canyon wall like a man trying to prove a private point to someone who wasn't even there to see it.

The thought bit into him like a cold wind, clear and cutting, finally giving his focus a place to anchor.

He straightened, pushed the bike the rest of the way to the access road, and decided—without quite admitting to himself that it was a decision—that he would be more careful next time.

Not slower, just more careful, and the distinction mattered.

Across campus, the natatorium carried the clean, sterile scent of chlorine, and the drumming of laps gnawed at the high ceiling, the sound refusing to fade. Splashes overlapped with breath, whistles cut across the air at irregular intervals, and the slap of water on tile rebounded from wall to wall.

Angela sat on the bleachers beside her roommate, Toni, her arms folded loosely across her knees ; the pool churned before her. Humidity clung to her skin and softened the edges of everything, including thought, until the whole room existed inside a light haze of heat and sound. Damp air coaxed frizz from the loose knot of Toni's dark curls while she glared at a macroeconomics textbook , her mouth pulled into a thin line as if the textbook were a personal enemy.

"I wonder who they are," Toni said, nodding toward the far side of the pool where a second group had begun to gather.

Angela followed her gaze.

The coach stood at the edge of the water with his whistle hanging at his chest, calling the team in with short, efficient gestures. Swimmers climbed out and went automatically for towels, shaking water from their arms and hair as they formed a loose semicircle around him. Behind them, another group stood apart, not quite integrated into the space and therefore impossible to ignore.

Strangers filled the deck.

One face, however, pulled at her memory.

Suzette.

Even at a distance, she stood out, not from any effort to draw attention, but from a stillness that carried its own force.

Angela's hands spasmed on the edge of the bleacher; she swallowed as her pulse hammered a jagged, uneven staccato at her collarbone—the physical ghost of a history she had never quite managed to outrun.

Toni glanced at her. "That's not a neutral face."

"I have a neutral face."

"You absolutely do not."

Angela didn't answer.

The whistle cut through the air.

"We're lucky to have some of the best swimmers in the country with us today," the coach called. "Anyone up for a hundred-meter challenge?"

Suzette leaned in and said something too quiet to hear. The coach nodded, then turned.

"Angela."

The name carried across the natatorium , a leaden weight that seemed to pull the oxygen from the air.

Angela hesitated only for a breath before she stood.

Toni squeezed her shoulder, a brief, firm pressure that felt like a grounding wire. "Try not to murder anyone," she murmured. "But if you do, I know where the blind spots in the pool's security cameras are."

Angela almost smiled. "No promises."

By the time she reached the pool deck, everything else had already begun to fall away.

The starting block anchored her with a familiar solidity, and for a moment the rest of her life receded, the dorm, the tension at home, the unfinished conversations. There was only the water, the lane, and the narrowing space before the horn.

She glanced sideways.

Suzette didn't look at her.

That made it sharper.

The horn sounded.

Angela dove cleanly, the cold snapping through her body and bringing everything into focus. Her stroke locked into its cadence almost immediately, pull, kick, breathe, each movement locking into place with the precision of long practice.

She took the early lead.

It wasn't a thought, but alignment.

Then, halfway down, the water shifted.

A presence crowded her—the subtle weight of someone matching, then gaining.

Suzette.

Angela pushed harder, but by the final stretch the difference was no longer subtle. When she hit the wall, it was over.

She stayed in the water, fingers curled over the edge, her chin just above the surface while her pulse hammered through her ribs. The noise of the room returned slowly, as if from a distance.

A towel settled over her shoulders.

"You almost had her," Toni said.

Angela didn't answer.

Footsteps approached.

"It hasn't changed, has it?"

Angela looked up.

Suzette stood there, not smiling, not triumphant. If anything, exhaustion settled in the lines of her face.

"I heard about your dad's shop," she said. "I'm sorry."

Angela had no answer for that.

"But my family's gym is on the line too," Suzette continued. "And I'm the only one left who can save it."

She hesitated, then added, "I don't have the luxury of being a good sport anymore."

Her gaze sharpened.

"Please don't get in my way."

Then she turned and walked off.

Toni crouched beside the pool. "Wow. She really knows how to do ominous."

Angela pushed her hair back. "She means it."

"Do you?"

Angela pulled herself out of the water. "I don't know yet."

But something in her had already answered.

She dropped onto her dorm bed later, still smelling faintly of chlorine, and stared at the ceiling while a thin crack in one of the tiles held her attention longer than it should have.

"You okay?" Toni asked.

"I just don't think I'm ready for college life yet."

Toni didn't shrug it off. She set her textbook aside and stood up, her movements suddenly deliberate. "Then don't be," she said. "If you're looking for a sign to stop playing at being a student while your head is already out there, this is it." She reached into her desk and pulled out a heavy, matte-black multi-tool and a weathered field rucksack. "Take these. The tool was my brother's—magnesium casing, industrial-grade—and the bag is waterproofed for the Sierras. It's better than the nylon thing you've been hauling around. I'll cover for you with the RA, too. I'll tell them you're at an overnight study session if they do a floor check. You just focus on the hunt."

Angela didn't laugh. She ran a hand over the heavy canvas of the rucksack, the weight of the gear making the decision feel real. Her attention drifted toward the desk, toward the coin.

Her gaze shifted to a faded trading card tucked into the frame of her mirror, the sleuth in the purple dress, a relic of the Saturday mornings her father had spent calling her "Danger-prone Daphne." The nickname had been a badge of honor, a way to recast her habit of stumbling into situations she wasn't prepared for as a kind of accidental bravery. He'd always told her she didn't find trouble; trouble simply recognized her as its favorite destination.

It sat near the lamp where she had left it, small enough to ignore if she chose to, heavy enough that she didn't.

She picked it up and turned it slowly between her fingers.

"I found this last weekend."

Toni leaned closer. "Wait—I've heard of these. Did you log it?"

Angela shook her head. "I don't want to find out it's not real."

Toni slid her laptop over. "We're fixing that."

The website wasn't a hobbyist blog; it was a sleek portal for something called the Apex Hunt. They spent an hour digging into Rex St. James—the billionaire heir turned "adventure architect" who had turned geocaching into a high-stakes global pursuit. Registration was a formal gauntlet, requiring a verified serial number, a multi-page liability waiver, and a passport scan. It was less a game and more a recruitment process.

Angela typed the code from the coin's rim. The screen shimmered, validating the entry, and a map of the globe unfolded with a single waypoint glowing in the dark. A photo of Rex loaded in the sidebar, confident, composed—a man who never had to worry about rent.

"Wow," Toni said. "He's gorgeous."

Angela allowed herself a small smirk. "He's a distraction."

"That was dangerously calm."

Angela rolled her eyes. "I'm not making a life-altering decision because someone photographs well."

She reached the final prompt: REGISTER ALIAS.

Angela typed: DAPHNE.

"Who's Daphne?" Toni asked.

Angela pulled out the card, its corners softened by years of being kept. "Because she finds trouble first," she said. "That's me out there."

Toni watched her with a sharp, expectant focus. "So, Daphne. What's the first move?"

Angela looked toward the framed photo of her mother. "I don't know."

But the uncertainty was already narrowing as she lowered her gaze.

A week later, they were back at Enrico's.

Sam slid into the booth, his silhouette softened by a faded, oversized hoodie that lacked the sharp, starched geometry of his school blazer. The white fabric and the permanent creases he'd carried like a forced identity were gone, replaced by something frayed and anonymous.

"No uniform?" Angela asked.

"I'm done with the costume," Sam said. "I'm trying something new."

She slid printed pages across the table. "What do you think?"

"I think it's stupid."

"I'm talking to Dad."

"He won't go for it."

"I thought we could do it together."

Sam's phone rang.

"Dad's not coming."

Angela nodded. "Let's just eat."

They didn't.

After a while, she said, "We should take him some."

Sam brightened. "Yeah."

A peculiar wrongness permeated the house the moment they walked in.

Stale air hung in the hallway, thick with something that hadn't moved in too long. Angela flipped on the lights one by one, revealing takeout containers, newspapers, clothes left where they had been dropped.

None of it was sudden. That was the worst part. It had accumulated—quietly, completely.

The television flickered somewhere deeper in the house.

Angela stood still, her hand tightening around the paper bag until the handles bit into her palm. She didn't realize her hands were shaking until the paper bag chattered in her grip. Her chest felt brittle, and a heavy, cold hollow opened in the pit of her stomach. This wasn't a temporary lapse; it was a slow, quiet sediment of days left unlived.

She moved toward the glow, Sam following close behind.

The coin in her pocket grew heavy.

Chapter 8: The Paper That Breaks It

The house was dim when Angela and Sam arrived, the only light a pale glow from the living room. Mike was hunched over his laptop, his face etched with shadows that deepened the lines around his eyes. He didn't look up at the sound of the door. He was too focused on the screen, his eyes scanning a map that pulsed with movement, his hands gripping the mouse as he tracked the shifting icons.

Angela watched him for a moment from the edge of the room, tracking the rigid line of his shoulders before she finally stepped into the light.

Mike jerked around, his eyes wide as he looked between them.

For a moment, none of them moved, then Angela lifted the pizza box slightly.

"We brought you pizza."

She kept her voice flat. She didn't lean on the doorframe as she usually did; she stood with her weight centered, her chin tilted just enough to catch the light from the hallway, her expression a sealed envelope.

"Since you were too busy to meet us at Enrico's."

Sam said nothing. He stood a little behind her, his gaze fixed on their father with a rigid stillness that made him seem older than he was.

Mike stood, a flush rising along the back of his neck as he glanced back at the open laptop screen. The moving map remained visible, icons pulsing on the dark background.

"Thanks for the pizza." His voice stayed level, though his eyes darted back at the screen. "I, uh… I just got home."

Angela extended the box. She let go the moment his fingers brushed the cardboard, stepping back before the heat of the pizza could transfer to her hands.

"Okay," she said, already turning toward Sam. "Let's go."

"Hey—wait."

Both of them paused.

Mike's eyes shifted toward the kitchen. "There's mail for you," he said. "On the counter."

He moved toward it, his back stiff as he stepped away from the open laptop. Unopened envelopes, folded advertisements, and loose papers cluttered the counter. He gathered a stack without sorting it and came back into the living room.

"There you go."

Angela took it and began flipping through the envelopes, her attention casual at first—bills, store circulars, a reminder about something neither of them had requested. Her fingers moved in a blur of habit.

Then they slowed.

A thicker document sat near the bottom, heavier than the rest, its edge visible even before she pulled it free.

She slid it out.

The word CONTRACT stretched across the top in bold, unmistakable print.

Mike's grip tightened on the pizza box, the cardboard buckling under his thumb. Angela didn't blink. Her thumb hooked into the corner of the page, the paper crinkling under a sudden, white-knuckled pressure as her gaze locked onto the final paragraph.

"Angela—" Mike began, stepping forward, one hand already reaching for the paper.

She pulled it back, just out of reach.

"No."

Her voice was steady, and the lack of a tremor made Mike flinch more than a shout would have.

"Let me finish."

Sam looked between them, his brow knitting as he searched their faces. "What is it?"

Angela didn't answer right away. Her eyes kept moving across the page, taking in the details with a speed that suggested she was already seeing the end of it.

When she spoke, her voice was barely a murmur.

"Dad's sold Mom's soaring school."

The sentence left a vacuum in the room. Mike stood paralyzed, the only sound the low, electric whine of the laptop fan and the rhythmic ticking of a cooling radiator.

She let the contract fall from her hands. It landed on the floor with a soft sound that still felt final.

Then she turned and walked toward the front door.

Sam lunged forward, catching the contract before it fully settled, flipping to the last page with urgency.

"It's not signed," he said. "It's not signed yet, Angela."

But she was already gone.

"Angela!" he called, running after her.

The front door opened and shut again, the sound echoing through the house.

Sam hesitated only long enough to turn back. He crossed the room, pressed the contract into Mike's hands, and then, without warning, wrapped his arms around him in a quick, tight hug.

Mike stood frozen as Sam pulled away.

"I love you, Dad."

Then he followed Angela out the door.

The walk back across campus felt like navigating a museum of a life she no longer recognized.

Earlier that morning, in her Aeronautics seminar, Angela had watched the professor draw a perfect, theoretical wing on the whiteboard, a shape that didn't have to contend with unpredictable gusts or the sudden drop of a thermal. The diagram rendered flight as a sterile math problem. Sitting in that plastic chair, she had felt the air grow thin and her chest tighten, as if she were something wild being taught how to exist inside a cage.

By the time she reached her dorm room, the decision had already taken hold.

She sat at her desk and turned the brass coin she'd salvaged over in her palm, tracing the alphanumeric code etched into its rim. On her laptop, the portal for the Rex St. James "Latitude Run" was a stark interface.

She entered the code, uploaded her passport, and signed the digital waiver.

The screen didn't offer a ticket, only a destination and a countdown.

Paris. Forty-eight hours.

She checked her bank balance: eight dollars and forty-two cents.

Sam sat on the edge of her bed, his rucksack already half-filled. "That won't even get us to the airport, Ang."

"I'm selling the vario," Angela said, her voice tight.

She pulled the carbon-fiber variometer from her flight locker, the precision instrument that had been her pride. Toni had already handled the negotiation with a junior on the soaring team; she dropped three hundred dollars in crumpled twenties onto the desk, her expression fierce. "He tried to lowball you," Toni said. "I told him I'd break his flight computer if he didn't bring the full amount in cash immediately."

It still wouldn't cover the gate fees.

She opened a bookmarked tab she hadn't touched since the funeral: her mother's frequent flier legacy. Maria had accumulated a fortune in miles on the international circuit, a ghost-hoard she'd never spent.

Angela booked two seats for Paris and a later leg to Venice, her mouse-clicks the only sound in the room as the mandatory taxes and gate fees devoured two hundred and eighty dollars of the variometer cash.

When the confirmation finally cleared, the balance on the screen sat like a stone: eight dollars. She smoothed the remaining twenty-dollar bill from the sale over the wood of the desk.

"The Latitude portal says there's a milestone stipend released once we check in at the first waypoint," Angela said, her voice dropping to a low calculation. "It barely covers a bunk and a transit pass for the next leg, and we only get it if we're on time. It won't buy a sandwich in a terminal. It won't pay for the train to the airfield today."

Sam reached into his pocket and pulled out a small, salt-stained envelope. He laid it next to her twenty. "I have the cab money," he said. "Saved it from the summer. Eighty-five dollars."

One hundred and five dollars in cash, plus the eight in her bank account. It was a pathetic ledger for a transcontinental crossing, but it was a number they could live with.

They had their seats.

Paris would be a city of long walks and shared bread.

Stacks of half-packed belongings crowded her side of the room. Clothes lay folded in uneven piles. An open textbook lay facedown on the rug, its spine cracked at a chapter on fluid dynamics. A half-empty coffee mug sat on the windowsill, a dark ring drying at the bottom—the wreckage of a Tuesday that would never finish.

Toni wasn't just standing by; she was rummaging through her own gear locker, finally pulling out a rugged, slate-gray storm shell. She tossed it onto Angela's bed. "Take it. It's high-grade Gore-Tex, and the weather in the Alps is trash this time of year. Don't let the coach see you wearing it if you ever come back."

Angela zipped her bag partway and paused, her hands resting on the fabric.

"I'm not ready for this place," she said. "Not like this."

Toni pushed her textbook aside. "He might not let you back on the team next semester. And your family, what about them?"

She looked at the open book. "I'm drowning in a major I hate just to keep my dad from yelling. I wish I had the guts you do."

Angela let out a breath that almost became a laugh. "It doesn't feel like guts. It feels like if I stay here, I'm just agreeing to something."

"To what?"

"To waiting. To letting everyone else decide what happens."

Silence settled between them.

"So what do you want me to tell people?" Toni asked. "If they come looking for you?"

Angela picked up the coin from beside her laptop and turned it once between her fingers before slipping it into her bag.

"Tell them I'm okay," she said. "And that I'll call when I reach the first waypoint."

Toni gave a short, incredulous laugh. "You're really doing this."

Angela nodded.

The room grew still, the silence deepening until the desk lamp's faint, electric hum was the only sound left.

She grabbed her keys, slung the backpack over her shoulder, and paused at the door.

Her gaze moved once more across the room—the bed, the desk, the life she had barely begun to inhabit.

Then she opened the door and kept going.

"Angela—at least text me when you get wherever you're dramatically heading," Toni called after her.

That almost drew a smile.

"Okay," Angela said, without turning.

Then she was gone.

Chapter 9: The Chase Begins

Angela traced the route again with her finger, following the red line that stretched across the map from Tucson to San Francisco.

On paper, it looked almost too simple. The line moved cleanly from one point to another, uninterrupted and without hesitation, stripped of the kinds of interruptions real movement always invited. It reduced distance to something abstract, something manageable enough to fit between two printed edges—a straight route, a visible destination, a story of cause and effect that assumed the person following it knew exactly what she was doing.

Only hours earlier, she had been sitting in the back of an Advanced Avionics lecture, as the professor traced the "inevitable" life cycle of a landing gear assembly. The air in the hall was recycled, heavy with the weight of years of diagrams and standardized testing. Her hands were grease-stained and steady; the future was clear: she was being trained to keep other people's dreams in the air while her own stayed grounded on a syllabus.

The departure felt less like a choice and more like a reflex, a sudden rejection of a life she had never chosen. Out here, it was nothing like that.

She folded the map slightly and braced it at the center console, her eyes flickering between the paper and the road as she adjusted her grip on the wheel. The desert was beginning to thin into longer, flatter stretches of highway, the terrain widening in front of her until the horizon pulled farther away with every mile. Familiar ridgelines had given way to land less named, less personal, as though she had crossed some invisible boundary between the life she knew and the one she had only imagined in fragments.

The Slurpee in her cup holder had started to melt. Each time she lifted it for a sip, the sweetness drifted faintly through the car. Her body was still too charged to settle into small comforts. Her attention kept returning to the road, to the motion beneath the tires, to the simple and undeniable fact that she was still driving west and not turning around.

For the first time since leaving campus, she allowed herself to sit with that fact instead of pushing past it.

She was doing this. She wasn't preparing for it or imagining it as a distant possibility. She had stopped using the idea of escape as a way to make staying feel temporary. She had actually left.

Her grip tightened on the wheel until the leather groaned. She didn't turn back. A restless heat climbed her arms, an electric current that refused to settle into either fear or excitement. There was no structure around her now, no schedule waiting to pull her back into place, no version of herself already arranged by other people's expectations.

The road did not care whether her decision made sense.

There was only distance, and whatever came next.

On the passenger seat, the map threatened to slide every time the road curved. Her phone sat beside it, silent for now. She had expected guilt to overtake her more quickly than this, expected fear to arrive in a clearer form. Instead, both hovered just outside whatever steadier resolve had taken hold of her since she started driving.

Maybe this was commitment, a decision made too quickly to second-guess properly. Or maybe it was only because she had not yet had to explain herself to anyone who mattered.

She pushed the thought aside and kept driving.

A green highway sign passed overhead. Another exit slipped by. Gas stations appeared and disappeared at intervals, their parking lots half-full of pickup trucks, minivans, and people whose days had not split in half the way hers had. The ordinariness of it all only heightened the strangeness of her own movement.

She was driving toward San Francisco because of a coin, a website, and a pull she still could not fully explain without sounding reckless even to herself.

The farther she went, the less that mattered.

The decision had already been made. What remained was the follow-through.

At a stoplight, she reached for her phone; the screen remained dark, and she did not unlock it. No new messages. No voicemail alert. Sam's face appeared in her mind—how he would look when he found her room empty and the truth finally landed—and the thought struck harder than she expected.

He would understand the pull of it more than anyone else. He would also take it personally, because he always did when something carried the sting of abandonment, even if he masked the wound with humor.

The light changed. She set the phone back down.

"I'll call," she said, gripping the wheel a little tighter, as though saying it aloud gave the promise weight.

Twenty miles passed, and still she had no real plan beyond reaching the city. Coordinates wouldn't give her a place to stay, and momentum alone wasn't a strategy. The recognition should have frightened her more than it did. Instead, it sharpened her. She had spent too long living inside other people's delayed decisions. Improvising her own didn't feel like chaos. It felt like relief. Even so, relief had limits.

At the next gas station, she pulled in, filled the tank, and stood by the pump while hot wind pushed at her shirt in uneven gusts. The mountains in the distance were flatter now, worn down by space. Inside, she winced at the cost of even the simplest supplies and chose a pen, a spiral notebook, and a single granola bar. Back in the car, she wrote three things on the first page:

Find the next coordinates. Do not run out of money. Call Sam.

Below them, she added a fourth:

St. James.

She had spent the last ten minutes on her phone, digging through forum archives and old news clippings. The name on the coin's edge belonged to Rex St. James, a reclusive billionaire who had turned his obsession with "forgotten geography" into an invitation-only global hunt known as the Apex Hunt. It was not just a game; it was the Great Meridian—a circuit of high-stakes navigation that required physical proof of legacy to even enter.

She reached the final prompt on the Apex Hunt's stark interface: REGISTER ALIAS.

Angela opened the coin more deliberately, prying the metal halves apart to reveal the slim tracking tag nested inside. She held the tag to the lens, then her father's old aviator ring, the metal gleaming in the dim car light.

The screen hummed and updated.

Registration confirmed. Contestant 412. Destination: The Iron Lady's Shadow.

The logistics of the next leg—San Francisco to Paris—loomed like a physical wall. She pulled into a rest stop, her thumbs hovering over the flight search. The prices for last-minute international fares were a mockery of her balance.

The heavy Pelican case in her backseat was filled with the calibrated torque wrenches and diagnostic sensors she'd spent three years assembling. Selling them was an amputation of her future, but she posted the listing to a technician's forum with a "local pickup only" tag for San Francisco, the price low enough to guarantee a bite.

Even then, it wasn't enough.

She dug through her email archives until she found the login for her mother's frequent flier account—a dormant legacy of miles from a life spent traveling for consulting jobs she'd never fully explained. There was just enough to bridge the gap for two seats, provided she paid the exorbitant taxes and surcharges upfront.

As she confirmed the payment, the remaining funds in her mother's emergency account shrank to almost nothing.

Eight dollars.

The number landed heavily. It wouldn't cover a taxi from the airport, let alone food for two. The financial drain was no longer just a hurdle; it was a ticking clock that would follow her through Paris and into whatever lay beyond.

There was no undoing it now. She had traded security for motion, for a chance she could not yet justify beyond instinct.

She closed the notebook, her hands unsteady on the wheel, and pulled back onto the road.

The phone in the console pulsed suddenly, sharp and insistent.

The Apex Hunt had updated, but the pin on the map was no longer stationary. It was drifting steadily toward the coast, shadowed by a flicker of changing altitude data.

Angela reached into the glove box and pulled out a weathered leather binder—her father's old cross-country navigation logs. She flipped through the dog-eared pages until she found the approach charts for the Bay Area. She cross-referenced the coordinates on the screen with the printed vectors, her mind working through the descent rates she'd studied in her avionics seminars.

The "Iron Lady's Shadow" wasn't a landmark. It was a flight path, a specific arrival currently moving through the city's crowded airspace.

If the target followed the standard landing pattern, it would be on the ground in less than ninety minutes.

The prize wasn't waiting at a fixed point anymore.

The game had changed.

It was no longer a search.

It was an intercept.

If she did not reach the city in time, the money she had just spent would become nothing more than the cost of a failure she had chosen.

She pressed harder on the accelerator.

Across town, the Tucson airport pulsed with movement.

The air carried the layered smell of jet fuel, floor wax, recycled air, and coffee gone stale in paper cups. Announcements drifted overhead in a practiced rhythm, blending into the steady movement of travelers through security lines and boarding gates. Conversations overlapped, luggage wheels rattled across tile, and every few seconds another voice rose with just enough urgency to cut through the noise before dissolving again.

Suzette walked ahead with Quinn, both of them moving with a pace that left no room for hesitation. Quinn carried a steady forward pressure, as if motion itself solved part of the problem. Suzette's focus was tighter, her energy contained rather than outwardly tense, though the strain showed in the way she held herself.

Tom lingered just behind them, his gaze moving in quick, assessing arcs that were never entirely random.

Near the boarding line, a small boy sat cross-legged on the floor, surrounded by candy and cheap toys. He rolled a matchbox car across the tile and laughed when it spun farther than he intended. His mother followed after it without thinking, leaving her purse and an open bag of treats near the chairs.

An opening appeared, but Tom's gaze drifted past the purse to a more lucrative target.

His eyes swept the terminal's high corners where the security lenses rotated in slow, sweeping arcs. He adjusted his path, moving into a blind spot created by a concrete pillar.

As he drifted past a traveler buried in a spreadsheet, he let his hand—clutching a slim, matte-black device—brush within inches of the man's coat. There was no physical snag, just a faint, phantom vibration in his palm. He stepped away, the device disappearing back into his sleeve, leaving the stranger's pockets untouched but his digital credentials mirrored.

"Get over here," Suzette called. "We're boarding."

Tom didn't break stride. He fell into step beside them as though nothing had happened.

Quinn glanced at him once and understood.

"You're unbelievable," he said quietly.

Tom gave him a look that suggested he took that as praise.

Suzette didn't ask, but the tightening of her jaw said enough. Confronting him here would cost time they didn't have.

At the gate, she handed over her boarding pass without looking away from the window beyond the agent's shoulder. Somewhere out there, the plane sat waiting, impersonal and necessary.

"You know this isn't just about training anymore," Quinn said, leaning closer.

She gave a slight turn of her head. "No?"

"It hasn't been since you saw that card."

Suzette took a moment before answering. "I don't like being behind someone I can't see."

"That's not the same thing."

"It is if they stay ahead."

Tom, already halfway down the jet bridge, tore open a bag of sweets he'd produced from a pocket and looked back at them.

"Are we getting on the plane or having a conversation about our feelings?"

Quinn shook his head and followed. Suzette came last.

Once airborne, they settled into the narrow confines of their seats. The hum of the engines filled the space, constant and inescapable. Tom tore into the sweets, the bag crinkling as he ate with careless volume.

Quinn leaned toward him.

"Why are you like this?" he asked under his breath.

Tom tapped his pocket. "Extra travel money."

Quinn stared at him. "What happens if someone saw you?"

Suzette shifted in her seat and closed her eyes briefly. "Enough. I'm not listening to this all flight."

Tom muttered something just loud enough to carry. "Don't start acting like Mom."

Suzette straightened immediately. "Don't make me."

The tension tightened.

Quinn glanced toward the aisle, aware of the passengers nearby. "Can we not do this here?"

Suzette leaned back again, though the edge remained in her voice. "I don't appreciate that."

Tom shrugged, dismissive.

Quinn exhaled slowly. "I'm sorry."

The apology held long enough to keep the moment from escalating.

After a while, Suzette pulled the Daphne card from her bag and turned it between her fingers, studying it.

"We're still the best team out here," she said. "Whoever left this thinks they're ahead of us."

Her gaze sharpened.

"They're not."

Quinn's gaze stayed on her for a moment before he looked out the window.

Tom said nothing, but the smirk remained.

They settled into a quieter silence, bound more by direction than by trust.

At St. Mary's Boarding School, the dormitory had gone quiet.

Late-afternoon light stretched across the ceiling as Sam lay on his bed, staring upward, his hands folded over his stomach as though stillness might bring order to his thoughts.

It didn't.

Everything moved at once, none of it resolving.

Angela had left.

And she hadn't called him.

The door opened.

Adam stepped in with his arms full of books, already uncertain. "So… are you going to help me?"

Sam didn't sit up immediately. "Depends. Do we have a deal?"

Adam glanced toward the hallway. "Those nuns terrify me."

"Then fail," Sam said. "What do I care?"

Adam stared at him, then exhaled. "Fine. I'll do it."

Sam pushed himself upright and opened the desk drawer, handing him a notebook.

"I already did the work."

Adam flipped through it. "When?"

"Lunch."

Sam stood, his focus narrowing. "Now we need a plan."

Within minutes, they were moving quickly but quietly, shaping pillows and books beneath the blankets into something that might pass for a sleeping body. It didn't need to be convincing, only enough to delay discovery.

Every sound in the hallway made Adam tense.

"I can't do this," he whispered.

"You just have to buy me time."

Sam held out his hand. "I need the cab money."

Adam hesitated. "Why tonight?"

Sam looked down. "I got a weird voicemail from my sister."

That was enough.

Adam handed over the money.

"You owe me," he said.

"I know."

"No, I mean financially and emotionally."

Sam almost smiled.

Before leaving, his gaze swept the room once, then returned to Adam.

"If anyone asks, you haven't seen me."

"That's the plan."

Sam slipped into the hallway.

By the time he reached Angela's dorm, something was already wrong.

The room was half-empty.

"Where's Angela?" he asked.

Toni leaned against the desk. "She went after hidden treasure." She added quickly, when he didn't react, "She's okay."

"Where?"

"San Francisco."

Sam reached for his inhaler, taking a quick breath to steady himself. "She didn't call me."

"She said she would."

That didn't help.

"When did she go?"

"This morning."

Too long.

Toni stepped closer. "She looked determined. Not panicked."

But he was already moving.

His phone buzzed with messages he didn't check. He called Angela instead.

Voicemail.

"You can't just leave me behind," he said, forcing his voice steady. "Call me back."

Nothing.

He kept moving.

By the time he reached the station, he wasn't expecting her to answer. What mattered was catching up.

"San Francisco," he said at the counter.

"One way?"

"One way."

"Traveling alone?"

"Going to my mom's."

The attendant studied him for a moment, then nodded. The ticket printed, and minutes later he was on the train.

As it pulled away, the distance between him and everything familiar stretched steadily.

He didn't know what he would find. He only knew staying had stopped being possible.

He sat by the window, phone in hand, his gaze fixed on the message screen.

I'm not staying behind, Ange. You don't get to just leave me.

He sent it.

Outside, the city gave way to distance. Inside, the motion steadied him.

Somewhere ahead, Angela was moving toward the same place as Suzette, Quinn, and Tom. The thought should have made everything larger. Instead, it narrowed everything into focus.

The chase had begun, and now he was part of it.

Chapter 10: The Presidio Cipher

The fog in the Presidio was a thick, wet wool that muffled the world, turning the towering eucalyptus trees into jagged ghosts. It didn't just obscure the view. It swallowed the sound of the city, replacing the distant drone of San Francisco traffic with a heavy, dripping silence that felt centuries old. Angela adjusted the strap of her pack, her fingers numb from the damp chill. Beside her, Sam was a small, shivering shape in a borrowed fleece, his hand never straying far from the pocket where his inhaler lived. He was breathing in measured, careful sips, treating the air like something expensive.

She pulled her phone from her pocket and checked the display. The blue dot representing their position was stuttering across the screen, shredded by the canopy above. The electronic interference from the city's grid, combined with the dense mist, made the digital map a liability. It was a flickering lie. She shoved the device back into her jacket and reached for the small, brass magnetic compass she had salvaged from the hidden compartment of her mother's trunk. The metal was cold, a familiar, honest weight in her palm.

"The GPS is useless, Sam. We have to trust the needle." Angela's words dissolved in the mist, stripped of their harmonic depth by the damp air. She watched the needle settle, pointing toward a North that felt miles away from the safe, sterile corridors of the flight academy. "The notes in those weathered flight logs said the pioneer's signal was at the base of the battery, aligned with the old mail route. We need to stay on the western ridge."

Sam nodded, his face pale against the dark green of the forest. He didn't speak. He was saving his air for the climb. They started up a narrow, mud-slicked trail that wound toward the cliffs. Every few yards, Angela stopped to check their bearing. The needle didn't judder like a sensor or lag like an app. It held its place, tethered to the earth's core by a force indifferent to fog or billionaire architects. A faint, high-frequency hum sang through the brass, a subtle tension that pulled at the skin of her palms. You didn't ask the world where you were; you waited for the world to speak.

A sharp snap of a dry branch echoed from the trees behind them. Angela froze, her hand snapping to Sam's shoulder. They crouched low, slipping behind the massive, peeling trunk of a blue gum tree. Through the shifting veil of white, a flash of high-visibility blue moved along the lower trailhead. It was a man in a technical windbreaker, a radio clipped to his shoulder. He wasn't a tourist. He moved with the predatory economy of someone being paid to find something. One of Suzette's scouts. The Hunt wasn't just a race anymore. It was a pursuit.

"They're here." Sam's voice caught, his words tapering to a whisper. The words were followed by a small, suppressed cough that he smothered with his sleeve. His eyes were wide, the pupils blown dark with a mixture of fear and adrenaline. "They must have seen us at the terminal."

"They're looking for a signal, not a person." Angela leaned in, her breath warm at his ear. "They're relying on the tech. As long as we stay off the main path and keep the compass steady, we have the advantage. The fog is our cover, not theirs."

They waited until the blue shape faded into the mist before moving again. Angela led the way, scrambling up a steep embankment where the earth was a tangle of exposed roots and crumbling shale. Her boots slipped, her shins striking the hidden rocks, but she didn't slow down. The pressure was a physical thing now, a pressurized tension in her lungs that matched the narrowing of the trail. She sensed the proximity of the bridge, the massive steel structure of the Golden Gate looming somewhere above them, its foghorns groaning like dying leviathans in the distance.

They came to a clearing where the trees gave way to a series of low, concrete structures half-buried in the hillside. The bunkers were scarred with graffiti and rusted iron, relics of a war that had never quite arrived on these shores. Sam stepped forward, his hands tracing the cold, pitted surface of a gun emplacement. He seemed to be reading a language only he understood. He had spent his childhood memorizing the schematics of the past because the present was too volatile to trust.

"This is it." Sam straightened, his eyes fixing on the bunker with a sudden focus. "Battery Boutelle. It's the highest point on this ridge. The early airmail pilots used the coastal batteries as visual waypoints before the radio beacons were established. If Rex is talking about a pioneer's signal, he's talking about the light."

He pointed to a rusted iron vent protruding from the top of the bunker. Angela climbed up, her fingers catching on the jagged edges of the metal. She reached into the dark, hollow space of the vent, her hand brushing something cold and plastic. She pulled it out. It was an old military ammo can, camouflaged with a layer of matte olive paint that had begun to flake away. It weighed on her arm, a capsule of intent left behind for those who knew how to look.

Inside the can, wrapped in a piece of oiled silk, lay a vintage aviation slide rule, its yellow finish tarnished by age. Angela didn't stop to admire the ivory-colored scales; a metallic click from the trail below—the snap of a radio being keyed—sent a resonance rattling through her teeth, a cold prickle that climbed the back of her neck. She gripped the tool, her thumb catching the sliding center bar. She aligned the coordinates from the logs against the bunker's fixed bearing, the numbers clicking into place under the cursor to reveal a heading that cut away from the main path. It was the physical manifestation of the math her mother had once performed in her head, now serving as their only reliable guide through the blind white of the ridge.

"It's beautiful." Sam's fingers trembled as they reached for the sliding center bar. He was shivering harder now, the exertion of the climb catching up to him. "Look at the cursor. It's been modified."

Angela held the slide rule up to the flat, gray light. Along the edge of the glass slide, she saw it. Tiny, microscopic etchings had been carved into the transparent surface, so fine they looked like scratches until the light hit them at the right angle. They weren't just marks. They were a sequence of letters and symbols, a cipher that didn't correspond to any standard aviation chart. It was a layer of information hidden within an instrument of calculation. A secret within a tool.

"It's a key." A sudden scent of ozone seemed to flare in the damp air, and a weightless float settled in Angela's stomach. "The coordinates we found in the logs were just the lock. This is how we read the next stage. Rex isn't just giving us a map. He's giving us a curriculum."

A thin, metallic whistle underscored Sam's next breath—a warning rather than a collapse. He stopped, one hand pressed hard to his sternum, the other already going into his jacket. He didn't wait for the world to narrow. He pulled the inhaler out, shaking it with a focused intensity that was more sobering than panic. Angela dropped the slide rule into her bag and was at his side in a second, her hand hovering near his back, giving him the space to manage the rhythm. He took the dose, his eyes squeezed shut in the damp air, and held it. He didn't double over; he stood rigid, a small figure anchored to the concrete, fighting a private war with the fog. After a moment, his shoulders dropped an inch. The whistle subsided, smoothed over by the medicine before it could turn into a scream of the lungs. He met her eyes, his face pale and damp with mist, but his gaze steady.

The fog continued to drip from the trees, indifferent to the small, human crisis unfolding beneath them. The world didn't stop because a child couldn't breathe. It only waited to see if he would get back up. Angela watched him, her eyes stinging with a sudden, sharp anger. She looked at the rusted bunker and the hidden ammo can, then at the bag where the slide rule lay hidden. This was the cost. It wasn't just her mother's legacy or her father's pride. It was Sam. He was twelve years old, and she was dragging him across a landscape of ruins and rivals because she didn't know how to exist without a goal to fly toward.

"I'm okay." Sam's thumb was white against the strap. He pushed himself back, his gaze anchoring on hers with a stubborn, fierce intelligence. "Don't look at me like that, Ang. I'm not going back. We found it. We found the cipher."

"You're exhausted, Sam. We need to get you out of this dampness." Angela tightened her grip on his shoulder, masking the tremor in her hands. She helped him stand, keeping her arm around his waist. He felt light, a frame of balsa wood covered in silk. "We have the rule. We'll find a place to study it once we're on the ferry. But no more climbing today. That's a pilot's order."

He nodded, leaning into her strength. They began the slow descent back toward the road, moving with a caution that felt like a retreat. The fog was beginning to lift, revealing the massive orange towers of the bridge as they tore through the clouds like the ribs of a giant. It was a beautiful, terrifying sight, a symbol of a city that had been built on the edge of the world.

As they reached the trailhead, Angela looked back one last time. The blue-jacketed scout was nowhere to be seen, but she knew he was still there, somewhere in the white void, waiting for a signal. She reached into her bag and touched the smooth, cold surface of the slide rule. It was a piece of the past, a tool for a future she couldn't yet see. She had the key, but as she felt Sam's uneven step beside her, she realized the lock was far more complicated than she had ever imagined.

The sky was still waiting, but for the first time, it felt less like a promise and more like a threat. Angela tightened her grip on her brother and stepped out of the trees, leaving the ghosts of the Presidio behind to find the iron gates of Alcatraz.

Chapter 11: The Island and the Theft

The coordinates for the Apex Hunt terminated in San Francisco.

Her bank balance was a static, mocking eight dollars and forty-two cents, a number that hadn't moved since the desert. The only thing keeping her upright was the three hundred dollars in cash she'd salvaged from the sale of the variometer in Arizona—a thin stack of bills meant to act as a buffer against the city's predatory gate fees and the constant, nickel-and-diming friction of the road.

The coordinates led deeper into the city. The pavement hummed with a low-frequency friction that prickled the base of her neck, a restless weight keeping her on edge. Traffic surged and stalled in uneven rhythms, buses hissed at curbs, and voices overlapped along crowded sidewalks in a mix of languages and tones that changed block by block. The city unfolded in dense, shifting patterns, but the logic of the coordinates grounded her every step.

Unlike the sparse reaches of Arizona, the city demanded a constant, pressing attention. There, distance did most of the work. Here, nearness did. Buildings pressed close, people crossed in front of one another without warning, and signals changed in rapid, stuttering shifts; the system relied on the necessity of split-second adjustments to avoid disaster. The adjustment grated. The sidewalk's restless flow ignored her; the city's impatience cared nothing for her belonging.

She boarded a streetcar and wrapped one hand around the metal pole. As it lurched into its climb, the cable's rhythmic pull brought a hollow float to her stomach, steadying her through the shift in balance.

Quick, unstable glimpses of the city slid past—storefronts, intersections, bursts of color, people in coats despite the time of year, a cyclist cutting between lanes as if traffic laws were merely advisory. Images dissolved before they could take shape. Faint reflections layered the windows, merging interior and exterior into a single shifting image.

The air sharpened near the ferry terminal. Signal bars ebbed on her phone as the city's network thinned at the bay's edge. Salt and diesel rode a wind colder and heavier than any in the desert, moving without its dry clarity. Wide and gray, the water shifted in heavy patterns beneath an overcast sky that muted the world. In the distance, Alcatraz rose from the bay, fixed and self-contained, its outline belonging to another time.

Angela stopped. The island loomed.

On the page, the clue for the Apex Hunt had carried a certain cleverness. Out here, it carried weight.

As she stepped onto the ferry, her pulse quickened and possibility narrowed to a hard, bright edge.

A spot near the side rail offered space to keep one hand on the bag at her shoulder as the ferry pulled away. Tourists clustered at the windows, their loud talk of prison lore ringing thin and distant. The island ahead and the folded paper in her pocket demanded her focus. There, the clue waited to justify her journey or expose the frailty of her assumptions.

The wind sharpened as the ferry pulled away, cutting through her jacket. She drew her jacket closer and glanced once back at the city, already softened by fog, then turned toward Alcatraz again and let the ferry carry her forward.

A dense stillness clung to the island. It wasn't silent—too many tourists moved through the halls—but the sound was trapped by the thick concrete walls. The flow of visitors pulled her through narrow corridors where footsteps echoed on concrete and aging paint. Fragmented voices from guided tours drifted past—dates, names, escape attempts—history survived only as clipped narratives, carrying more force as warnings than as stories. Somewhere deeper in the building, a metal door slammed, and the sound carried farther than it should have, stripping the air of softness for several seconds.

The farther she went, the more the place resisted being just another stop on a map.

A damp chill filled the cell blocks. Light failed in the corridors, leaving the far ends in deep shadow. Visitors moved with instinctive restraint, their voices dropping to a hush.

The crowd's momentum carried Angela only as far as the first corridor.

Deeper into the prison, the coordinates led to a row of identical cells. She slowed. The dimness of the cells gave way. Rusted bars, narrow bunks, small shelves, metal toilets fixed into corners with nothing but function in mind. Sameness met her everywhere, offering resistance instead of guidance.

Nothing stood out.

She made a second, slower pass. She searched the doorframes and the dust-heavy corners beneath the bunks. The shadows yielded nothing.

Still nothing.

Her jaw tightened, shoulders rising with the urge to move faster, to force a solution through momentum alone. Her initial momentum thinned, eclipsed by the weight of a misunderstood clue.

She stepped back and pressed her lips together, forcing herself to stop before impatience turned into carelessness.

Rushing wouldn't help.

She reached into her pocket and unfolded the paper.

THE BIRDMAN OF ALCATRAZ.

She read it once.

Then again.

This time, she stopped forcing an answer and waited for the words to settle.

"The Birdman." Angela let the name hang in the heavy air.

The answer separated itself, a quiet shift. It wasn't the prison or the cell, or even the confinement itself. It was what remained attached to it, the legacy bound to his name rather than the place where he had been kept.

She turned.

A sharp turn led back through the corridors, a retreat into the open air. Wind and the cry of seabirds cut through the silence of the prison. The path led downward, the uneven pavement of the northern slope meeting her boots as fog rolled over the ridge and swallowed the lighthouse.

The island dissolved into partial views and shifting edges. She strode past tourists lingering at plaques. Self-consciousness flared and vanished; pretending she was here for anything else was pointless.

Tucked below the main paths, the sanctuary sat visible but easy to overlook.

Angela stopped.

Birds moved through the enclosure in restless patterns, some lifting in a startled rush while others circled or settled again, the motion constant without ever resolving into stillness. Her pace slowed, a cautious approach intended to leave the birds undisturbed. Weathered boards and fencing lined the perimeter. The wind shifted, bringing the sharp scent of salt, wood, and feathers.

Under the damp weight of the fog, the search stretched on.

The birds kept moving, and the fog warped the world. Nothing held steady.

Yellow ink bled into a weathered barricade, forming a sequence of coordinates just outside the direct line of sight—easy to miss, impossible to ignore.

Her hands steadied, the frantic edge of her pulse easing into something more controlled.

She stepped closer, committing the numbers to memory before reaching for her notebook.

Behind her, the birds startled upward, their wings striking the air in a rush that broke the moment's stillness. She turned halfway, alert; nothing moved beyond the shifting flock.

Still, the sound carried.

She inked the coordinates with precise strokes, checked them once, then again, and closed the notebook.

A sudden, sharp weight in the air—the discordant pressure of another presence nearby—drove her toward the exit.

From a distance, Suzette lowered her binoculars.

A flash of blue had been enough. Now, with the details clear, recognition clicked.

Angela.

"I know who our Daphne is." Suzette handed the binoculars to Quinn.

He adjusted them and followed her line of sight, tracking Angela's movement while Tom leaned in beside him.

"So she's the one." Tom leaned in at the railing.

Suzette nodded. "She's been ahead of us since Arizona."

Quinn tracked her through the lenses, his knuckles whitening on the frame. "Then she's better than lucky."

Tom shifted his weight. "We taking it from her now or later?"

"Later." The ferry's wake churned white on the gray bay.

They didn't move closer.

Every tracked movement deepened their advantage.

Every minute spent watching her bought them time.

If Angela had already solved the Great Meridian stage of the Apex Hunt, there was no reason to interrupt her before she reached the Latitude Run.

"She'll realize eventually." Tom turned from the railing.

"Then we make sure it's too late when she does." Suzette didn't turn from the shoreline.

Quinn lowered the binoculars and studied her. "You know her well enough to predict her?"

"Well enough." Angela's silhouette stood out on the distant deck. "She's disciplined, but she's focused on the horizon. She won't see the hand in her pocket until the doors are already closing."

Tom smiled. "Convenient."

Suzette didn't return it. "Only if we're better."

Quinn turned once more toward Angela. "Then let's be better."

The fog thickened as Angela boarded the return ferry, softening the island to a ghost of an outline. The wind sharpened, driving cold through her jacket.

She sat near the railing and wrote the new coordinates into her notebook again, the repetition grounding her. One version. Then another in the margin.

Her phone buzzed in her pocket.

Sam.

The screen glowed, her thumb hovering.

She should answer.

But the conversation was already unfolding, and she didn't have room for it yet, not while the coordinates were still fresh or the next stage still taking shape.

She slipped the phone back into her pocket and stood, drawn toward the railing as the ferry pulled away. The city flickered through the fog in gray fragments. The water's rhythmic sway steadied her, anchoring her thoughts.

As the ferry neared the terminal, the crowd drifted toward the gangway in a slow, dense tide. Angela kept her hand near her shoulder strap, her focus on the approaching skyline. The fog gave them cover. Quinn moved first, his steps unremarkable, blending into the flow of passengers.

In the sudden bottleneck of the exit, he brushed past her—a firm, anonymous contact. With the practiced grace of a shadow, his fingers found the side-zip of her bag, a movement shielded by the drape of his own coat. Quinn palmed the GPS in a heartbeat. He didn't glance back. He found Suzette and Tom near the stern and held the device out. Suzette took it, turning it once in her hand.

"This is what she's using."

Tom leaned in. "So now we are too."

Suzette nodded. "Now we're ahead."

By the time the ferry bumped on the pilings, Angela's hand went to secure the device. Fingers met only an open zipper and cold air. Panic flared, a hard thrum that vibrated through her teeth, cold and metallic. She tore through the bag in a frantic, escalating search—the GPS had vanished.

She spun, but the deck and the passengers moving for the exit offered no clue. Her pulse hammered, her focus splintering as the world moved too fast. The thief had taken the one thing that mattered. A calculated strike; they knew the device's value. Eyes had tracked her from the start.

She dug deep into her bag, searching for any other loss, and her hand brushed a photograph tucked into the notebook's sleeve. A fresh crease marred one corner. She picked it up. Her breath caught. The image held her.

Her phone rang.

This time, she answered.

"Hello?"

"Where are you?" Sam's voice was a brittle wire over the line.

"San Francisco."

"I know. Me too."

Angela froze. "What?"

"I mean where in San Francisco?"

She stood, the movement jarring the phone at her ear. "What do you mean you're here? How did you get here? Is Dad with you?"

"No. I took the train."

"What were you thinking?"

A pause, then, "I wasn't going to stay at school by myself."

Despite everything, a small breath escaped her that almost became a laugh.

"I'm getting off the ferry from Alcatraz."

"Good. The sign is right here. Don't move."

She shook her head, a faint smile breaking through.

Of course he was already there.

She gathered her things, cinched the strap of her bag, and moved toward the exit.

They found each other near the entrance.

She crossed the distance and pulled him into a tight embrace before she could stop herself.

"You are in so much trouble." Angela didn't let go of him.

"I was going to tell you I was running away." Sam looked at his boots. "Then you beat me to it."

Her expression shifted. "What about Dad?"

"He probably doesn't know yet."

"That's not funny."

"I couldn't stay there."

He stood before her, a study in exhaustion.

"You have to go back."

"Only if we go back together."

"I can't. I found the next coordinates for the Apex Hunt."

She showed him the notebook.

Sam frowned. "Where's the GPS?"

"Someone took it."

Surprise didn't touch his face. Instead, he swung his backpack around, revealing a tangle of charging cables and the slim, dark weight of a tablet he'd liberated from the school's tech lab. He pulled a folded paper map from the mess and spread it between them.

"A map doesn't need a signal." Sam spread the paper on the bench. "And the tablet can act as our new GPS once I find a way to power it up. I also have the Milestone Credit—the four hundred Rex authorized for clearing the island. Combined with the legacy miles Mom left behind, we can move. The credit handles the international taxes and terminal fees that usually keep those miles grounded."

Angela's gaze sharpened. "That's a corporate leash, Sam. Blood money."

"It's a tiny unlock." He met her eyes. "We use it to get to the next stage, then we wait for the next drop. We use his money to beat him."

"Then we establish a ledger," Angela said, her voice hardening with a sudden, pragmatic focus. "The miles get us the seats, but the credit handles the heavy lifting—the predatory fees and the fuel surcharges. That's the corporate leash; every time we clear a terminal, they see our location. For the food, the local rooms, and the things that keep us off the grid, we use the cash—the three hundred I have left from the variometer and the cab money you've been hoarding. We'll have to sell the tablet or the spare optics once we land. We buy the distance with Rex's crumbs, but we buy our invisibility with our own. We keep the two pools separate, Sam, or we won't make it past the first border."

With the map lying open between them, she turned back to him. For the first time since the ferry, the next step was possible again.

"You brought all this from boarding school?" The tangle of electronics drew her gaze.

"I didn't want to get lost trying to find you." Sam gestured to his backpack. "And we'd need more than a phone if things got complicated."

That made her smile.

Then his expression shifted. "You're really okay?"

She hesitated. "Mostly."

"That's not an answer."

"It's the one you're getting."

He accepted it.

"Fine. But no more disappearing."

"Then no more taking trains across states without telling anyone."

"That depends." Sam waited for her nod. "Are you going to keep doing this without me?"

"Probably."

"Then we understand each other."

They bent over the map together while the city moved around them. Then Angela straightened. The scale of the Latitude Run loomed. "We have to move. Not just to the next block, Sam. We're heading east. Way east."

The journey that followed was a grueling exercise in endurance, a sequence of blurred departures fueled by the pittance of the 'Milestone Credits'—those sterile digital vouchers that absorbed the terminal fees and fuel surcharges that their legacy miles didn't cover—and the hollow patience of the standby list. They landed in Paris exhausted. Ten days remained, the morning sun glaring through the terminal glass. The air inside Charles de Gaulle was stale, smelling of jet fuel and recycled oxygen, and a headache throbbed behind Angela's eyes.

They drifted toward the RER station, their movements sluggish and imprecise. At the ticket kiosk, the screen was a blur of French. Focus fractured; her fingers fumbled as the line behind them grew. A man leaned against a pillar twenty paces away, the shadow of a low cap swallowing his face. He held perfectly still, watching them through the reflection of a shop window.

The air thickened with the metallic tang of ozone, a sudden static charge that raised the fine hairs on her arms. He lifted a hand to his ear, a subtle, practiced motion—a predator closing a circuit.

'Move,' she whispered, her voice cracking.

She gripped Sam's sleeve, hauling him toward the platform just as a train screeched to a halt. The doors hissed shut, leaving the man behind, a silent sentinel receding into the gloom. The near-miss sent a jolt of ice through her veins, a reminder that their delirium was a vulnerability being measured in real-time.

They lost the first night to a cramped cabin over the Atlantic, and the second to a frantic dash through Venice, where they paused only long enough to verify the meridian on the damp stone of the city's heart. The twenty-hour marathon toward Darwin fractured what remained of their internal clocks. On the third day of transit, the sun rose twice—once over the Mediterranean and again over the Indian Ocean—turning the cabin into a grey, airless purgatory. By the time they reached the final leg toward Sydney, the equator faded into memory and the clock winnowed their remaining time to seven days.

They weren't just traveling; the horizon locked in their vision as they outran their own collapse on the fumes of sheer momentum.

Chapter 12: The Shadow of the Golden Gate

The fog didn't just sit over the water; it owned it. It moved in thick, wet lungfuls, swallowing the base of the pylons until the Golden Gate Bridge seemed to float without a foundation. From the overlook, the orange steel was a series of geometric ghosts. Angela stood with her hands deep in her jacket pockets, her fingers tracing the cold rim of her mother's silver locket. The air here was heavy, tasting of salt and old machinery, a sharp departure from the thin, scorched oxygen of the Arizona desert. It felt like a physical weight, a pressure that signaled the end of the world they knew and the beginning of something unmapped.

Beside her, Sam was a small, restless shadow. He wasn't looking at the bridge. He was hunched over the tablet they had bartered for, his face illuminated by the harsh blue glow of the screen. The light made his skin look translucent, highlighting the dark circles beneath his eyes that had deepened since they left the Presidio. His thumb hovered over the Apex portal, the interface a clean, predatory grid of data and maps. A notification sat at the top of the screen like a digital taunt.

Initial Stipend: $250.00 USD. Status: Active.

"He's watching us," Sam said. His voice was small, nearly lost beneath a low-frequency hum that seemed to pull at the fine hairs on her arms. "The second I logged into the transit terminal, the funds cleared. It's an advance, Ang—two hundred and fifty dollars. We don't get the next drop until we hit the first waypoint in Paris. It wasn't a bank transfer; it was an unlock."

Angela looked away from the bridge and toward the screen. The digits on the screen seemed to shimmer, a sum that felt too heavy for the thin air of the overlook. In the hangar, two hundred and fifty dollars was a set of tires or a week of groceries. Out here, against the scale of a global hunt, it was a pittance—a handful of crumbs meant to lead them from one trap to the next. It was a digital leash. Angela ran the mental ledger, a grim calculation of their remaining autonomy. The three hundred dollars from the sale of the variometer had already been thinned by gate fees and the ride from the Presidio, leaving Sam with a small roll of untraceable cab money for the gaps in the grid. Her own bank account, with its mocking balance of eight dollars and forty-two cents, was a rounding error. They were surviving on Carlisle's charity now; every time they used the credit for a baguette in Paris or a train ticket in Venice, a server in a Carlisle Industries basement would strobe with their coordinates.

"It's a tracking beacon," Angela said. Her voice remained level, but her fingers tightened on the silver locket in her pocket, the cold metal a hard, unyielding pressure on her skin. "He isn't just funding the trip. He's mapping the trajectory."

Sam clicked his inhaler, the sharp, plastic sound echoing off the concrete wall of the overlook. "Suzette's team won't be using the portal credits. They have corporate backing. They'll be moving through private accounts, ghosting the system while we're lighting up the map like a flare."

He turned the tablet toward her, showing a schematic he had been laboring over. It was a breakdown of the inertial reference unit they had traded earlier. The lines were jagged, filled with Sam's handwritten annotations. "The gear we're taking, the stuff from Mom's old kits, it's all analog, Ang. If the altitude sensors on the flight to Paris are calibrated for modern avionics, our scavenged tech might not even sync. We're flying on hardware that belongs in a museum."

Angela reached out, resting a hand on his shoulder. Through the fabric of his thrifted hoodie, she could feel the rigid line of his shoulders, a tremor that reminded her of a plane caught in a crosswind. "It's not about the sync, Sam. It's about the truth of the air. Mom didn't need a digital interface to tell her when she was losing lift. She felt it in the floorboards."

She looked back at the bridge. The massive cables were held in a state of perpetual agony, a balance of tension and compression that kept the whole structure from collapsing into the bay. It was a masterclass in controlled stress. That was what they were now, she realized. They were the suspension cables, stretched to their limit between the life they had abandoned and the one they were trying to buy back.

"The bridge doesn't move because it's stiff," Angela said, her voice dropping into the register she used when they were pre-flighting a bird. "It moves because it's balanced. We do the same. We use his money because we have to, but we don't trust the map it gives us. We trust the compass."

Sam looked up at her, his eyes searching hers for the same hairline fracture in her resolve that he felt in his own. He found only the unwavering, horizon-fixed stare of a pilot who had already committed to the dive. He sighed, a jagged sound that ended in a small wheeze. "The flight leaves in four hours. International terminal. We have to clear customs with a suitcase full of vintage avionics and a brass sextant. They're going to think we're either crazy or dangerous."

"We're both," Angela said. Heat rose into her face, tightening her jaw as she lifted her chin. "That's why we're still in the hunt."

The wind shifted, bringing the smell of diesel from a passing tanker far below in the shipping lane. It was a heavy, industrial scent that reminded her of the hangar, of her father's grease-stained hands and the stack of liquidation papers on the kitchen table. The $250 credit wouldn't stop the auction, and it certainly wouldn't stop the rot. Only the prize could do that. Only the end of the line.

"Mike's going to find out," Sam whispered. "He's going to see the account activity eventually. He's a ranger, Ang. He knows how to follow a trail."

"Let him follow it," she replied. "By the time he catches up, we'll be over the Atlantic. He can't ground us if he can't reach the cockpit."

The mention of their father sent her stomach into a cold, weightless float, the kind of hollow gravity that comes when the engines cough and die. She could almost see him standing in the empty hangar, the fatigue etching deep lines into his face as he realized the keys to the Jeep were gone. He would be looking for the maintenance logs, looking for some explanation for why his children had vanished into the fog. He wouldn't find it in the books. The only record of where they were going was written in the ciphers Sam was currently decrypting and the sensory memory of a woman who had died in the dirt of a desert she loved too much.

Sam shut down the tablet, the blue light vanishing and leaving them in the grainy orange glow of the bridge's lamps. "The Presidio scout saw us, Ang. If they're already in San Francisco, they'll be at the airport. Suzette isn't going to let us just walk onto a plane to Paris."

"She won't have a choice," Angela said. She stepped away from the railing, her boots striking the pavement with a finality that ignored the way the cold iron bit into her palms; she swallowed, her throat suddenly dry. "They're professionals, Sam. They play by the rules of the race. We're playing by the rules of survival. It's a different kind of math."

Her gaze lifted to the orange towers one last time. They were leaving the soil of the only country they had ever known, crossing a boundary that couldn't be repaired with a simple return flight. The Golden Gate was a gate in truth, a threshold that demanded a price for passage. For Angela, the price was the safety of her father's silence and the comfort of the Arizona horizon. For Sam, it was the fragile stability of his health and the predictable logic of his schoolbooks.

"Get the bags," Angela said. "We're done searching."

Sam nodded, stuffing the tablet into his pack with a determined jerk of his arm. He adjusted the strap, his small frame seeming even thinner beside the massive engineering feat behind him. He might have passed for a child playing at a man's game, but when he met her eyes, his expression held a precision that belonged to someone much older. He was a Santiago, and the Santiagos didn't fear distance. They feared the ground.

They walked back toward the rented car, their shadows stretching long and thin across the overlook. The city's collective drone shuddered behind them, a pressurized engine of millions of lives, none of which mattered to the coordinates they were following. As they drove away, the bridge vanished into the fog, leaving only the memory of its orange glow and the weight of the digital leash tightening around their necks. The air in the car was silent, save for the way the inhaler's seal gnawed at the quiet—a plastic heartbeat drumming through the cabin.

The transition across the Atlantic was less a journey and more a slow, pressurized erosion of the self. By the time they reached the RER station beneath Charles de Gaulle, the world was a smear of fluorescent light and damp concrete. Ten days remained, a number that burned behind Angela's eyes with every throb of the leaden fatigue that comes from fifteen hours of recycled oxygen. Beside her, Sam was a ghost of himself, his breathing sounding like dry leaves skittering over pavement, his small frame taut with the electric tension of a delirium that made every footstep a feat of will.

At the ticket kiosks, the crowd was a churning tide of wool coats and cutting elbows. Angela fumbled with the terminal, her fingers thick and clumsy as she tried to navigate the French prompts. The load of her pack—laden with the brass sextant and the jagged, analog remnants of her mother's flight kits—seemed to double with every passing minute. As they came to the turnstiles, a man in a charcoal overcoat moved with a sudden, predatory efficiency, clipping Sam's shoulder. The boy stumbled, his bag swinging wide and the dense metal gear inside clanging on the barrier with a resonance that hummed through her nerves at a jagged, metallic frequency.

The man didn't offer a traveler's apology. He paused, his gaze dropping to the bag, then snapping up to Angela's face with a calculation that was too cold for a commuter. In that heartbeat, the haze of exhaustion vanished, replaced by a jagged spike of adrenaline. It was the same stillness she'd seen from the scout at the Presidio. She didn't wait; she gripped Sam's collar and hauled him through the gate, the metal bars catching her hip as they dove toward the platform. They threw themselves into the closing doors of the blue line train, the smell of ozone and old electricity swallowing them as the station slid away, leaving the man in charcoal a dwindling, motionless silhouette on the tile.

Chapter 13: Market Street Scramble

Market Street smelled of ozone and damp asphalt. The noise was a pressurized current; Sam's hands spasmed on the straps of his backpack; he swallowed as his pulse drove a sharp, uneven rhythm more piercing than the ozone. The San Francisco fog had descended into the canyon of buildings, mixing with the heat of the tech bazaar to create a humid, electric soup. Sam adjusted the straps of his backpack, aware of the load of the tablets and chargers. He pressed his hand to the hard, plastic lump of his inhaler in his pocket, checking it was there for the tenth time that hour.

Beside him, Angela moved with a coiled, kinetic energy, her gaze cutting through the crowd for a break in the pattern. She didn't watch the neon signs or the throngs of commuters; instead, her index finger gave a minute, rhythmic twitch on her strap, an instinctive adjustment for a breeze that hadn't yet rounded the corner. She navigated the bazaar by the pressure of the crowd's wake, her body angling into the slipstreams as if reading an invisible thermal.

Sam shouldered past a row of hollowed-out servers that leaned like skeletal remains on bins of tangled fiber-optic cables, keeping pace with Angela as she wove through the maze. The bazaar was a digital reef where the husks of the last decade's innovations went to die, and the high-pitched whine of cooling fans vibrated through Sam's teeth with every step.

Here, the noise was a wall, a low-frequency thrum of a thousand conversations that made the silence of the Arizona hangar feel like a memory of another life.

"Keep your head down." Angela leaned in, her voice lost beneath the rhythmic clatter of a nearby mechanical keyboard. "We find the collector, we drop the sensor, and we get to the terminal. We don't have time for a tour."

Sam nodded, his jaw working as a hard knot of muscle jumped at his cheekbone, and kept his eyes fixed on the cracked screen of his phone. The green dot for the cache was twitching on Sam's phone, flickering and uncertain. Every time they passed a transformer, the signal buckled, the connection fraying until the screen froze. "If this thing drops signal one more time," Sam muttered, his thumb jamming the refresh button, "I'm throwing it into the creek." The tracker his mom had salvaged was struggling with the interference, the icon stuttering against the canyon walls. To a normal geocacher, it was a trophy. To the man they were meeting, it was a missing piece of a vintage flight simulator. To the Santiagos, it was two tickets to Paris.

The green dot finally settled as they reached a stall built into the gutted fuselage of an old cargo plane. Angela stepped over a discarded landing strut, her hand trailing over the cold, riveted skin of the craft as they searched for the collector's mark. Tucked behind a stack of ancient cathode-ray monitors, a man sat with his fingers dancing over a tablet. He didn't look up as they approached the makeshift hatch, his eyes narrowing behind thick, rectangular frames as if he'd forgotten what the sun felt like.

"You're late." The man didn't look up, his voice thin and dry like old parchment. "The market moves. Prices don't stay still for laggards."

Angela didn't flinch. She reached into her bag and pulled out the sensor, setting it on the counter made from a salvaged wing-flap with a deliberate, metallic click. She didn't recite the serial numbers or the history she'd found in her mother's logs. Instead, she pulled a circular flight computer from her pocket and spun the silver disks, calculating the unit's accuracy against the collector's readout. She used the slide rule to bridge the gap between salvage and survival, her fingers moving with a mechanical precision as she proved the machine's worth.

"It's a 702," Angela said, her palm flat over the metal as if checking for a heartbeat. "Gyros are true. You won't find another one this side of the Mojave."

Leaning forward until his nose was inches from the metal, the collector studied the device. He reached out to touch it, but Angela pulled her hand back just enough to keep it out of reach. The man let out a short, wet laugh. He looked at Angela, then at Sam, measuring the dust on their jackets and the tired lines around their eyes. He knew they were running. He just didn't know what they were running toward.

"It's worth five hundred." The man's eyes didn't leave the metal. "Maybe six if the ports aren't corroded."

"It's worth fifteen hundred." Angela leaned over the counter, her shadow cutting across his screen. "You have a buyer in Tokyo who's been waiting months for this serial number. I know how your manifests work. I grew up in a hangar, not a cubicle."

Sam stepped back, letting the technical jargon wash over him. He found a corner where the signal didn't drop every five seconds and flipped open his tablet, leaning his shoulder against the riveted aluminum of the fuselage. While Angela fought for their survival, Sam went looking for the ghost in the machine. He navigated the bazaar's firewall with frantic, muscle-memory precision, his thumbs dancing over the glass with a desperate fluency. He wasn't looking for shortcuts or easy answers anymore; he was hunting for the digital footprints of Rex St. James.

Formidable as it appeared, the Carlisle Industries server was a fortress that possessed a service entrance. Sam dug through the company's boring money files, his heart thumping in his ears. He found a tab for 'Acquisitions' and spotted a list of GPS numbers. He knew those numbers by heart. They were the markers for home.

A hollow opened in Sam's chest as he leaned on the stall's metal skin, his eyes fixed on a digital contract dated three years ago. It wasn't just a land survey; it was a predatory buyout plan bearing the signature of Harrison St. James, Rex's father. He scrolled through the maps, realizing their land sat on a vein of lithium—a score the Carlisle empire had been eyeing for years. To them, the soaring school was just an obstacle to be cleared, a thin layer of history masking the wealth beneath the red dirt.

A cold weight dropped in Sam's gut as his hands spasmed on the edges of the tablet. The Hunt wasn't just a game; it was a final, cruel vetting process for Rex, and they were participating in their own liquidation. His attention shifted to Angela, who still held her stalemate with the collector. She stood with her chin set and her shoulders squared, but she was small beside the corporate machinery he saw on the screen.

"Sam." Angela's voice broke through his spiral. She didn't wait for him to look at his phone; she was spinning the disks on her flight computer again, her eyes tracking the alignment of the scales. "Is twelve hundred enough for the baggage fees and the shuttle?"

Sam closed the tab, his fingers shook. He forced his voice to remain steady. He couldn't tell her yet. If she knew they were already losing the ground beneath their feet, she might stop flying. He needed her to keep her eyes on the sky.

"We're still four hundred short," Sam said, his voice thinned, brittle with exhaustion. "That's... that's a gap we can't close in time." His gaze drifted to their bags, then to the headsets clipped to the straps. They were high-end Bose units, the ones their mother had bought them for their first solo flights. They were more than gear. They were the way they heard the world when everything else was too loud.

Angela followed his gaze. She looked at the headsets for a long time. The silence between them was a heavy, unyielding weight. Angela didn't look up, her gaze fixed on the worn leather of the ear cushions as she pushed the headsets across the brushed aluminum counter. She reached down, unclipped the headsets, and laid them on the counter next to the sensor. The leather ear cushions were worn smooth from use, holding the shape of their heads and the echo of a thousand radio calls.

"These too." Angela met the collector's stare, her voice a jagged edge. "Everything. Just give us the cash."

The collector's eyes narrowed, catching the neon light behind his thick frames, and he offered no further argument. He reached under the counter and pulled out a stack of hundred-dollar bills, counting them out with a dry, rhythmic snap of paper. The paper was crisp and smelled of ink and old pockets. Angela took the money and shoved it into her jacket without looking at it. She turned away from the counter before the man could pick up the headsets. She didn't want to see him touch them.

"Angela, look—guards." Sam signaled toward the entrance of the warehouse with a sharp jerk of his chin. "They're scanning the crowd like they're looking for a stall in the pattern. If they spot us, we're grounded. We have to move." A group of men in dark, tactical jackets had just entered. They weren't tourists or traders. They moved with a synchronized, purposeful gait that Sam had seen in security footage of Carlisle's private firms. They were checking IDs, their eyes scanning the faces in the crowd with the cold focus of a searchlight.

Angela grabbed Sam's arm, pulling him into the shadows behind a row of server racks. As the guards fanned out, she fished her circular flight computer from her pocket once more. She didn't check a screen; she spun the silver disks by touch, calculating the remaining weight-fees for their gear against the stack of cash in her jacket. She needed to know if they could even afford the gate fees before the searchlights found them. She didn't look back. They ducked through the shadows of the warehouse. The smell of burning solder and old plastic was thick here, a stifling shroud. Sam felt the phantom itch of a tightening chest and reached for his inhaler before the sensation could bloom. He took a quick, quiet hit and dragged the medication deep into his lungs, refusing to let his body become the thing that slowed them down.

They found a side exit that led into a narrow alleyway choked with trash and the hum of industrial air conditioners. The transition from the bazaar's neon glow to the gray light of the alley hit Sam like a plunge into freezing water. Angela kept running, her boots splashing through puddles of oily water. They didn't stop until they reached the mouth of the alley, where the street opened up into the chaotic flow of Market Street once again.

"They're following us, aren't they?" Sam's voice thinned, his heart thudding in his ribs in a frantic, uneven rhythm. "I can't make us disappear, Angela. It's like we're trim-locked. We're just a signature on a sweep, and I can't find the ceiling. My hands won't stop shaking."

"It doesn't matter." Angela stepped into the street to flag down a passing taxi, her movements sharp and jagged. She threw their bags into the back seat and pushed Sam inside before climbing in after him. "We have the money. We have the coordinates. The rest of it is just noise."

Merging into the river of traffic, the taxi pulled away from the curb. Sam looked out the back window. The men in the dark jackets were standing on the sidewalk, their figures shrinking as the car accelerated. They didn't chase. They just watched, their presence a lingering promise of a confrontation they had only postponed.

Sam looked at his hands. They were empty. No headsets, no connection to the air, just the cold weight of the tablet in his lap. He thought about the files he had seen, the signatures of the men who wanted their desert land. He looked at Angela, who was staring out the window at the fog-shrouded peaks of the city. She was holding the gold coin in her pocket, her thumb tracing the rim in a relentless loop.

Though the city functioned as a trap, the sky remained an exit. They were flying toward Paris on a budget of sacrifice and secrets. Sam leaned his head against the cold glass of the window, watching the streetlights blur into long, distorted lines of yellow and white. He realized then that the Hunt wasn't about finding a treasure. It was about seeing who was left standing when the world stripped everything else away.

Looming against the gray horizon, the airport appeared as a cluster of white lights in the distance. It was a gateway to a world they couldn't afford, drawing power from a legacy they were losing. Sam closed his eyes and tried to remember the sound of the wind through the cockpit, back when the sky was theirs to breathe for free and the ground was a choice rather than a threat.

A dense stillness filled the taxi. Only the rhythmic, metallic click of Angela's thumb against the coin's gold rim broke the hush.

Chapter 14: Beneath the Lanterns

Grant Avenue opened before them in a wash of color and movement.

Angela and Sam passed beneath the ornate gate marking the entrance to Chinatown, its carved details rising high above the street with a presence, ornate and ceremonial. The structure framed the shift from one part of the city to another; stepping beneath it was less a crossing of an intersection and more an entry into a space governed by a different tempo. Stone lions stood on either side, their expressions fixed and watchful, as though they had spent decades observing one generation after another pass beneath the same arch without ever needing to move.

"Mom would have loved this." Angela stopped beneath the gate, looking up at the carved details.

The thought came without effort, and because of that it landed harder. Maria would have looked up first, taking in the gate before anything else, lingering to catch the details everyone else missed. She would have wanted to know the history of the lions, the names of the streets, what festival was happening and why, and she would have bought too much food from different stalls because choosing only one was a kind of failure.

Sam glanced up at the lanterns overhead, then at the crowds moving beneath them. "She would've talked to everyone."

Angela's smile held, thin but real. "And somehow all of them would've answered."

Beyond the gate, the street unfolded into something louder, brighter, and thick with life. Lanterns stretched overhead in long strands, their red surfaces catching the afternoon light and shifting in tone each time the breeze moved them. The air carried incense, fried dough, roasted meat, sugar, oil, something floral, something unfamiliar and sharp, all of it layered together until it became impossible to separate one scent from another. The Autumn Moon Festival filled every available space, pressing people together into a slow-moving current of color, sound, and motion.

Music drifted in from somewhere ahead, then gave way to a burst of cheering before settling again beneath the larger hum of voices. Nothing about the street was still; it breathed with a heavy, restless intent.

Sam slowed, his gaze flickering over the pressing crowd. His shoulders tightened. He was in his own clothes now—a thrifted hoodie and worn jeans—having left the starched expectation of his school uniform in a trash bin back in Sausalito, but his chest was a cage a size too small. It was the same claustrophobia that hit whenever Mike spoke of the academy. His breathing shifted. The hitch in his ribs would have stayed hidden to anyone else, but she had been tracking his rhythm since the ferry.

"Check that out." Sam nodded toward a group of performers farther down the street.

Drummers stood in a loose line, their hands driving a percussive thunder that hammered through the pavement. The sound wasn't just an auditory experience; it was physical, a series of low-frequency pulses that tightened the skin across her sternum. Nearby, acrobats moved in controlled bursts, folding and leaping with precision that drew cheers each time someone landed. A martial arts demonstration occupied another section of the street, the performers cutting through the layered noise with deliberate movements, each strike distinct against the softer chaos around it.

Angela smiled at the shift in Sam's focus, grateful for anything that drew him outward instead of deeper into himself. She pointed toward a storefront where fish circled in shallow tanks and rows of hanging poultry lined the window.

"You hungry?"

Sam angled away. "Not even a little." Angela didn't push it. The Mobilization Credit Rex had issued—a five-thousand-dollar 'unlock' meant to cover their needs across three continents—carried weight. It was a corporate leash, blood money that made every meal feel like a transaction with a ghost.

They both laughed, and for a moment the tension eased enough to let them move forward without carrying all of it.

Angela unfolded the paper map again, forcing her eyes to settle on the small print. The absence of the GPS closed in here, where every street branched into several others and the crowd made orientation difficult. Her phone offered little help; the signal drifted and faltered, and the map app flickered, guessing instead of knowing. She smoothed the paper in her palm and traced the streets again, checking the sign at the corner, then the map, then the block numbers, letting the coordinates narrow the possibilities until the path began to resolve.

"Slow down a second." Angela pressed the map flat to the base of the lamppost.

Sam leaned closer. "You think it's here?"

"I think it's close."

They moved another half-block, weaving through the crowd until they reached a pagoda-shaped lamppost just outside the densest flow of people. It did not look important at first glance, and that was part of what made it stand out.

Angela stopped. "This is it."

Across the street, inside a narrow bakery with fogged windows and warm light, Rex watched.

He sat near the front with a cup of tea cooling beside one hand, his posture loose enough to appear casual if anyone saw him at all. No one did. Festival traffic flooded the bakery—families carrying boxes of pastries, tourists ordering by pointing, and older regulars who looked as though they had been sitting at the same tables for years. The place was perfect: visible without drawing attention, positioned so the clue site remained in clear view without inviting a second glance.

The location fit the clue precisely, rewarding attention over speed. Anyone could reach Chinatown once the coordinates pointed to San Francisco. The question was what kind of person kept looking after the street had already offered its spectacle.

When an older couple stopped near the lamppost, Rex leaned forward, curiosity sharpening his focus.

They circled the base slowly, one of them holding a GPS device and squinting at the screen as though effort alone would improve its accuracy.

The man tapped his GPS screen. "This has to be it."

The woman gestured to the lanterns swaying overhead. "It's the festival. That's what the clue said."

They circled again, repeating the same movements as though repetition might reveal what attention had missed.

"I can't keep doing this." The woman swayed, reaching for her husband's arm. "I'm getting dizzy."

Rex allowed himself the smallest smile as he lifted his cup. The puzzle was doing exactly what it was meant to do.

Then Angela and Sam stepped into view.

He set the cup down.

Angela and Sam approached the lamppost with their attention narrowed enough that the surrounding crowd blurred. Sam paused, his breathing catching with a dry, uneven sound. The familiar, tightening sensation of being watched too closely returned, the air turning thin just as it did whenever Mike's overprotectiveness began to feel like a physical weight. He reached for his inhaler, taking a quick breath and then another, focusing on regaining control before he nodded.

Angela stepped toward the couple, her eyes fixed on the air shimmering around the grate. "You're looking at the wrong elevation."

The man didn't look up, instead shifting his heavy shoulder to bar her from the lamppost. "This is a Geopoet line, kid. We don't do handouts or hints. Go find a virtual on the pier and stay out of the way of the pros."

"The 'pros' have been walking in circles for ten minutes." Sam stepped into the man's space, his shoulders squaring.

The woman, Margaret, adjusted her glasses, her gaze scanning them with a clinical chill. "Twenty years in the circuit, and we've never seen your tags. We don't share coordinates with amateurs who stumble onto a site by accident. Move along."

Joe tapped his high-end GPS unit, his lip curling. "The signal is coming from the pillar. It's a dead-drop. If you think you know better than the satellites, prove it. Or better yet, let's make it interesting. You find it without your screen, we talk. You fail, you hand over that paper map and clear out of our sector."

Angela didn't move. She stepped closer to the lamppost, closing her eyes as she reached out. Her fingers hovered just inches from the iron surface of the post, then dropped toward the cold metal of the sewer grate. This was her listening touch—a way of letting the world's frequencies translate through the fine tension in her skin. The heavy transit of subterranean water and the percussive cadence of the festival drummers anchored in the hollow of her throat, but beneath it all, a sharp, artificial staccato surfaced—a thin, ozone-scented hum that prickled the back of her neck.

"The moon isn't the lantern." Angela pointed toward the gutter, where the red light of the lanterns bled into the runoff. "It's the reflection in the runoff. You're looking for the cache 'below illumination,' but you're looking up. It's a distinct float in the stomach right here, tethered to the third bar of the grate."

Joe's skeptical sneer faltered. He looked at the grate, then at the paper clue in his hand. "The kid's right, Joe." Margaret leaned closer to the iron grate. "The coordinates are centered on the drain, not the post."

Joe looked back at Angela's hand. The hidden geometry shivered beneath the iron. "How could you possibly feel a proximity trigger through iron?"

"I listen." Angela met his eyes. "Now, do we talk, or do I just take the cache and go?"

The territorial tension broke, replaced by a reluctant, sharp-edged curiosity. Margaret stepped back, allowing Angela space. "Show us."

Across the street, Rex leaned forward just enough to follow the shift. This was the part that mattered—the players who could hold spectacle and function at once, who could see beyond what was presented.

Angela crouched beside the grate and shifted it aside. The smell that rose from below was immediate, but she didn't flinch. She leaned forward, her fingers trailing the metal until they snagged the cord she already anticipated. She pulled, and a small box emerged. She didn't hand it over, holding Joe's gaze until he gave a short, begrudging nod—a silent acknowledgement of her right to be there.

Rex committed the scene to memory, then stood, left cash on the table, and slipped out the back.

At her touch, the box gave way.

Inside were smaller containers marked the same way: Moon cake.

Despite the plain packaging, the cakes were pressed into patterns, their surfaces detailed with intricate, traditional pressings.

"Looks good." Margaret broke hers open.

"Check for a clue first." Sam held his hand out for the box.

Joe looked at the grate. "You've got a knack for the resonance."

"Apparently she does." Sam offered a sharp, knowing look to the older couple.

They searched through the packaging, but nothing revealed itself. Angela turned the cake in her hand and broke it apart.

Margaret paused, then reached into her mouth and pulled out a heavy, matte-metallic coin with a surprised laugh. A faint heat throbbed in her palm.

Angela opened hers and found an identical tracking coin.

"There aren't any coordinates." Angela turned the coin over; the beacon's internal signal stirred a rhythmic, insistent warmth through her palm. "Just a code."

The man nodded. "We're the Geopoets—Margaret and Joe."

"I'm Angela. This is my brother, Sam."

Margaret studied them. "You two seem good at this."

"We're learning." Angela met Sam's eye.

She slipped one of her Daphne cards into the larger box before returning everything to its place.

Sam shook his head. "Her alter ego."

Angela replaced the box beneath the grate and set the cover back into place until it sat flush again.

Margaret let out a breath. "Thank you. We wouldn't have found it."

Joe lifted his coin. "Let's see what's next."

Inside the bakery, the noise softened into something warmer and more contained. They gathered around a small table while Joe opened his laptop and waited for the connection to resolve.

Her phone weighed in her pocket, but she didn't reach for it.

A message appeared.

CONGRATULATIONS. BON VOYAGE.

Margaret leaned closer. "This is the last U.S. clue."

Sam's attention shifted to the countdown. "We're running out of time. Twelve days left, and we haven't booked a flight."

Joe clicked again, then looked at Sam's phone and Angela's paper map. He didn't offer the tablet. Instead, he leaned in, his voice dropping. "You're good, Angela. But Paris isn't Chinatown. You'll need a dedicated GPS and two tickets that don't exist on a student's budget." He tapped a weathered finger against the table. "There's a vintage Founders' Token on the third-story cornice of the Bank of Canton. I'm too old for the climb, and the Geopoets need that trophy to stay in the circuit. Retrieve it, and I'll book your passage. Fail, and you're just kids playing a game you can't afford."

A new line appeared.

A passage to India. Rue 72.

The next stage took shape even before she understood it.

Her phone buzzed.

Dad.

She ignored it.

Sam's phone rang next.

"Where are you?" Mike's voice crackled through the phone, distorted and thin.

Sam covered the phone and looked at Angela. "He knows."

Angela held out her hand. "Give it to me."

"Hi, Dad."

"What is going on?"

"I told you about the geocache. I'm following it."

"Where are you?"

"San Francisco."

A pause.

"Put Sam on the phone."

She handed it back.

Sam looked at the screen for a moment, then ended the call.

Angela stared at him. "Why would you do that?"

"He's just going to tell us to come home."

Her phone rang again. She answered, her grip tightening on the casing. "I'll send him back. I promise."

Sam flinched before he could hide it.

Then he turned and walked out.

"Sam—wait."

Angela followed him into the street, pushing through the crowd as the noise and movement pressed in from all sides. Sam moved with desperate strides, as if he could outrun the reach of Mike's voice. But the harder he pushed, the more the air seemed to solidify into the suffocating pressure of home—the weight of a life where every breath was scrutinized for weakness. He slowed, then stopped, bracing himself against the wall as his lungs seized. Angela reached him and guided him down, placing the inhaler in his hand.

Angela leaned in until her forehead touched his. "He's not here. Breathe."

He focused on the expansion and contraction of his lungs, dragging air in while she stayed beside him, one hand resting against his back until the tension began to ease.

The festival surged around them in a tide of noise and motion, providing a grounding weight in which he finally found his breath again.

After a moment, he looked up.

"We stick together."

Angela nodded. "We stick together."

When they returned, the street had already absorbed their absence. The drummers played, the lanterns shifted, and the crowd moved on as if nothing had changed. The climb had been a cold, vertical exercise in desperation. Angela ignored the vertigo, her fingers finding purchase in the narrow masonry while Sam stood as a small, nervous sentinel in the crowd below. When she finally pried the brass token from the shadows of the cornice, the high, cold frequency of the metal vibrated through her teeth—the first thing she had truly earned since her mother's death. She had descended with the grit of the city under her nails and pressed the metal into Joe's palm. He didn't smile, but he had handed over the ruggedized tablet and a digital confirmation of a brutal itinerary—a sequence of connections that treated human endurance as an afterthought. Paris, Venice, and then a staggering twenty-two-hour transit to Darwin. It was a map of exhaustion.

But something had.

Suzette and her team were already there, lifting the grate and retrieving what remained. They vanished, taking what was left and disappearing into the crowd before Angela and Sam could reach them.

The loss settled.

"The map is such a potato." Sam's thumb stabbed at the screen as his breathing smoothed. "It's got zero chill. We need a real waypoint, Angela. Something that actually connects to India."

"Did you hear what they said?" Angela turned to him. "Last U.S. clue."

Sam pulled two passports from his bag and held them up.

"I came prepared."

Angela laughed despite herself. "You planned this?"

"I thought we might need them."

She studied him, then shook her head. "Do you have any money?"

He did.

Not much.

But enough to matter.

Later, near the Wharf, they counted it together while the bay wind pushed cold through the thin cotton of Sam's hoodie.

"Four thousand, eight hundred and twelve dollars." Angela stared at the balance on the tablet.

Sam adjusted the weight of the device Joe had given them, its screen casting a pale, clinical light over his fingers as it searched for a signal through the fog. "Enough for the trains and some hostels, maybe. But if we run out, we're stranded."

Angela looked at the screen.

Paris.

Then she reached for her phone.

Her mother's voice filled the silence.

Angela stilled, her breath catching.

"He never changed it." She didn't look up.

The beep sounded.

"Dad." She gripped the phone until the plastic bit into her palm. "Just listen. We're going to keep going. I'm sorry I didn't ask, but I need this."

A pause.

"You're just like your mother."

"That's not a bad thing."

"Come home."

She closed her eyes.

"Not yet."

The line went dead.

She stood there a moment longer, the wind pushing against her hair.

In the car, Angela stared at the glowing screen of the tablet. The confirmation for Flight 418 was a victory that tasted of brick dust and adrenaline. She hadn't relied on a ghost's inheritance or a stroke of luck; she had traded her safety for a piece of the sky, leaving them dependent on the finite credit Rex had provided—a tether that tracked their every move.

By the time they reached the terminal, the adrenaline of the flight from Chinatown had curdled into something colder. A cavern of glass and white noise, SFO served as an indifferent machine for moving people from the lives they knew to the lives they were choosing. At the gate, Angela stared at the digital display: Flight 418 to Paris-Charles de Gaulle.

Not until the physical weight of her passport pressed into her palm did the reality hit. This was the 'dropping out' her father had always feared, the impulsive streak he blamed on her mother's side of the family. Seeing Sam curled into a plastic chair with his hood pulled low, they were no longer just players in a game. They were fleeing.

The silver locket beneath her shirt rested heavy, a cold anchor at her skin.

When the gate agent's voice crackled over the speakers, calling for the first rows to board, a sudden urge struck Angela to turn around, to call Mike, to admit they'd gone too far. But then Sam lifted his head, his eyes wide and searching. There was no going back.

The journey became a hollowed-out vacuum of recycled air and the engine's low churn gnawing at the cabin. Time ceased to be a linear progression and became a nauseating loop of plastic trays and fitful, upright sleep. Outside the cabin windows, the sun refused to set, then vanished, then rose again in a blinding, premature arc that felt like a personal affront to their internal clocks. Eleven hours over the Atlantic, chased by a nine-hour jump into the future, left Angela's consciousness lagging several miles behind her physical body—a ghostly tether stretched thin across the ocean.

By the time they cleared customs at Charles de Gaulle, the world had tilted on a broken axis. It was mid-morning in France, but her body insisted it was the dead of a San Francisco night. The terminal lights buzzed with a predatory sharpness that made Angela's skull ache, and her depth perception had frayed; her fingers missed the edge of her bag, grabbing only empty air. It hit the floor with a dull thud, spilling receipts and maps across the linoleum. She stared at the mess, her thoughts moving with the viscous drag of deep-sea water. Beside her, Sam leaned against a pillar, his face the color of parchment and his movements the jerky stutters of a body forced through eleven hours of recycled air and a nine-hour theft of time.

Sunday, 10:42 — 12 Days Remaining

When they stepped into the morning air of Paris, the remaining four thousand dollars on the Mobilization card was a terminal diagnosis. They stood at the RER station, staring at a fare gate that required a piece of Rex's soul to pass. Angela's stomach cramped, a sharp reminder that they hadn't eaten since the flight's meager offerings. Her hands shook as she pulled the card from her pocket, the plastic cold and clinical. It was their only lifeline, a corporate leash that reduced her to a pet being led toward a bowl. She tapped the card against the reader, the gate clicking open with an indifferent mechanical chirp, every cent spent a breadcrumb left for the man who was pulling their strings.

But they were still moving.

As they walked through the terminal beneath unfamiliar signs and drifting announcements, Sam glanced at her.

"You really think we can win this?"

Angela met his eyes, then faced forward.

What waited next was larger than anything they had faced before.

But turning back no longer felt like caution.

"I think we have to try." The crowd surged past them, an indifferent sea of strangers.

Chapter 15: Airborne Anchors

Viewed through the harsh terminal glass, the gate at SFO felt final, an end to everything they had known. Behind them lay the neon grit of Chinatown and the hollowed-out feeling of the windowless office on Mission Street where Angela had bartered her mother's signature avionics kit—a master set of precision tools—for two standby seats, a decommissioned tablet, and enough surplus cash to satisfy the international taxes that would have otherwise grounded them at the gate. Sam sat on a terminal bench, looking at the massive nose of the Boeing 777 through the floor-to-ceiling glass. They were dropping out of the only world that knew their names, running away from the gravity of a life that had already collapsed. When the final boarding call echoed through the vaulted ceiling, a sudden, leaden lurch settled in Angela's gut, a weight that seemed to pull her through the floor before the climb had even begun. There was no safety net, only the jet bridge.

The plane was packed, the cabin air recycled and stale. At thirty-five thousand feet, the world below was nothing more than a scattering of distant lights. Angela sat in the middle seat, her knees pressed into the rough fabric of the chair in front of her. Thin and tasting of recycled plastic, the air carried the sour, unwashed scent of three hundred bodies in close quarters. Her skin felt filmed with a fine layer of cabin grease, her hair matted at her neck. It was a sterile environment that had long since stripped away the heat of the Arizona desert, leaving her shivering in the unnatural chill of the vents. Every joint ached with a deep, rhythmic throb, a physical protest against the cramped economy seat that felt less like furniture and more like a cage.

She pulled her phone from her pocket, the screen casting a harsh, blue glow across her face. She opened the banking app, watching the Mission Street transaction settle into its final sum. Eight dollars—the pittance remaining after the airline had finished extracting the fuel and security fees that always clung to 'free' passage. The number was a shock—until the salvaged tablet chirped with a notification from the Apex portal: Stage One Transit Confirmed. Mobilization Credit: $5,000. It was a lifeline that felt like a leash. Every mile the plane covered was a mile further from any safety net, and the pull of that digital tether tightened through her chest, harder than the G-force of any takeoff. Angela's chest constricted, something cold settling deep that no amount of lift could counteract. They were halfway across the Atlantic, miles beyond the point where a return trip was a simple matter of turning around. They were committed to the trajectory, whether the fuel held or not.

Beside her, Sam was a small, pale ghost. His hoodie was stained with spilled juice from the first leg of the trip, the fabric smelling of stale sugar and travel-grime. He looked gaunt, the dark circles under his eyes like bruises across his translucent skin. On his lap, the salvaged tablet lay like a heavy, cold stone, its screen a spiderweb of fractures. It was a crude replacement for the equipment they'd lost, a piece of digital wreckage that Sam had spent the last four hours trying to coax into a GPS receiver. His head leaned back against the headrest, his eyes closed, but his jaw was tight. Every few seconds, a soft, whistling sound escaped his throat. It was the sound of air struggling through narrow passages, a mechanical failure of the body that sent a cold needle of adrenaline spiking through Angela's nerves. She watched the rhythm of his chest, counting the seconds between inhalations. It was too fast. Too shallow.

Don't fight the air, Sam, she thought, her own lungs tightening in sympathy. Let it tell you what it wants.

She reached out and placed a hand on his arm. His skin was clammy, despite the warmth of the cabin. He didn't open his eyes, but his fingers curled into the fabric of his seat. His pulse ran fast and uneven. He was a twelve-year-old boy who had been uprooted from everything stable and thrust into a world of coordinates and high-stakes gambles, and now the very air was betraying him.

Angela's fingers tightened on the boy's arm. "Sam. Look at me."

He opened his eyes. They were wide and glassy, reflecting the flickering light of the seatback movie screens around them. He reached for his pocket, his hand trembling as he fumbled for his inhaler. Angela took it from him, her movements steady and practiced. She shook the canister, the sound of the ball bearing inside a sharp, rhythmic click. She held it to his lips, and he took a deep, shuddering hit of the medicine. He held his breath, his face turning a deeper shade of gray before he finally exhaled, the tension in his shoulders dropping just a fraction.

"It's the altitude." Sam locked his fingers onto the edge of the tablet. "The pressure is wrong."

"We're in a pressurized cabin, Sam. It's the same as being on the ground."

Sam looked up at the cabin ceiling. "The machine knows. It knows we're hanging by a thread. I can feel the thinness. There isn't enough between us and the nothing."

Angela didn't have an argument for that. She knew the feeling of the nothing. She had felt it when the hawk struck her canopy, when the sky stopped being a partner and became a vacuum. She reached into her jacket and pulled out a small, crumpled photograph. It was a relic, something she had taken from the hangar office before they left. It showed Maria Santiago standing in front of a white sailplane, her flight suit unzipped to the waist, her hair a wild, windblown halo. She wasn't smiling for the camera; she was looking past it, up toward a horizon that only she could see. There was a lightness in her posture, a sense of belonging that made the heavy machinery behind her look like an afterthought.

Angela pressed the photo into Sam's hand. "Look at her. She used to say that the plane is just an anchor if you don't know how to use the wind. But if you learn to listen to the pressure of the air, the whole sky is a bridge."

Sam traced the edge of the photo with his thumb. Worn down by years of handling, the paper felt soft beneath his thumb. "Dad's going to hate this. He's going to hate that we're here."

"Dad's been holding his breath for five years, Sam. He thinks if he stays still enough, nothing else can break. But that isn't how it works. You can't save a plane by keeping it in the hangar forever. The seals dry out. The fuel turns to varnish. It dies anyway."

"But what if we don't find it? What if Suzette gets there first?"

Angela looked at the flight map on the screen in front of her. The little digital airplane was a tiny, lonely icon crawling across a vast, blue void. "Then we'll have been in the air. That has to count for something."

She closed her eyes, and for a moment, the hum of the jet engines faded into the clean, sharp whistle of a glider's wings. She remembered her first solo flight. She had been sixteen. The instructors had always told her to watch the instruments, to trust the dials over her own senses. But when she was finally alone in the cockpit, the instruments felt like a distraction. She had closed her eyes for a heartbeat (a dangerous, impulsive thing to do) and felt the lift in the seat of her pants. It was a physical tug, a pull toward the sun. She had banked the plane because the air demanded it, not the dial. In that moment, she wasn't a girl in a machine. She was a body in space, moving with a geometric precision that felt like the only truth she had ever known. It was freedom, absolute and unbroken. It was the only time she had ever felt entirely safe.

Vanished now, that sense of freedom had been replaced by the crushing weight of a digital leash, a stomach that roared with a hollow, acidic hunger, and a brother whose every breath sounded like a grinding gear.

* * *

In San Francisco, the sun was just beginning to burn through the morning fog, lighting up the glass facade of Carlisle Industries. Rex St. James sat in his father's office, a space that felt like a museum of corporate conquest. A massive obsidian desk dominated the room, and the air was cold. On the wall, a digital map of the world displayed the real-time locations of every active participant in the Carlisle Hunt. Thousands of dots flickered across the continents, a swarm of ambition and greed that Rex had set in motion to prove he could create something his father couldn't control.

He leaned forward, his eyes fixed on a specific cluster of data. Most of the top-tier teams were moving in predictable patterns, following the established hubs of international travel. They were the professionals, the ones with corporate sponsors and logistics teams. But one account was different. It was registered under the name Daphne, a name that felt like a deliberate obscuration. The team had been a non-entity until forty-eight hours ago, when they had suddenly leaped from a quiet sector in Arizona to the heart of San Francisco, and then, inexplicably, onto a flight to Paris.

"Show me the registration details for Daphne." Rex's shadow stretched long across the obsidian desk.

The computer chirped, and a window opened on the secondary monitor. The name on the credit card used for the initial entry fee was Michael Santiago. Rex felt a cold prickle of recognition at the back of his neck. He knew that name. It was buried in the archives of his father's acquisition files, a small aviation company in Arizona that had been flagged as a liability years ago. Santiago. Maria Santiago had been the name on the flight logs, a woman who had been a legend in the soaring community before her crash.

He tapped a few more keys, pulling up the passenger manifest for the flight to Charles de Gaulle. There were two Santiagos on the list. Angela and Samuel. They weren't professionals. They didn't have a support team or a corporate jet. They were kids traveling on the proceeds of a desperate liquidation, moving with a desperate, frantic speed that bypassed all the logic of the algorithm.

Rex watched his unblinking reflection against the city lights. "Why are you running, Angela?"

He watched the dot representing their flight as it crossed the mid-Atlantic ridge. His father's analytics had predicted that this phase of the hunt would be dominated by Suzette Saunders and the Carlisle-backed teams. They had the math. They had the resources. But the math didn't account for the kind of momentum that comes from having nothing left to lose. The Santiagos weren't just playing a game. They were trying to outrun a tragedy, using the hunt as a vehicle for their own survival.

Rex stood up and walked to the floor-to-ceiling window. Below him, the city was a grid of order and commerce, a world built on the idea that everything had a price and a place. He looked at his own reflection in the glass, the tailored suit and the expensive watch, and felt a sudden, sharp pang of envy for the girl in the middle seat of a commercial airliner. She was in the air. She was moving toward a legacy that had a name and a face, while he was just a ghost in his father's machine, monitoring the progress of people who were actually living.

He turned back to the screen. He could shut them down. He could flag the account for suspicious activity, or he could tip off Suzette to their location. It would be the professional thing to do. It would ensure the hunt stayed within the parameters his father expected. Instead, he reached out and touched the screen, his finger resting on the tiny, flickering dot of the Santiago flight.

He touched the screen where the flickering dot pulsed. "Keep going."

* * *

As the flight entered its final stretch, the cabin lights dimmed. Angela leaned her head against Sam's, the photo of their mother still clutched between them. The whistling in his chest had subsided, replaced by the heavy, rhythmic breathing of deep sleep. She watched the moon reflect off the vast, dark expanse of the ocean below. It was a lonely view, a reminder of how small they were in the grand architecture of the world.

She thought about her father, sitting in the empty house in Arizona, surrounded by boxes and the silence of a life that had been packed away. She knew he would see the bank statement eventually. He would see the withdrawal and the coordinates of their journey, and he would feel that cold, airless void opening in his chest all over again. He would think she was being reckless. He would think she was repeating the mistake that had killed her mother.

But he was wrong. This wasn't a repeat. This was a correction.

Angela shifted her weight, feeling the slight vibration of the plane through the floorboards. She thought about the philosophy of the listening touch. It wasn't about a lack of control; it was about a different kind of mastery. It was the ability to feel the tension in the wings before they snapped, to hear the change in the wind before the storm arrived. Her father had tried to ground them to keep them safe, but safety was a lie. You were never safe; you were only ever in balance or out of it.

As the first hint of dawn began to grey the eastern horizon, Angela's grip tightened on the armrest until the plastic groaned. She didn't turn back. They were over the water, suspended between two worlds, with no way to go but forward. The bank account was empty, and the air was thin, but for the first time since the crash, she didn't feel like a replica of a tragedy. She felt like a pilot.

Angela leaned her forehead against the cool vibration of the window. "We're almost there, Sam."

Beginning its long, slow descent, the plane brought a shift in pressure that popped painfully in Angela's ears. When the wheels finally struck the tarmac, the nine-hour flight hit her like a physical blow. Her equilibrium fractured; the floor of the terminal seemed to pitch like the deck of a ship. At the RER station, the kiosk glowed with a demand for twenty-three euros for two tickets to the city center. Angela stared at the screen. She didn't reach for the pathetic handful of coins the exchange booth had yielded for her final eight dollars; instead, she swiped the Hunt's digital credit, the transaction clearing in silence. The hunger in her gut was a sharp, localized cramp, and Sam was swaying on his feet, his face the color of wet ash.

Stepping out of the station, the air was heavy and damp. The jet lag settled into her bones, making her limbs feel filled with lead. Her eyes were bloodshot, the world vibrating at the edges of her vision. They were in Paris, but they were filthy, exhausted, and vibrating with the frantic energy of the owned. The coordinates and riddles she had banked on were blurring; the math of the Hunt was dissolving into the fog of a body that hadn't known a bed in thirty-six hours. She wasn't just navigating a new city; she was trying to outrun a collapse that was already written in the tremor of her hands.

Chapter 16: The Parisian Shadow

Angela hit the cobblestones of the Marais with the scout's radio-static still ringing in her ears. The buildings leaned over the narrow streets, dense and pressing, thick with the scent of yeast from the boulangeries and the damp, mineral breath of ancient limestone. It was nothing like the open horizons of Arizona; here, the sky was a jagged ribbon of blue caught between slate rooftops. Every window was an eye. Every shadow had a purpose.

She kept her hands deep in the pockets of her jacket, her fingers tracing the edge of her mother's brass compass. It rested cold and solid in her pocket.

Sam walked half a step behind her. He was hunched over a tablet that was tethered to a small, hand-soldered box in his pocket. The device hummed there, a steady, insistent vibration he felt with every step. His thumb moved across the screen in a rhythmic, obsessive pattern, trying to weave a shroud of noise around them. The city was a sea of invisible chatter, a flood of signals that Rex St. James could use to find them in the crowd.

"The city is too loud," Sam muttered, his thumb flying across the tablet's screen as he adjusted the box in his pocket. "The air is too crowded. If she's watching, we're pinned to her map like moths. There's no room here to slip between the cracks."

Angela didn't look back. The glass of a shop window reflected the street: a woman in a silk scarf buying a baguette, a man in a dark coat reading a newspaper. Nothing was out of place, yet something in the air shifted. The same tension preceded a storm front moving over the mountains. The atmosphere changed. The world held its breath.

"We need to get off the main thoroughfare." Angela turned into a side street rank with wet trash and expensive perfume.

They moved deeper into the labyrinth. The Marais was built for secrets, a grid of private courtyards and hidden gardens—remnants of a nobility that valued its privacy above all else. A sharp tingle sparked across her fingertips, and the horizon locked in her vision. No thermals or wind shifts now; only the break in the rhythm of the crowd, the person moving with too much intention.

He stood near the entrance to the Place des Vosges, using a stone pillar for cover, his attention fixed on a tourist map. He wore a blue technical jacket. The fabric had the same dull finish and heavy seams as the gear worn by the scout back in the Presidio. It was a uniform of professional intent. He wasn't a tourist. He was a tracker.

"Sam." Angela kept her eyes on the shop window. "Blue jacket. Ten o'clock. Don't look."

Sam didn't look up from his tablet, but his shoulders stiffened.

"He's there in the glass," Sam whispered, his voice cracking. "He's not just following us. He's erasing where we've been. Like we were never there at all."

A cold stone settled in Angela's stomach. Suzette hadn't just followed them to Paris. She had hired local assets to do the heavy lifting. The Hunt was no longer a race between pilots and explorers. It was a corporate operation with a local footprint. They were being hunted by people who knew these alleys better than they knew their own names.

"The clue from Rue 72," Sam whispered, his eyes fixed on the tablet. "That thing in the memoir about the Passage to India. If we can reach the courtyard behind the old post office, we might be able to cut the thread. But he's right on us."

Angela grabbed the strap of Sam's backpack and pulled him into a sudden sprint. They bolted past a flower stall, the scent of crushed lilies trailing behind them. The man in the blue jacket didn't shout. He didn't run. He straightened up and spoke into a small microphone clipped to his collar.

They dived into a narrow passage that was barely wide enough for two people. The walls were covered in layers of faded posters and graffiti. Her boots thudded over the cobblestones. Sam's breathing became a ragged, rhythmic whistle as his lungs strained in the damp Parisian air. The city was a cage today.

"Almost there." The pursuit crowded behind them, a displacement of air rather than sound. The scout was closing the gap without breaking a sweat.

They burst into a small, sun-drenched courtyard. It was a pocket of silence in the middle of the city. A single chestnut tree stood in the center, its leaves turning a brittle gold. The space was enclosed by high stone walls and wrought-iron balconies. There was only one way in and one way out. It was a beautiful trap.

Sam collapsed against the trunk of the tree, his chest heaving. He fumbled for his inhaler, the plastic clicking at his teeth. He took two quick draws, his eyes closed as he waited for the medicine to open the cage of his ribs. The towering history of the Marais dwarfed him.

Angela stood by the entrance, her back to the cool stone. Shadows deepened on the opposite wall. A moment later, the blue jacket filled the mouth of the alley, pausing with his silhouette cut clean against the bright street beyond. He didn't enter the courtyard. He held there, a silent sentinel marking their location. He was waiting.

"He's just holding his position," Sam said, his voice thin as he straightened. "He knows we're trapped. He's a beacon for the rest of them."

Wrought-iron balconies loomed over the courtyard. The Passage to India wasn't a physical route. It was a reference to the mail planes that once flew from France to the colonies. The memoirs spoke of a post office of the soul where the letters were never delivered. They were filed in the stone.

A stone basin of a dry fountain stood in the corner of the courtyard. Carved into the rim was a series of coordinates and a small, weathered symbol of a winged envelope. It was a marker for the Aéropostale pilots, a piece of forgotten geography hidden in plain sight.

"The cache isn't in the streets. It's in the history of the building itself."

She reached into the basin, her fingers searching the crevices of the mossy stone. A loose brick near the base slid out with a gritty protest, revealing a small, metal cylinder. It was cold and heavy, wrapped in the same lead foil they had used in the catacombs to dampen their signal. She tucked it into her jacket next to her compass.

"Got it." Angela tucked the cylinder into her jacket. "Now we just have to leave."

But the victory was hollow. The man in the blue jacket was still there, a dark shape at the end of the tunnel. His presence was proof they were no longer invisible, but data points on a screen moving through a city that had become a participant in their pursuit. A constant, low-level tremor rattled her hands—the physical tax of the Hunt.

"We need a new way out." Sam's thumb slipped, leaving a smear on the glass, and he hissed a frustrated breath. "There's a basement door to the Metro. If I can get the lock to click, the stone will swallow our trail. Down there, the stone will blind them. It'll just be the dark."

The scout remained a dark shape at the tunnel's mouth; Sam was a study in frantic, focused motion. The Hunt was changing them. It was stripping away the last of their innocence and replacing it with a hard, tactical competence. They were learning to move like shadows in a city of light. They were learning that in a game this big, there was no such thing as a safe place.

"Do it." Angela watched the mouth of the alley. "Before his friends arrive."

As Sam worked on the lock, his fingers steady despite his ragged breath, a familiar thrum of a distant engine vibrated the air. It wasn't a plane, but the rhythmic pulse of the city itself. She closed her eyes. The air shifted. The pressure was dropping. A storm was coming, and in the darkness of the Parisian tunnels, they would find their next thermal. The door clicked open with a dull, mechanical finality. They stepped into the darkness, leaving the man in the blue jacket behind. The Parisian shadow was long, but they were learning how to walk within it.

Chapter 17: Passage

Sam leaned his full weight against a support pillar, his chest hitching in the stagnant, humid air of the station. The eleven-hour haul from San Francisco, followed by a frantic layover and the nine hours they had surrendered to the eastward sun, meant they had been in transit for over thirty hours. It was Tuesday morning, but Sam's internal compass was still spinning somewhere over the mid-Atlantic Sunday. It had turned his bones to lead and his thoughts to glass, his skin filmed with the sour, recycled grease of a middle-seat sleep.

He pressed his palm to the turnstile, but his motor skills lagged; the metal arm refused to budge. Behind them, the line of commuters shifted with growing impatience, heels tapping on tile in a rhythm that carried more intent than sound. "It won't recognize the ticket," he muttered, his gaze fixed on the unyielding metal. Every failed scan landed like a physical blow to their dwindling resources; they had seventy euros remaining from the sale of their mother's vintage watch, a pathetic sum the city seemed determined to swallow whole.

Angela caught his sleeve, her own throat tightening with the station's thick scent of burnt rubber and damp limestone. "Try the next one. Just breathe, Sam." Her stomach gave a sharp, hollow twist—a reminder that their last meal had been a shared packet of airline pretzels somewhere over the dark Atlantic.

When they finally reached the sidewalk, the nine-hour leap across time zones had left Angela's internal clock shattered. The world lacked solidity; the city did not so much appear as loom into place, pale and intricate. The sun was a cold, white coin climbing toward its zenith, a relentless marker of the hours they were burning just to stay upright. Her mind was still anchored in a Pacific midnight, and the Parisian light felt abrasive across her gritty, unwashed eyes. The cloying humidity settled over her, making her clothes cling in a way that felt like a second skin of travel-grime.

The light was different here. It filtered through pale stone and narrow streets that held onto it rather than throwing it back, giving everything a muted, lived-in glow. Buildings were less interested in impressing than enduring, their facades worn in ways that suggested time had passed through them patiently rather than violently. Cars moved more slowly than they did at home, as though the city had settled on a pace long before they arrived, and the people navigating the streets moved within that rhythm without needing to think about it. Voices rose and fell in unfamiliar patterns that Angela could not follow, yet she listened all the same. The air carried coffee, old stone, and the suggestion of rain that had not quite fallen.

For a moment, she surrendered to the sight, letting the clue, the timer, the race, and even the thought of others on the same trail fall away, until all that remained was Paris itself and the unlikely fact that she and Sam stood there together, in a place their mother had never shown them and neither of them had expected to reach this way.

Then the reason they had come settled back into place.

Sam unfolded the paper and read the clue again, his voice a dry rasp worn thin by the miles. "A passage to India. Rue seventy-two."

Angela held the GPS against the map; the French syllables were grit behind her eyelids. Her focus, frayed by the flight and the heavy weight of the nine-hour time jump, slipped. A sharp jolt struck: she had been studying the wrong section, her brain stalling as it tried to reconcile the digital glow with the ancient, solid reality of the street. It took three attempts to force the map into focus, the lines blurring like ink in water. She steadied herself and traced the map again, forcing her attention to slow as the city spread before her in a pattern structured at first glance and then grew more complicated the longer she studied it. Broad avenues broke into smaller streets, which folded into narrower ones that curved just enough to disrupt her sense of direction if she lingered too long.

"It's divided into districts," she said, tracing the lines. "Arrondissements. We need to narrow it down."

Sam leaned in, his eyes narrowing despite the fatigue in his posture. "The map is glitching," he said, frustration surfacing as his thumb tapped the glass in a restless, twitching rhythm. "It's like we're stuck in a loading screen. We just need one big-deal landmark. Something that screams India."

"Or a business." Angela scanned the storefronts. "A restaurant, a cultural center, anything that points us the right way."

Sam nodded. "Rue seventy-two could be anywhere."

Angela glanced up and studied the movement around them. Tourists paused openly, checking maps and lifting cameras, while locals moved with practiced certainty, adjusting their path without hesitation. Somewhere between those two groups, she and Sam existed in a third category—neither grounded nor entirely lost, but moving forward on a logic that only made sense because they had committed to it.

She stepped toward a man passing by and held out the map, shaping the question in the stiff syllables of hesitant French. Her voice felt like it belonged to someone else, a recording played at the wrong speed.

"Inde? Route… des Indes?"

He paused, studied the map, and after a moment pointed toward a section before continuing on his way.

Angela turned back. "That looked like the eighteenth."

Sam followed her finger. "North?"

"Yeah."

She folded the map, leaving one edge open for quick reference, and turned to move.

Then she stopped.

Sam's breathing had shifted.

It was not yet serious, but it carried the first signs she had known long before he named them himself. The strain of the airport, the train, the distance, and the pressure of keeping pace had begun to accumulate.

Across the boulevard, the Geopoets ducked into a taxi. If she flagged the next car, they could beat them to the eighteenth and reclaim the lead. But Sam's face had gone a brittle, translucent gray. The choice felt like a physical weight: the race, or her brother. She watched the taxi pull away, letting the advantage vanish.

"We're walking," she said, taking Sam's bag and slinging it over her shoulder. A taxi was a fantasy for people with a dwindling stash and a future that didn't involve counting every cent for a crust of bread. "He pointed to the eighteenth. We'll take it steady."

Sam did not argue, and the absence of resistance told her she'd made the only choice that mattered.

They walked together at a pace they could sustain, the urgency settling into something more deliberate. The city unfolded around them in quiet layers, revealing itself through repetition rather than spectacle. Cafés extended onto sidewalks in rows of small tables, the scent of roasting beans and buttered pastry mocking Angela's empty stomach. She kept her eyes fixed on the pavement, avoiding the menus that listed prices she could no longer afford to even consider. Waiters moved between them with practiced ease, balancing trays through narrow spaces. By the time they reached the fringes of the eighteenth, the shadows had begun to stretch long and thin across the limestone, the afternoon light deepening into the color of aged parchment. The day was hemorrhaging time they couldn't afford to lose. Cups touched saucers with small, contained sounds. Chairs scraped against stone. Laughter rose from a doorway and dissolved beneath the hum of passing traffic.

Balconies lined the upper floors, their ironwork repeating in patterns that shifted subtly from street to street. Some were newly painted, others softened by time. Laundry hung from a few windows. Flower boxes crowded others so fully they were less decorative than determined.

Fragments of conversation drifted past—French, English, something else she could not place—and the lack of understanding did not distance the city. If anything, the city became more complete, existing without any need to explain itself to her.

Then Sam slowed.

Angela followed his gaze.

The Eiffel Tower rose in the distance, cutting into the pale sky with a presence that made everything else feel briefly secondary. It was farther away than it first appeared, but distance did not diminish its effect.

For a moment, everything else receded.

Sam reached for her hand. "I really miss Mom."

Angela let the words settle before answering. "I know."

He kept looking at the tower. "She would've loved this."

Angela nodded. "She would've made an itinerary with color coding."

"And backup plans," Sam added.

"And made us wake up too early," Angela said, a faint laugh slipping through.

He squeezed her hand. "But I'm glad we have each other."

She squeezed back. "Always."

He hesitated. "I wish Dad understood that."

Angela looked down the street before answering. "I think he does. I just don't think he knows how to show it without feeling like he's losing something."

"Like what?"

"Control." Angela watched a pigeon bank along the gray stone. "Or maybe us."

Sam considered that, then said, "That seems like a terrible strategy."

The corner of Angela's mouth quirked. "Yeah."

They began walking again.

The eighteenth district shifted around them. Streets narrowed, buildings pressed closer, and sound gathered rather than dispersed. Music reached them before its source did, layered with percussion and voices that suggested a gathering just out of sight.

They turned the corner and stepped into it.

The festival filled the street in overlapping waves of color and motion. Women in bright saris moved in clusters, their fabric catching light and shadow with each step. Men carried offerings through the crowd with measured care. Children wove between them. Incense drifted through the air, mixing with food, smoke, and traffic.

At the center, a chariot crawled forward, draped in flowers and carrying a bronze figure of Ganesh, its presence reshaping the flow of the street around it.

Angela stopped, caught by recognition.

"I think we're on the right track." Angela squinted into the afternoon glare.

Sam exhaled, the sound nearly lost to the crowd. "Yeah. That's not subtle."

He pointed toward a building just beyond the procession.

Angela checked the GPS again.

It matched.

This time, she did not move immediately. Instead, she studied the crowd, letting her attention settle.

Angela caught his arm. "Wait."

Sam turned. "What?"

"We weren't first at the last one." Her voice was low, tight. "If anyone's close, they'll be here."

Sam scanned the area more deliberately now, taking in faces, movement, patterns. Nothing obvious revealed itself.

"You think they're here?"

"I think we should assume we're not alone."

Near the entrance, two figures stood apart from the festive swirl. The woman, Margaret, held a heavy leather-bound logbook like a shield, while Joe stood beside her, his gaze tracking the procession with a proprietary air. They were the ones she'd seen in the taxi; they had arrived with time to spare.

"You're late." Margaret's fingers clamped down on the heavy leather logbook. "And you're in the way. We're not here to hand out participation trophies to everyone with a smartphone. Move on."

Joe shifted his weight, his broad shoulders barring the entrance to the small alcove where the cache was hidden. "This isn't a race for the uninitiated, girl. You're just vibrating at the wrong frequency. Go back to the tourist traps."

Angela didn't argue. She stepped into the narrow space between them, her palm finding the rough, humid limestone of the wall. She closed her eyes, letting the 'listening touch' sweep past the surface noise of the crowd. She felt the way the drumbeats weren't just sound, but a physical weight pressing into the stone's pores.

"It's a closed loop." The resonance vibrated in Angela's own chest. "The architecture is funneling the sound. It spirals up the arch and gets caught in the masonry. You're standing here waiting for the resonance to hit the keystone, but you've missed the shift." She opened her eyes, fixing Margaret with a tired, sharp intensity. "The air changed thirty seconds ago. You're listening to the echo of a ghost. The cache is already active."

The tension held for a long moment, the festival swirling around their static tableau. Margaret looked at the arch, then back at Angela, a flash of genuine, competitive heat in her eyes. She clicked open the logbook's heavy latch.

"Most people just see the saris." Margaret's voice dropped to a begrudging murmur. She pulled out a small metal tag and a geobug. "You have the ear for it. A pity. I was hoping you were just another tourist."

She handed the items over as a challenge rather than a gift. Joe stepped aside, his gaze lingering on Angela with a newfound, wary respect. Angela placed her Daphne card in the basket as they moved, and Sam caught the geobug as Margaret released it.

They exchanged a look with the Geopoets that wasn't quite a truce, but a recognition of shared weight, before the older couple vanished into the crowd.

Inside the internet café, the shift in atmosphere was immediate. The noise of the street fell away, replaced by dimmer light and the low hum of aging machines. The air carried a ghost of dust and coffee.

Angela sat at a terminal, her fingers leaving smudges on the sticky keys. Her vision swam, the fluorescent hum of the café vibrating in the back of her skull. They had paid for ten minutes—a calculated sacrifice from their meager funds—and the countdown in the corner of the screen felt like a timer on their very survival. She logged the geobug with trembling hands and waited.

The screen refreshed.

A message appeared.

EZRA POUND ISN'T A PRISONER.

Beneath the text, a digital travel voucher for the night train to Venice pulsed with a steady, clinical glow. The Hunt was paying their way now, but the charity felt like a leash.

Sam didn't hesitate, though his eyelids were heavy enough to look painful. "Venice."

Angela looked at the voucher, her mind already calculating the cost of another ten hours spent upright in a rattling train car. "If the rumors about the final legs in Australia are true, we're looking at nearly forty-eight hours of transit after Venice. The globe is going to eat two full days of our lives in one bite, Sam. We'll cross the date line and lose a Wednesday entirely. Twelve days sounds like a lifetime until you realize the map is stealing half of them."

He looked at her, his expression unreadable behind the haze of exhaustion. "Can we?"

She looked at the screen, then back at him.

"We'll figure it out."

It wasn't certainty, but it was enough. Outside, the sky had bruised to a deep violet, the first stars of the Parisian night blinking into existence. Eleven days remaining, and half the world still left to cross.

Chapter 18: The Bone Cathedral

Angela led Sam down the spiral staircase, her palm flat to the damp limestone to steady the boy's descent. Every step swallowed more of the Parisian afternoon, drawing them into a silence that shivered with the weight of the earth—a mineral-tasting quiet that muffled the frantic pulse of the Metro. It was the opposite of the sky. In a cockpit, she could feel the wind's current tightening the skin of her palms, but here the atmosphere closed around their lungs like a damp shroud, stagnant and heavy.

Sam clung to her shadow, his breath held in a careful, measured rhythm. The humidity settled into his chest like a hand. He didn't complain, but Angela could hear the effort in the way he placed his feet, the cautious focus of a boy monitoring his own internal pressure. He was trying to be silent, trying to be a ghost among the six million already in residence. She slowed her pace, matching her stride to his careful tempo.

The "Passage to India" clue had felt like a riddle until Sam connected it to the old aviator's memoir they had found in the Presidio. The pilot, a man who had flown the postal routes in the twenties, had written about a "Bone Cathedral" where the secrets of the earth were kept safe from the wind. It was a poetic description of the Catacombs, a place where the air never changed and the coordinates of the past remained fixed. Angela felt the gold coin in her pocket, tucked deep inside a pouch lined with scavenged lead foil. It was a small, hard reminder of the stakes, its tracking pulse muffled by the metal skin she'd wrapped around it. Eight dollars. That was all they had left in the world above.

They reached the bottom, where the tunnels opened into a labyrinth of stacked femurs and hollow-eyed skulls. The walls were constructed of the dead, a meticulous, terrifying geometry of calcium. Angela adjusted the beam of her flashlight, the circle of light dancing over the rows of teeth and empty sockets. The light felt intrusive, a violation of a peace that had been earned over centuries. She looked at Sam. His face was pale, his eyes wide as he scanned the walls for the marker.

"The memoir said the third junction past the well." Sam pressed his ear to the cold limestone. "Near the alcove that looks like the prow of a ship."

"Or a cockpit." A subsonic thrum produced a hollow float in her stomach that had nothing to do with the cold. "Pilots see the world in different shapes, Sam."

They moved deeper into the ossuary. A chill rose from the floor, smelling of wet lime and ancient, forgotten dust. It was a suffocating environment for a boy who needed the world to be wide and open. Sam stopped, leaning against a pillar of skulls to pull his inhaler from his pocket. The sharp, medicinal hiss of the aerosol was an alien sound in the cavern, a proactive strike through the heavy air. He took a long, steadying breath, his eyes closing as he maintained the clear pathways in his lungs.

"We can turn back." Angela watched the rise and fall of his chest, her guilt a nameless weight. "The Hunt isn't worth you getting sick."

Sam shook his head, his eyes snapping open. They were bright with a fierce, stubborn intelligence. "We aren't turning back. I have the shafts mapped on the tablet's local cache," he said, gesturing to the pack where the device sat insulated by lead foil. "It's blind navigation without a live link, but the geometry is already in the memory. We're closer than you think."

He was right. They were always closer than she thought, and always further from safety than she liked. A distant sound echoed through the tunnel, a heavy, rhythmic thud that didn't belong to the dripping water or the settling of the earth. It was the sound of boots. Heavy, professional boots, striking the stone with an arrogance that suggested they didn't care who heard them. Tom and Quinn were in the labyrinth.

Angela switched off the flashlight. The darkness was absolute, a thick, velvet void that seemed to press against her eyelids. She reached out and found Sam's shoulder, her grip firm and grounding. They stood still, listening. The footsteps were approaching from the north, echoing through the corridors in a way that made it impossible to judge their distance. The professional teams didn't solve clues; they tracked the persistent electronic heartbeat of the contestant coins, homing in on the radio-frequency pings that turned the hunt into a digital harvest. They followed the scents of those who did the actual thinking.

"Hide-and-seek among the dead." Sam's fingers tightened on her sleeve, his knuckles brushing her palm.

Angela pulled him into a narrow crevice between two stacks of bones, her hand tightening against the lead-lined pouch in her pocket. If the foil had a single tear, if the signal bled even a ghost of a frequency into the cold air, they were found. In Sam's pack, the tablet lay like a heavy, cold stone, its heartbeat silenced by the same metallic shroud. The skulls watched them with indifferent gazes, their secrets long since surrendered to the earth. She could hear Tom's voice now, a low, resonant rumble that carried the casual cruelty of a man who viewed the Hunt as a hunt in the most literal sense. He was talking about the microfiche, his words punctuated by the metallic clink of gear.

"The girl has the touch, but the boy has the lungs." Tom's boots clicked against the limestone, the sound ringing through the gallery. "They won't stay down here long. Find the alcove. If they aren't there, we wait by the exit."

Angela felt a cold spark of anger. It was a familiar sensation, the same one she felt when the wind tried to push her off course or when her father talked about selling the hangar. She waited until the footsteps faded toward the next gallery, then clicked the light back on, keeping the beam low. They moved with a new urgency, navigating the tunnels with a predatory focus. They weren't just searching anymore; they were escaping.

They found the alcove ten minutes later. It was a small, recessed space where the bones had been arranged in a sweeping, aerodynamic curve. To a historian, it might have looked like a religious shrine. To Angela, it was the shape of an open-cockpit biplane, the ribs of the dead forming a fuselage that protected a central stone shelf. In the center of the shelf sat a small silver tube, its surface polished and bright against the dull gray of the limestone.

Angela reached out, her fingers inches from the metal, when a sharp, plastic clatter echoed through the bone. Sam had fumbled his inhaler, the canister skittering into the open corridor. He froze, his hand pressed flat to his chest, fighting the instinctive urge to gasp; he wasn't wheezing yet, but the fear of it hung around him like a visible shroud. The silver tube was right there, a single motion away, but the light was widening and Tom was coming. Angela turned her back on the clue, lunging to catch her brother and dragging him into the deepest shadow of the stone fuselage just as Tom's boots struck the entrance. The microfiche remained on the shelf, a silver target in the center of Tom's searching beam.

"Give it over, Angela." Tom stepped into the entrance, his calm more threatening than a shout. "You've done the hard work. Let us handle the rest. Your brother looks like he's about to collapse. Don't make this more difficult than it needs to be."

Angela stepped in front of Sam, her fingers locking white-knuckled around the hilt of the multi-tool in her pocket. It wasn't much of a weapon, but it was a point of leverage. "The Hunt is about the gap between the gear and the person, Tom. You're all gear. You don't know how to read the air, even when it's standing still."

Tom took a step forward, his shadow looming large against the walls of bone. "I don't need to read the air. I just need to read the room. And right now, there's no way out for you."

Angela looked at Sam. He wasn't looking at Tom; he was looking at the ceiling, his eyes following a ghostly drift of dust. He gave her a small, sharp nod. He had found the ventilation shaft he had mentioned earlier. It was an undocumented auxiliary shaft, a narrow vertical chimney designed for airflow rather than passage, but it was their only chance. Angela knew the way the wings hummed in the bones of her inner ear, a frequency that lived in the tension of her skin, wasn't just for flight. It was for finding the openings the world tried to hide.

"The thing about the dead, Tom." Angela stood her ground in the looming shadow. "They don't like to be crowded."

She grabbed a heavy, loose femur from the wall and hurled it at the flashlight in Tom's hand. The impact was loud, a sharp crack of bone on plastic. The light flickered and died, plunging the corridor back into a chaotic, shifting darkness. In the vacuum of light, Angela lunged for the shelf, her fingers closing over the silver tube by memory alone. Tom cursed, the sound of his scuffle echoing as he tried to find his bearings.

"Now."

She grabbed Sam's hand and ran, not back toward the main entrance, but deeper into the alcove. Sam led the way, his instincts for the subterranean world far sharper than her own. They reached the base of the shaft, a narrow chimney of soot-stained brick. A series of rusted iron rungs were bolted into the masonry, disappearing into the dark above like the spine of a buried giant. Angela positioned herself beneath Sam, her hands guiding his feet and her shoulder acting as a living platform to take his weight when his breath caught. The climb was a struggle of friction and muscle, a slow, agonizing ascent through a space that didn't want them. Her shoulders scraped against the cold brick, the nylon of her jacket tearing, as she hoisted him through the narrowest bottlenecks, his small, rattling gasps echoing in the tight vertical tomb.

They emerged into a small, gated courtyard near the edge of a park. They breathed in a draft of cool, sweet oxygen that tasted of rain and the city's exhaust. Angela collapsed onto the grass, her lungs burning, her hands covered in a fine, white dust. She looked at Sam. He was gasping, his chest heaving, but he was smiling. He held up his hand, the tablet's screen suddenly bright. Now that they were clear of the lead-lined pouches, the device chirped, finding its voice again in the city's mesh. He'd managed to keep hold of the flashlight, too.

The sun was setting, casting long, violet shadows across the Parisian rooftops. The city was beautiful and indifferent, unaware of the struggle that had just unfolded beneath its streets. Angela reached into her pocket and felt the silver tube. It was safe. They had the microfiche, and they had each other, but the narrow escape had stripped away the last of the Hunt's illusion. It wasn't a game anymore. It was a pursuit where the safety of the participants was an afterthought to the prize.

"We're in second place," Sam said, reading the fresh data as his breathing leveled. "But we're the only ones who know what's on that reel."

Angela stood up, brushing the dust of the dead from her jeans. She looked at the sky, where the first stars were beginning to burn through the twilight. The wind moved through the square again, a steady, predictable current that promised momentum. They had survived the cathedral, but the real test was still waiting for them in the lagoon. The sky was waiting, and for the first time since the crash, Angela felt like she was ready to answer it.

The sun was setting, but the dark stayed in their lungs.

Chapter 19: Across the Lagoon

"You okay?" Angela asked quietly.

Sam adjusted the strap of his bag, his movements smaller and more deliberate. "Yeah. Just need a minute."

Angela let the pause remain, allowing it to exist without forcing them forward. The lagoon moved beside them in a steady rhythm, water striking stone in a sound that seemed to settle deeper than the surface. The city itself felt as though it breathed through that motion, exhaling a briny scent that carried age and repetition in equal measure. Each passing boat sent a subtle tremor through the ground beneath them, a reminder that nothing here rested on anything entirely fixed.

She stood at the edge of the water and drew in a slow breath, holding it just long enough to feel the difference before releasing it.

The air was cooler here, damp without heaviness, carrying salt beneath a more complex layering of stone, water, and time. Out across the lagoon, Venice rose in soft, shifting layers. Boats crossed in intersecting paths, their wakes stretching and dissolving into one another. Reflections broke and reformed with each movement, never holding still long enough to settle into certainty, yet never collapsing into chaos either.

The entire place felt suspended, held together by motion rather than structure.

Angela let herself take it in fully for the first time since they arrived, allowing the urgency of the hunt to loosen just enough that she could feel where she stood.

Then she brought her attention back.

They had not come to stop.

They found a water taxi along the dock, its paint worn through in places where years of use had revealed older layers beneath. The driver took them in with a brief glance and gestured toward the seats without question.

Angela stepped in first, adjusting her footing as the boat shifted beneath her. Sam followed, lowering himself carefully and leaning back slightly to open his breathing.

The engine turned over, sending a low vibration through the frame of the boat and into the soles of their shoes as they pulled away from the dock.

At first, the water resisted them in uneven jolts.

Then the motion smoothed.

Angela waited until Sam's shoulders relaxed before reaching for the map.

The GPS flickered in her hand as she adjusted the angle, aligning it with the paper. Venice resisted simplification. Streets did not behave as expected. Paths that appeared connected dissolved into bridges or dead ends. The city had grown by accumulation rather than design.

She stopped trying to force it into a straight line.

"Let's start with the clue again," she said.

Sam leaned forward. "Ezra Pound isn't a prisoner."

Angela repeated it quietly. "So we've been thinking about it wrong."

Sam nodded. "Not where he was held."

"Where he wasn't," she said.

"Or what he wasn't," Sam added.

Angela felt the direction settle.

She pulled out the guidebook and read more slowly this time, letting context shape the answer.

Pages turned beneath her fingers.

Then she stopped.

"Here," she said, turning the book toward him. "San Michele."

Sam leaned closer.

"It used to be separate," she said. "Set apart. Controlled."

"Contained," Sam said.

"But now it's a cemetery," she continued. "Not a prison."

Sam's expression shifted. "And Ezra Pound is buried there."

The answer settled without resistance.

Angela closed the book. "San Michele, please."

The driver gestured toward a low, crumbling section of the island's perimeter. "I can put you on the north bank. It is closer to the poet's corner, but the ledge is narrow. You must be quick."

Angela looked at the pursuing boat, then at Sam. He was leaning heavily against the gunwale, his face drawn and waxen in the salt spray. If she took the north bank, she could reach the grave before the others even docked, but Sam would never make the climb.

"The main gate," she said, her voice steady.

"Angela, they're right behind us," Sam whispered.

"Then they'll have to wait," she said, tightening her grip on his arm. "We're staying together."

The driver shrugged and adjusted course for the public landing.

Behind them, Venice receded.

Ahead, the island began to take shape, its form defined more by separation than by connection. Where the city spread outward, this place held inward.

Angela watched it closely.

Beside her, Sam noticed. "You think this is it?"

She held the question a moment, then nodded. "I think we're right."

Behind them, another boat followed.

Suzette stood near the edge, her balance adjusting naturally to the movement beneath her. She raised the binoculars briefly, confirming the lead boat's direction.

"They've got something," she said.

Quinn frowned at the GPS. "The coordinates aren't resolving."

"Then stop trying to resolve them," Tom said. "Follow them."

Suzette considered it, then nodded. "We stay back."

The driver adjusted their course.

The distance narrowed.

Angela felt it before she saw it—the change in the water, the echo of another engine, the subtle shift in pattern.

She turned slightly.

A boat.

Sam followed her gaze.

"We're not alone," she said.

He nodded once.

They moved forward without rushing, without speaking. Ahead, San Michele came into clearer view.

Whatever waited there, they would meet it together.

Chapter 20: Murano Glass Dead-drop

The Venetian lagoon was a masterclass in resistance. Unlike the invisible currents of the Arizona sky, the water was heavy, a green and opaque muscle that fought back against every stroke of the oars. The strain in Angela's shoulders was a slow burn, anchoring her to the present. They had bypassed the sleek, chrome-heavy water taxis for a weathered wooden boat, its hull scarred by years of salt and collisions with stone. It was slower, but it was quiet. In a city where every engine echoed off the canal walls, silence was the only armor they had left.

Sam sat in the bow, his laptop balanced on his knees, shielded from the spray by a yellow rain slicker. His face was pale, his breath ratcheting in a shallow wheeze that sent a sudden, weightless float into Angela's stomach, her breath hitching in sympathy with his. The dampness of Venice was a weight on his lungs, a thick humidity that couldn't be coughed away. He didn't look up as they passed a vaporetto, the wake tossing their small craft like a piece of driftwood. He focused on the map, his thumb tracing the jagged coastline of Murano.

"Three minutes," Sam said. He fought with his glasses, which were fogging in the salt air, wiping them on his slicker with a frustrated huff. "It's like a low-visibility approach. If Rex didn't lead us into a stall, the furnace guys take their break at ten. We've only got twelve minutes before they start the—the annealing thing. The cooling part."

Angela nodded, digging the oar deeper. A fine tension sparked in her fingertips, the oar's low frequency telegraphing the lagoon's hidden landscape. The water's subtle resistance guided her, her index finger twitching against the wood in a phantom correction for a breeze that hadn't reached the hull yet—the way the stick once whispered about a coming gust before the wings even shuddered. There were ripples that spoke of hidden pylons, and swirls that betrayed the passage of a larger vessel just out of sight. It was a different kind of navigation, grounded and gritty. She missed the three hundred and sixty degrees of the sky, the way the world fell away beneath the wings of her glider. Here, the world was a labyrinth of brick and reflection, closing in on them with every turn.

They slipped into a narrow side canal, the light disappearing as the high walls of the industrial district rose around them. The smell changed. The rotting salt of the lagoon was replaced by the dry, metallic scent of extreme heat and the phantom tang of ozone. Murano was an island of fire, a place where sand was forced into clarity through the sheer will of the furnace. Angela tied the boat to a rusted ring set into the stone, her movements quick and practiced. Sam moved first—and immediately chose wrong.

He turned into a narrow passage that pinched into shadow, the walls close enough to flatten the sound of their steps. "This way," he said, already moving, his confidence just a fraction ahead of the data.

Ten steps in, he stopped.

Something didn't line up. Not visually—acoustically. The space swallowed too much. No echo bleed from a main canal. No engine noise carrying through the brick. It was a pocket, sealed off from the larger flow.

"...no," he said, quieter now.

Angela didn't speak. She watched him recalibrate.

Sam stepped back out into the open, turning in a slow half-circle, not looking at the streets but past them—listening for pressure, for movement. "This place isn't laid out," he muttered. "It's... layered. Like airflow. You don't follow the path, you follow where things open."

He angled toward a different bridge, one that didn't look like the fastest route.

"They'll cover the obvious approach," he added, almost as an afterthought. "We go where it doesn't make sense." Angela followed without question.

"Stay close," she whispered. "And watch your breath. The heat inside is going to be dry."

Sam closed his laptop and tucked it into his bag. He looked at the looming silhouette of the factory, his eyes narrowed, his gaze sharpening into the same needle-point focus he used on a difficult equation. He had ceased to be a passenger; he was the navigator of their survival. They moved toward a side entrance, a heavy steel door that stood slightly ajar to let out the staggering heat of the interior.

The transition was a physical blow. The air inside the furnace room was a shimmering wall of gold and orange, tight with the subsonic roar of the gas burners. It was a cathedral of industry, the rafters lost in a haze of smoke and flickering light. Sweat sprang to Angela's skin instantly. To her left, long rows of cooling kilns—the lehrs—stretched into the shadows. The workers had just stepped away, their tools leaning against the brickwork like discarded weapons.

"There," Sam said, pointing toward the third kiln. "The clue mentioned the heart of the ruby. I read on a forum that they use real gold to get that color. It's like a high-spec turbine—expensive, but if it's trim-locked by the heat, it just shatters."

They hurried toward the kiln. The heat radiating from the metal housing was enough to make Angela's eyes water. Inside the cooling chamber, dozens of glass vessels sat in various stages of completion. They were beautiful, translucent shapes of crimson and violet, but they weren't looking for beauty. They were looking for a failure.

Angela's hands hovered over the glass, her palms catching the frantic, microscopic pulse of the cooling shapes. Her mother's hands had once read a hot engine the same way, finding hairline fractures in the metal's resonance. She moved past a set of perfect vases, her fingers stopping near a heavy, misshapen orb of deep red glass. It was flawed, a thick bubble of air trapped near the base, distorting the light.

"This is it," Angela said. Her voice was small beneath the roar of the burners. "It's too heavy. The balance is off."

She reached for a pair of insulated tongs resting on a nearby workbench. With an unwavering hand, she tilted the cooling glass. Hidden within the thick, ruby-colored base was a small, dark shadow. It wasn't an air bubble. It was a heat-resistant tag, fused into the glass while it was still molten. She tapped the base with the tongs, the sound a dull, heavy thud instead of a clear ring.

"Quinn's teams have more money, better gear," Sam muttered, his eyes darting toward the main entrance. "But they're just redlining the approach. They aren't looking for the structural fatigue."

Angela carefully shattered the base of the flawed orb against the edge of the workbench. The glass gave way with a sharp, crystalline snap, showering the floor in red shards that looked like spilled wine. She reached into the debris and pulled out the tag. It was a small slip of blackened titanium, etched with a set of coordinates that glittered in the firelight. It was cold to the touch now, a hard piece of the future won from the fire.

A shadow cut across the floor. Angela went still as stone, her solar plexus tightening as her hand closed over the tag. At the far end of the workshop, three figures stood in the doorway. They weren't tourists, and they weren't glassblowers. They were young, dressed in dark windbreakers, their faces as unreadable as unworked stone, the look of men who measured their lives in the simple mathematics of a paycheck.

"Quinn's scouts," Sam whispered, his words catching in a throat that had suddenly gone dry as the desert floor. He reached for his inhaler, his fingers trembling.

The scouts didn't rush. They moved with the unhurried precision of predators, fanning out to block the primary exits. Their familiarity with the layout suggested they had been waiting for the Santiagos to do the heavy lifting. One of them, a tall boy with a jagged scar across his eyebrow, held out a hand, gesturing for the tag.

No weapons stood in the workshop, only the tools of a trade she didn't fully comprehend. The room resolved into a series of rapid-fire strikes—the distance to the side door, the speed of the scouts, and the exit angles. The horizon locked in her vision with the same electric clarity of the cockpit—the moment the air thins at altitude and survival relies on a single, sharp turn. She didn't have a glider, but she had the heat.

"Sam, get to the door on the count of three," she said, her voice dropping into a low, iron tone.

"What are you doing?"

"Reading the room."

She grabbed a heavy iron glass-mold from the bench, its surface still radiating a dull, dangerous heat. As the scouts closed the gap, she didn't run. Instead, she swung the mold with everything she had, slamming it into a rack of empty metal blowpipes. The sound was deafening, a discordant, metallic crash that vibrated through her teeth, echoing through the high-ceilinged room like a gunshot. The scouts flinched, the sudden violence of the noise shattering the measured tread of their advance.

Before they could recover, Angela kicked over a bucket of water used for cooling the tools. The water hit the hot floor near the main furnace, erupting into a blinding, white wall of steam. It was an artificial cloud, a sudden loss of visibility that she navigated by memory and instinct. In the white-out, the world became a matter of memory and instinct.

"Now!" she shouted.

She grabbed Sam's arm and pulled him through the fog. They moved by touch, their feet finding the gaps between the workbenches. The scouts were shouting, their voices muffled by the hiss of the steam and the roar of the fires. Angela pushed through the side door, the cool air of the alleyway hitting her face like a benediction.

They didn't stop to look back. They sprinted through the maze of narrow passages, their boots echoing on the damp bricks. Murano was a series of sharp corners and dead ends, a place designed to confuse the uninitiated. But Angela kept the image of the lagoon in her mind, a fixed point of navigation. She led them toward a low bridge, then down a flight of moss-covered steps to where their boat was still moored.

Sam collapsed into the bow, his chest heaving as he fought for air. Angela untied the rope and shoved off, the wooden hull groaning along the stone. She took the oars and heaved with a desperate, surging pull, the boat cutting through the dark water of the canal. Behind them, the factory was a glowing ember against the gray Venetian sky.

They reached the open lagoon just as the sun began to sink, the water turning the color of the ruby glass they had left behind in shards. The coordinate tag was a solid weight in Angela's pocket, a promise of momentum. Sam's breath was finally returning, his eyes fixed on the low, brick-walled expanse of San Michele. It was a short crossing from Murano, barely a kilometer of choppy green water, a passage between the living fire of the furnaces and the silent stone of the dead.

"We got it," Sam said, his voice a rasping shadow of itself. "We actually got it."

Angela didn't answer. The light hit the water, the surface shimmering with a deceptive, shifting clarity. They had the coordinates, but the city was still a maze, and the professional teams were no longer just watching from the sidelines. The game was hardening, shedding the clean layers of intelligence for something more primal—a contest of who was willing to leave the most wreckage in their wake.

The sky was turning a bruised purple, the same color as the shadows in her mother's old flight logs. Angela adjusted her grip on the oars, her palms raw and stinging. She steered toward the white Istrian stone of the Cimitero vaporetto stop, avoiding the churning wake of the larger boats. The lagoon was vast, but their world had shrunk to the narrow stretch of water between the glassworks and the graves.

The water didn't offer a path, it only offered a choice.

Chapter 21: The Edge of the Water

The scent of the lagoon—salt, diesel, and something ancient like wet stone—clung to the back of Angela's throat. They had left the sulfurous heat of the Murano glassworks behind only minutes ago, a short passage across the open lagoon—a crossing into another era. Their weathered wooden boat pitched in the wake of a passing transport before Angela pulled it toward the Cimitero stop. She tied the boat to a rusted ring set into the stone, the hull knocking along the salt-stained pylons. San Michele was separate from Venice; the frantic chatter of the city died into the rhythmic, heavy movement of water against moss-slicked brick. The separation was more than geographic, a quality quieter and more deliberate, as though the island had accepted stillness long ago and continued to choose it every day since.

Narrow paths wound between carefully tended graves, their lines precise without rigidity. Stone markers rose in varied forms—simple slabs worn smooth by years of weather, small domed structures catching pale light at shifting angles, wrought-iron enclosures delicate enough to cast lace-like shadows across the ground. Some graves were marked with newly placed flowers, while others held framed photographs, small ceramic crosses, glass votives, or objects holding the memories of lives in ways language could not contain. Names stood in marble and granite, some deeply cut and clear, others fading at the edges where time had softened the letters.

Above it all, the sky opened wide and pale, uninterrupted by the close architecture of the city. The air was altered, carrying sound more gently; everything moved with a measure of care for what had already come to rest.

A shift took hold the moment her feet touched the stone.

The urgency that had carried her across continents shifted, settling lower and steadier, guiding her now with a more controlled sense of direction. The island would not respond to haste.

Beside her, Sam inhabited the same gravity. He did not speak, but his steps slowed as they moved away from the dock, his breathing deliberate against the heavy dampness of the lagoon—a weight that pulled him back to the airless dormitories at St. Jude's, where every breath had been a negotiation with the walls. One hand brushed the strap of his bag in a small, grounding motion that had become familiar over the past ten days.

They had only just begun along the path when someone passed them heading in the opposite direction.

The young woman moved quickly toward the water taxi launch, her pace controlled but purposeful, having already found what she came for, leaving no reason to remain. She paused briefly by a neglected grave near the path, her hand reaching out to straighten a fallen copper vase before the water taxi arrived. The gesture was small, a momentary softening of the tight inward focus she carried. Then her phone vibrated. She answered it with a sharp, defensive motion, her face hardening into a familiar mask—the look of someone whose worth was being negotiated in real-time. "I'm at the dock, Father," she said, her voice brittle. "I won't let the legacy slip. I know the cost of failure." She stepped onto the boat without looking back, her spine rigid with a weight that had nothing to do with the container she held.

She reached the dock. "She was here for the cache," Sam said.

The young woman vanished into the crowd at the taxi launch.

They were not first.

The truth settled without the sharp edge it might have carried earlier. The frustration that might once have followed was absent, replaced instead by something steadier. This was the shape of the game now. They had moved beyond empty spaces and waiting clues; they were part of a pattern formed by others moving with the same intention, and each new location made that more visible.

"Then we're close," she said.

They moved deeper into the cemetery, their pace measured, their attention shifting from urgency to observation.

The details offered themselves to a slower pace: the spacing of graves, the clusters of family plots, and the variations in layout that suggested intention rather than accident. The clue would not reveal itself to someone who expected it to announce itself.

A step behind, Sam read the names, dates, and fragments of lives compressed into carved lines. Now and then, he paused a moment longer at a photograph or a pair of dates marking lives cut short. It added a different weight to the island, compressing the game into something smaller and stranger by comparison.

A salt-edged quiet settled between them, as heavy and immutable as the island's damp stone.

The island carried its own rhythm, and without a conscious mark of the transition, they had both adjusted to it.

Margaret and Joe.

They stood shoulder to shoulder, but as Angela approached, their posture stiffened into a territorial line. It wasn't the easy greeting she had expected; it was the bracing of rivals who had claimed the ground first.

"You're trailing haste into a sanctuary," Margaret said, her voice devoid of its usual warmth. She stepped slightly to the left, obscuring the base of the stone. "You're just a collector of coordinates, Angela. You don't have the ear for the poetry beneath the dirt."

Joe didn't look up. "The Geopoets don't share the rhythm with those who only run. If you can't hear the island, why should we help you find the next verse?"

Angela stopped. The rejection was a physical barrier. She knelt, pressing her palm flat to the damp, moss-rimmed base of the monument. She let the stone's vibration sink into her skin until it hummed through the marrow of her hands. The slow, rhythmic shove of the tide moved through the island's pilings and the heavy, silent patience of the earth.

"The stone is shivering," Angela said softly. "It's the pressure of the lagoon, not the cold. It's an anchor for a city that's slowly pulling away. That's why the container is here. It's the one place the salt can't reach."

Margaret remained unmoved, her hand shielding the base of the monument. "A child can follow a GPS," she said. "But we've spent years learning the breath of these islands. If you can't tell us what this stone is holding, you don't deserve what's hidden beneath it."

Angela did not pull back. The vibration revealed a specific, hollow resonance, a cavity tucked beneath the north corner. "The shivering is uneven," she said, her voice dropping. "There's a dead spot by the left footing—a pocket of air trapped against the cypress roots. That's where you've been looking, isn't it? But you're looking for a box, and you should be looking for a void."

Joe finally looked up, his eyes widening with recognition. He exchanged a look with Margaret. "She isn't just reading coordinates," he said. "She's diagnosing the decay." He stepped back, granting her space as a rival rather than a guest.

The name on the headstone was clear.

Ezra Pound.

Near the base of the grave, positioned with enough care to blend among flowers and personal offerings, sat a waterproof container. It did not draw attention to itself. To anyone not looking for it, it might have passed as another object placed there in remembrance.

But there, nestled against the stone, it was undeniable.

Joe bent slightly, reaching toward it with quiet confidence.

The air tightened.

Behind Margaret and Joe, another presence closed the distance.

Quinn stepped forward first, his expression easy and his tone light enough to pass as casual. "Looks like we're all chasing the same thing."

Margaret turned, her gaze sharpening back into a defensive edge. "The hunt is over for you, Quinn."

Joe didn't look at him, his body shielding the stone like a barricade. "The meter is ours, Quinn. You're out of your depth."

Suzette and Tom were already approaching, moving past Quinn.

Their pace did not belong in a place like this. It was too direct, too coordinated.

"Wait," Angela said, but the moment had already begun to move faster than her voice.

Tom reached the container first, lifting it in a single decisive motion without hesitation. Suzette moved beside him immediately, her focus narrowing to the container even before it was fully secured.

At the same time, Quinn stepped into Joe's space, a calculated intrusion. Joe braced his shoulder against him, but Tom's sudden, low reach bypassed them both. Margaret lunged for the container, her fingers catching the lid before Quinn's arm swept her back. In the brief, sharp struggle for the ground, the space had changed.

Margaret stumbled slightly, Joe caught her arm, and in the brief moment it took for them to regain balance, the space had changed.

"They've taken it!" Joe shouted, his voice cutting sharply through the quiet of the island.

Sam moved at once.

He didn't hesitate or calculate. He stepped directly into Tom's path, forcing him to stop as momentum met resistance in a sharp, immediate collision.

The container shifted between them, each reaching for it in rapid succession. Tom twisted. Sam braced. Shoes scraped against stone. For a brief instant, the struggle balanced on a single unstable point.

Then the container slipped free.

It struck the ground between them with a hollow crack.

Sam reached for it first.

Tom shoved him back.

Tom's strength overwhelmed him. Sam stumbled, caught himself, and came forward again before the loss of balance had fully registered. He kept moving, pushing forward with a direct determination that closed the gap created by force.

That disruption, brief as it was, gave Suzette the opening she needed.

She stepped in with practiced precision, bent, and lifted the container before either of them could recover. In one smooth motion, she opened it and scanned the contents, selecting without hesitation. What mattered to her disappeared into her hand at once, while the rest fell away as irrelevant. Some items scattered across the stone. Others bounced and rolled toward the edge. A few slipped over and vanished into the water below.

The act cut more sharply than the theft itself. It went beyond winning. It was refusal, a willingness to discard anything outside the narrow line of victory.

Suzette lifted her gaze.

It settled on Angela with calm certainty.

"I thought you would have learned by now," she said evenly. "You don't win against me." Her gaze dropped to the churned water where Sam had disappeared, and for a fleeting second, the mask fractured, revealing a hollow exhaustion that mirrored Angela's own. "Some of us don't have the luxury of coming in second, Angela. My father didn't raise me to survive a loss."

There was no anger in her voice.

That made it worse.

Then she turned.

Tom struck once, fast and direct, with the flat of his arm.

Sam lost his footing.

The scene collapsed into a single compressed moment—the break in balance, the absence where he had been standing, the shift of his body away from stone and toward open water.

Then came the splash.

Sam disappeared.

Angela moved without thinking.

As he broke the surface, gasping, she was already in the water, the lagoon's chill snapped through her clothes, locking her muscles. The water was heavy, an immediate and invasive weight.

Sam's body was a heavy, unyielding weight.

Time stretched.

"Sam," she said, her voice tight but steady. "Stay with me."

She reached him and caught his arm, turning his weight toward the edge. Every movement became functional, stripped of everything unnecessary. She pulled, adjusted, braced, refusing to waste motion. His body resisted only in the way exhaustion resists—through heaviness, through delay, through the terrifying uncertainty of not responding immediately.

When she pulled him onto the stone, her hands moved with a clinical, practiced rhythm. She performed the specific, rhythmic percussion her mother had drilled into them, a sharp sequence to clear his lungs, ignoring the monks to focus on the exact tilt of Sam's chin. It was a sequence Mike had spent years trying to suppress, yet as the water leave Sam's lungs, its necessity was absolute.

Around them, the quiet of the island broke. Voices rose. Footsteps approached. Somewhere behind her, Margaret called for help, her voice controlled even in alarm.

The monks arrived quickly, their presence bringing calm rather than urgency. They moved with quiet efficiency, bringing blankets, guiding people back, speaking softly as they worked. One knelt beside Sam and spoke to him in Italian, the tone steady enough that the meaning did not need translation.

Sam coughed. Air returned in a sharp, uneven pull. Angela found his inhaler and pressed it into his hand. He took the medicine in a long, desperate draw, fighting the panicked tightening in his ribs—a familiar smothering—not by the water, but by the crushing weight of his father's constant, hovering anxiety.

"I'm here," she said.

He nodded once.

Suzette stood back from the others, close enough to see, far enough that she didn't have to be part of it.

Water ran from his clothes across the stone in thin lines that caught the light before disappearing into the seams.

Joe's voice cut through the moment.

"The coin—it's still there."

Angela turned.

The container had drifted just beyond the edge, one remaining coin caught against its side.

Sam's attention snapped to the container. His voice was rough but steadier than expected. "You can get it."

The memory of how quickly control could fail stalled her.

Then she nodded.

"Stay with him," she said.

Margaret touched her arm in acknowledgment.

When Angela entered the water again, she moved differently.

There was no rush, no wasted motion. Each stroke was controlled, measured against the current. The container drifted farther as she approached, nudged by a distant wake.

Then the coin slipped free.

It vanished beneath the surface.

Angela drew one breath and followed.

The water closed over her. Light dissolved into a muted green haze, and the world beneath lost proportion. Shapes blurred. Distance shifted. Her lungs tightened before she reached the spot.

Still, she reached.

Her fingers closed around metal.

The certainty of contact cut through everything else.

She pushed upward, broke the surface, and turned back toward the stone.

When hands reached down to pull her up, she was already shivering.

But the coin remained in her grasp.

Later, inside the quiet warmth of the retreat house, everything slowed again.

Inside was dry stone, warm light, and a hush that shaped how people spoke—a jarring stillness after the cold water.

Sam sat wrapped in blankets, a ceramic cup warming his hands as color slowly returned to his face. His hair lay damp against his forehead, and now and then a shiver passed through him. Angela sat close, her own blanket pulled tight, exhaustion settling into her in heavy layers.

Joe approached, the retrieved coin balanced on his palm.

"We've spent our lives studying the meter of this place," he said, his voice gravelly. "But we've been too caught up in reading it to ever make the jump. You didn't hesitate."

He pressed the metal into her hand. "This isn't a gift, Angela. It's an acknowledgment."

Margaret stepped closer, her expression shifting into something deeper, more respectful.

"Then keep it as a reminder," she said. "Not of the cache, but of the moment you stopped being a collector and became part of the stone."

The coin rested heavy in her palm, no longer mere proof of progress. It felt tied instead to the water, to Sam, to the moment when everything had nearly gone wrong.

She accepted it.

For a moment, neither of them moved.

The quiet of the room held, dense and complete, as if stepping out of it would set everything in motion again. Angela turned the coin slowly in her hand, its weight settling deeper the longer she held it.

Beside her, Sam's breathing had steadied, though a faint unevenness remained, a trace of the water that hadn't fully left.

At the airport, the goodbye unfolded quietly.

Margaret embraced Angela with steady warmth. "We'll see each other again," she said, not as comfort but as fact.

"I know," Angela said.

Joe shook Sam's hand with quiet seriousness. "Take care of each other."

"We will," Sam said.

When they stepped apart, nothing was finished. It was a pause in something still continuing.

Later, Sam stretched across a row of seats as the first flight climbed into the night, sleep taking him quickly. The tenth day ended in the low hum of jet fuel and pressurized air, leaving them only two days to cross the world. His breathing had settled into something steady.

Angela sat nearby, the coin turning slowly in her hand.

She opened her laptop and entered the tracking number. The page refreshed.

Uluru, Australia.

She stared at it. Another continent, another distance, another decision.

For a moment, she didn't move. Then she closed the laptop.

When she called her father, the panic in his voice was already a roar. In his study, Mike stood surrounded by the heavy, airless silence of the life he had built to protect them. He was holding a microfiber cloth, his knuckles white against the mahogany of his desk. "The tickets are booked for New York," he said, his voice brittle. "The feed was live, Angela. He was under for forty seconds. You're coming home."

"He's breathing," she said, her voice shaking with cold but gaining strength. "I used the percussion. The 'Elena strike.' It's the only reason he's here, Mike."

Mike looked at his hands, raw from the bleach he'd been using to scrub the baseboards of a house already sterile. On his desk lay Elena's final flight log, the leather cracked. He'd been obsessively indexing it, trying to map her last movements to find a mistake he could finally fix. Instead, his gaze fell on a note she had scrawled in the margin: Protection is a form of pruning; do it too much, and nothing grows. We provide the oxygen, Mike, but they have to learn to process the thin air on their own. He looked at the sterile, safe walls of his office. He had been presiding over a slow, quiet drowning. He had tried to keep them safe, but he had only succeeded in keeping them stagnant.

A man leaning against the terminal glass nearby adjusted his phone. Beyond the glass, a plane sat grounded in a distant hangar and a sparrow lay still on the exterior ledge. "She's right, Mike," he said, loud enough for the satellite link to catch. "You can keep them in the hangar, but it won't help them when they're over the water. Let the girl go."

A mechanical hush followed, the line humming with a low-frequency vibration like an engine idling deep within a hangar.

"Rex?" Mike's voice was barely a whisper, thick with sudden, jagged conflict.

"Send them to the Outback, Mike," Rex said, then walked away. "Or you'll lose them anyway."

Another silence stretched, heavy and long.

"I'm re-routing the tickets," Mike said finally, his voice sounding older, more resolute. "Australia. Finish it. I'm booking a flight to Darwin now—I'll be there for the final leg. Just… keep using her techniques, Angela. Keep him safe until I get there."

Later, standing in line for coffee she did not really want, the movement of the airport settled around Angela.

"Scusi."

She turned. It was the man from the terminal glass.

"I know you," he said, his posture composed.

Angela gave a tired smile. "You seem to know my father, too."

He studied her briefly, his eyes sharp but not unkind. "I knew Elena," he said. "She wouldn't have wanted you to go back to that house yet."

Then he stepped away, vanishing into the flow of the terminal.

Sam returned a few minutes later.

"Do you know who that was?" he asked.

She shook her head.

"That was Rex St. James."

She turned, but he was already gone.

Still, something had shifted, not dramatically, but enough.

Sam glanced up at the departure screen and stopped.

"He did it," he said. "The itinerary just updated. Australia."

Angela blinked, then laughed, the sound breaking through something that had been holding too tightly.

The journey that followed was a grueling exercise in endurance, a forty-hour sequence of connecting gates and the stale, recycled breath of a dozen time zones. They chased the sun across the Mediterranean and lost it somewhere over the Arabian Sea, watching the world dissolve into a sequence of terminal lights and altitude-deadened silence. The sun rose again, white and clinical, as they crossed the equator on the long haul toward the southern hemisphere. By the time the wheels finally touched the tarmac in Darwin, the eleventh day had surrendered to the twelfth, and the window of the race had narrowed to its final, jagged margin.

The heat of the Outback met them first, dry and immediate—the scorched greeting of their final day, carrying dust and sun-scorched eucalyptus. Red earth stretched toward a horizon that offered no shade, a vast expanse that rendered the remaining hours of their deadline both urgent and infinitesimal. The horizon sat low and uninterrupted, held in a silence so dry and vast it drank the sound from their breaths.

Sam leaned on the window. “It’s greener than I thought.”

The greenery scrolled past, vast and indifferent. “It still feels like home.”

They drove forward together, the road stretching ahead.

After a moment, Sam glanced over. “Think we’re behind?”

The map in her lap matched the vastness of the horizon.

Distance was no longer something to overcome.

“Yeah,” she said.

Then she smiled.

“But we’re still in it.”

A notification pulsed on the dashboard as the satellite signal settled. Angela reached for it. A message from Margaret and Joe appeared, sent from a station behind them. The photo showed them wind-burned and smiling, standing before red dust and distant windmills. Joe held a sign that read “Next Chapter,” while Margaret pointed toward the horizon.

The image of red dust and windmills gave way to the road stretching ahead.

The distance no longer isolated. It connected.

They were still moving—

and now they were not moving alone.

Chapter 22: The Darwin Layover

Angela shoulder-barged the terminal doors with the recycled chill of the cabin still clinging to her skin. The Darwin heat hit like a physical weight, a sodden wool blanket heavy with the scent of salt and rotting mangroves—the antithesis of the Arizona desert and a cruel joke to bodies already hollowed out by three continents in six brutal days—the clock already bleeding into the seventh. There was the eleven-hour crossing to Paris, a frantic blur in Venice, and the bone-deep erosion of a forty-hour sequence of budget connections through crowded Asian hubs to reach the Top End. Angela's clothes were stiff with the salt of Venice and the grime of a dozen terminals, her skin filmed with a layer of grit that no airport sink could scrub away during their frantic, sleepless layovers. In the hangar at home, the heat was a clean, sharpening stone—a dry weight that tasted of creosote and scorched oil—paring everything down to its essence. Here, the humidity settled like a thick soup, adding layers to everything it touched. It clung to the skin, seeped into the lungs, and turned the simple act of breathing into a deliberate, conscious effort. Moisture bloomed on her forehead before they even cleared the terminal doors. The sun was a white-hot coin hammered into the center of the sky, marking a Tuesday they had nearly missed entirely during the transit across the International Date Line. It was a living heat, one that didn't just burn but consumed.

Sam walked beside her, his movements sluggish, his chest already tightening in the saturated air. Each breath felt like pulling wet wool through a narrow straw, a labor that had begun the moment the cabin pressure equalized with the Darwin swelter. They were halfway through the twelve-day window Rex had granted, and every hour spent in a pressurized cabin was a theft of their remaining time. He was shivering despite the heat, his body unable to reconcile the Darwin noon with what his nerves insisted was Venice midnight, his stomach a clenched, aching knot after days of partitioned airline snacks and lukewarm airport tap water. They hadn't eaten a real meal since a stale baguette in a terminal at De Gaulle. His inhaler was a permanent fixture in his right hand, a small plastic talisman against the crushing humidity. He didn't look at the palm trees or the sulphur-crested cockatoos that shrieked like rusted hinges as they circled the airfield. His eyes were fixed on the cracked screen of his phone, watching a small, pulsing blue dot that represented a high-priority hitchhiker cache. It was a beacon Rex St. James had released specifically for the elite tier of the Hunt, a digital flare that had appeared on their radar the moment they touched Australian soil.

"It's moving," Sam said, the words hitching behind a thin, wet rattle in his lungs. "The signal is drifting with the tide, or maybe the wreck is settling. It's Tuesday afternoon, Ang. If we wait for the morning flight to Alice Springs, we'll have less than five days left to find the rest. It'll be submerged or gone."

Angela looked at her brother. The circles under his eyes were the color of bruised plums, and his skin had a translucent, waxen quality that worried her. She thought of their father, Mike, and the rigid, fearful silence he had maintained since they left. He would want them to sleep. He would want them to find a sterile hotel room with recirculated air and heavy curtains. But Mike wasn't here. He was a ghost in her phone, a series of unread messages that she couldn't bring herself to open because she knew the weight of his caution would ground her faster than any engine failure.

"We aren't waiting," Angela said. She adjusted the strap of her pack, feeling the gold coin shift in her pocket. "The sky is shifting, Sam. Can you feel it? The pressure is dropping. If we don't move now, the weather will make the decision for us."

They bypassed the taxi stand, heading instead for a gravel lot where the vehicles were more rust than paint. The man behind the counter had skin like cured leather and eyes that didn't miss the way Angela's hand hovered over the card reader. When the machine let out a sharp, mocking beep of rejection, the silence in the shack grew teeth. The flights through the European legs had scoured the proceeds of her mother's vintage watch to nothing; they were surviving now on the meager stipend Rex released with each logged waypoint. It was a tether, not a fortune, and the card reader's refusal to acknowledge their digital credit was a final, cruel hurdle. They were starving, vibrating with a fatigue so deep it felt structural, and their remaining funds were locked behind a Hunt interface that felt more like a cage than a bank. Angela looked at Sam's gray, trembling face and knew they were at the edge of collapse. With a hollow feeling in her chest, she unclipped the silver flight wings from her collar—her father's wings, earned in a sky that felt a lifetime away—and set them on the counter. The man studied the silver, his thumb tracing the worn feathers, before sliding a set of keys toward her and pointing toward the north, a gesture that encompassed the entire, untamed horizon. The drive was a blur of gray-green scrub as the afternoon light began to lengthen and yellow over standing water, the road narrowing until the asphalt gave way to a corrugated, iron-rich washboard that rattled Angela's teeth and sang a metallic vibrato through the steering column. She kept her hands loose on the wheel, letting the truck find its own path through the ruts, much like she would let a glider find the center of a thermal.

The wetlands began where the trees grew legs. The mangroves stood in the brackish water like an army of spiders, their roots interlocking in a chaotic, impenetrable weave. Angela parked the truck where the track dissolved into a muddy bank. The silence that greeted them was absolute, broken only by the high-pitched whine of mosquitoes and the distant, rhythmic thrum of a bullfrog. It was a heavy, expectant quiet, the kind that preceded a strike.

"The beacon is three hundred meters in," Sam said, pointing his phone toward the dense heart of the swamp. He wiped sweat from his eyes, his thumb smearing the screen. "The signal is jumping—it's hitting something massive and metallic just ahead."

Angela looked at the water. It was the color of weak tea, opaque and still. She knew about the crocodiles here. She had read the warnings in the airport, the colorful signs that treated the apex predators as a local charm rather than a death sentence. A familiar tightening seized her chest, accompanied by the copper tang of fear, the same cold spike of adrenaline that had pierced her when the main spar of her mother's plane groaned under the load. It was the instinct to turn back, to choose the safety of the shore over the uncertainty of the current.

She stepped into the water anyway. The mud swallowed her boots with a wet, sucking sound—a cold invitation. The water proved surprisingly warm, a tepid bath that offered no relief from the stifling humidity. Sam followed, his breath coming in shallow, rhythmic whistles. He was fighting the instinct to gasp, knowing the heavy, spore-laden air would only lock his airway tighter if he forced the intake. He held his phone high, a digital compass guiding them through a labyrinth where every tree looked identical to the last. They waded through knee-deep muck, their eyes scanning the surface for the telltale ripple of a snout or the blink of a prehistoric eye. Every floating log was a threat; every snapping branch was a warning.

They found the wreck at the edge of a small clearing where the mangroves had failed to take hold. It was a Mitchell B-25, the old bomber's spine broken and half-submerged in the mire. The aluminum skin was a map of oxidation, the original olive-drab paint long ago bleached to a ghostly, mottled gray. It was the skeleton of a great, prehistoric bird that had fallen from the sky and been forgotten by time. The wings were sheared off, resting like tombstones in the mud, and the nose had collapsed into the tea-colored sediment, giving the aircraft a look of profound, eternal exhaustion.

Angela stopped, her breath catching in her throat. The history of the impact was etched into the twisted metal. It wasn't just a wreck; it was a memory of a failure. She reached out and touched the jagged edge of the tail fin, her fingers tracing the rivets. The metal didn't hum, and there was no sharp ping of cooling components; it was cold and dead, a stark contrast to the vibrating energy of the sailplanes she loved. This was what happened when the air stopped listening.

"The signal is coming from the starboard engine," Sam said, his voice echoing strangely against the hollow metal. He pointed a trembling finger at the rusted mass. "It's buried deep in the housing. We have to get up there."

The engine was a mass of rusted cylinders and tangled wiring, perched precariously on a section of the wing that still clung to the main body. It sat several feet above the waterline, a height that required Angela to climb the slick, unstable fuselage. She looked at Sam, who was struggling to maintain his footing in the shifting mud. He was leaning forward, hands on his knees, his shoulders heaving in a desperate struggle to find oxygen in the soup of the swamp. The humidity had become a physical barrier, and the whistle in his windpipe was growing sharper—a thin, high note of distress he tried to damp down with sheer will.

"Stay here," Angela commanded. "Keep an eye on the water. If anything moves, anything at all, you shout. Do you hear me?"

Sam nodded, his eyes wide and dark. He leaned against a mangrove root and took a long, preventative draw from his inhaler, the hiss of the medication lost in the drone of the swamp. Angela turned back to the plane. She found a foothold in a jagged tear in the aluminum and hauled herself up. The metal groaned under her weight, a low, metallic protest that vibrated through her boots. She didn't think about the structural integrity of the sixty-year-old airframe. She didn't think about the salt-weakened rivets or the way the fuselage tilted toward the water. She only thought about the movement, the precise application of force required to keep her balance.

The cockpit was a cavern of shadows, the instrument panel stripped of its dials and switches. It was a hollow skull, its eyes staring blankly at the canopy of trees. Angela crawled along the spine of the wing, her hands slick with a mixture of sweat and old hydraulic fluid. The smell of the wreck was overwhelming now, a mix of stagnant water, bird droppings, and the faint, lingering scent of scorched oil. It was the smell of a machine that had been forced into the earth.

She reached the engine. The beacon was tucked behind a rusted inspection plate that was held in place by two stubborn, corroded screws. Angela reached into her bag and pulled out a multi-tool, her hands shaking. The jet lag was a physical weight, a literal lag in her synapses that made her hands move seconds after her brain commanded them. A sudden wave of vertigo, born of a dozen time zones and the hollow ache of hunger, made the fuselage seem to tilt beneath her. Her hands, slick with sweat and the residue of travel, slipped against the tool. She jammed the screwdriver into the first screw and turned. It didn't move. She tried again, putting her shoulder into the effort, her boots slipping on the curved surface of the wing.

Easy, Angela, she heard her mother's voice, a soft whisper in the stagnant heat. *Don't fight the metal. Listen to it. Find the gap between the rust and the steel.*

She took a deep breath, drawing the leaden weight of the swamp into her lungs. She closed her eyes for a second; the plane tilted, and the wind moved through the hollow fuselage. She adjusted her grip, shifting her weight to find a more stable center. She pressed the tool home and turned with a slow, steady pressure. The screw gave way with a sharp, crystalline crack. The second one followed moments later. She pried the plate loose, revealing a small, waterproof cylinder nestled among the dead cylinders.

"Got it!" she yelled, her voice breaking the stillness of the swamp.

She slid back down the wing, her heart pounding in her ribs. She hit the water with a splash, the mud rising up to meet her. Sam was already there, his hand outstretched, his face lit with a frantic, desperate energy. Angela handed him the cylinder, and they waded back toward the higher ground, their movements hurried by the darkening sky. The sun had dipped below the horizon, leaving the wetlands in a state of bruised purple twilight.

They sat on the tailgate of the truck, their stomachs cramping in a synchronized rhythm of deprivation while the mosquitoes swarmed. Sam unscrewed the cap, his fingers clumsy with exhaustion. Inside was a small piece of vellum, the paper surprisingly dry and crisp. There were no coordinates on it, no numbers to plug into a GPS. There was only a single line of elegant, hand-drawn script, out of place in the rugged Australian landscape.

The Rock is a Mirror.

Sam stared at the words, his brow furrowed in concentration. He turned the paper over, looking for a hidden map or a secondary clue, but there was nothing else. The warning was as stark and singular as a mountain peak.

"The Rock is a Mirror," Sam repeated, his voice barely a whisper. "He's talking about Uluru. But it's a monolith. It's solid stone. How can a rock be a mirror?"

Angela leaned back against the cab of the truck, looking up at the first stars beginning to pierce the thick haze. She thought about the way the light hit the

Arizona desert at dawn, the way the shadows stretched and morphed until the ground looked like a reflection of the sky. She thought about the way a pilot judged altitude not by the ground itself, but by the way the light played off the horizon.

"It's not about the stone, Sam," Angela said, the realization settling in her chest like a stone in a pool. "It's about the perspective. Everyone is going to go to Uluru and look at the rock. They're going to climb it, search the caves, look at the paintings. They're going to treat it like a destination."

"But Rex wants us to look at the reflection," Sam finished, his eyes brightening. "The shadow. Or the light it bounces back. If the rock is a mirror, then the clue isn't on the rock. It's in what the rock is showing us."

The realization shifted the space between them. The hunt was no longer just endurance or technical skill. It had become a game of perception, a challenge to see the world as something to be read rather than taken at face value. Rex St. James wasn't just hiding caches; he was forcing them to look differently. He was teaching them to read the landscape the way their mother had taught them to read the air.

Sam leaned his head against Angela's shoulder, his breathing finally leveling out into a ragged but steady rhythm, though the tightness in his bronchi remained a dull, warning ache. The humidity persisted, a dense, unyielding presence, but it no longer felt like a threat. It was just another element to be navigated, another layer of the atmosphere they had to understand before they could move through it.

"We're going to win this, aren't we?" Sam asked, his voice small beneath the vastness of the Australian night.

Angela looked at the wreck in the distance, a silver ghost fading into the blackness of the mangroves. She thought of her mother, and she thought of her father, and she thought of the empty hangar in Arizona that was waiting for a reason to be full again. She reached out and took Sam's hand, her grip certain and strong.

"We aren't just going to win, Sam," she said, her voice a low, steady hum that matched the rhythm of the rising wind. "We're going to find the truth of it. The sky is waiting."

She started the truck, the engine turning over with a roar that shattered the silence of the wetlands. As they drove back toward the city, a plume of fine, cinnamon-colored silt rising in their wake, an internal compass shifted within her. The Darwin layover had been more than a detour. With only five sunsets remaining until the Hunt's final bell, every mile through the red dust was a gamble against the approaching dawn. It had been a hardening, a tempering of their resolve in a climate that didn't care if they survived. They were no longer the grieving children who had left the hangar. They were something sharper, something more attuned to the subtle shifts of the world. The Outback was ahead of them, vast and indifferent, but for the first time since the crash, Angela wasn't afraid of the landing. She was looking for the light.

Chapter 23: Under the Rock

Angela eased the car off the highway and onto the access road leading into Uluru–Kata Tjuta National Park just as the afternoon light sharpened into something almost blinding. Ridges the color of rusted iron and dried blood stretched to the horizon, shimmering under a sky scrubbed of its moisture. Up here, she moved by the rules of the air, not the earth. Clusters of spinifex grass bristled through the surface in low, defiant bursts, and every so often a desert oak stood alone against the sky, its dark silhouette emphasizing the vastness surrounding it.

Even from miles away, Uluru was no mere landmark. It did not reveal itself gradually or invite interpretation; it simply existed—immense, grounded, and entirely indifferent to the presence of those who came searching for it. The stone wasn't just something to be approached; it felt like a presence that had already decided its place long before they arrived.

Beside her, Sam shifted in his seat, his gaze moving between the horizon and the GPS in his hand, then back again as though the device might offer some explanation for the view.

"Why do you think he gave such an obvious location?" he asked, his voice quieter than usual, worn down by travel but sharpened again by curiosity.

Angela slowed at the entrance. Activity surrounding the rock vied with the stone itself for her attention. A line of rental cars had gathered near the trailhead, their arrangement uneven but purposeful, each one marking the presence of someone who arrived with the same intent.

"Maybe it only looks obvious," she said after a moment. "Maybe he's counting on people to stop thinking once they recognize it."

Sam considered that, then looked back toward Uluru, his eyes narrowing slightly. "So the obvious answer is wrong."

"Or incomplete," Angela said. "Same difference."

They pulled into the lot and stepped out into the heat, which wrapped around them like a heavy, unseen shroud. Sam immediately turned his face into his shoulder, the desiccated air catching in his throat with a sharp, warning tickle. It carried the scent of parched eucalyptus and the metallic tang of sun-beaten stone, a dry weight that pulled the moisture from their skin and replaced it with the thrum of the desert's own pulse.

Angela paused just long enough to let her body adjust, then let her attention fan outward.

Visitors had gathered near the base of the rock, their voices drifting in the open air, swallowed by the immense, humming silence of the scrub. Off to one side, several members of the Anangu community stood watching, their presence quiet but unmistakable, observing without intervening yet never blending into the background. A nearby sign requested that visitors respect the site, remain on the ground, and recognize the cultural significance of where they stood.

Not everyone was listening.

Quinn was already partway up the rock, his boots rasping against the sun-baked arkose as he searched for footholds in a way that suggested experience without restraint. Suzette followed not far behind, her pace measured but determined, her focus fixed upward with an intensity that shut out everything else. Lower down, Gia lingered on the slope, her movements more cautious, each step tested before she committed to it, while at the base Etienne managed the rope, his stance steady but his attention divided between the climbers above and the growing strain in his hands.

Sam shaded his eyes. "They're climbing it."

The scene revealed more than action; it betrayed the assumption behind it. In that pause, the answer separated itself from the spectacle. The rock was too obvious, too central, too charged with meaning to be treated as nothing more than a climbing surface. Rex might build a challenge around attention and nerve, but he would not design a clue that required players to ignore the place itself.

"I don't think the cache is up there," she said.

"They seem pretty confident."

"They also seem like the kind of people who confuse obvious with correct," Angela said.

Sam let out a breath that caught in a dry, shallow wheeze—a sound that might have been a laugh if it weren't so strained—then glanced briefly at his phone. The signal bars were hollowed out, as dead as the scrub, and he slipped it away again. His hand hovered for a moment over his inhaler, not quite touching it. It was a reflexive check he'd learned in the cramped, airless halls of the boarding school, where every breath was something he had to ask permission for.

"We don't even have gear," he said.

Angela was already reaching into her backpack. "I remember something from that article about Rex," she said, pulling out a folded page and handing it to him.

Sam skimmed it quickly, his eyes moving across the text before lifting back toward Uluru.

"He said he'd like to rappel here," Angela added, "but he won't, out of respect."

Sam nodded once. "So he wouldn't put the cache somewhere that requires climbing."

"Exactly."

He checked the GPS again, a frown deepening. "It's reading close to the base," he said. "Really close."

"Then it's not on the rock."

Sam didn't argue. Instead, he reached for the compass and unfolded the map, turning it slowly until the orientation aligned with what they were seeing. "After that ion storm, I don't trust this thing completely," he said, rapping the GPS. "I think you're right."

They began searching the ground instead.

Angela moved first, circling outward from the base with deliberate care, forcing herself to ignore the obvious paths others had already taken. She searched for subtle disruptions in pattern—placements that did not quite belong. The ground resisted her at first, offering nothing but repetition: stone, scrub, shadow, each blending into the next in a way that punished impatience.

Sam followed her lead, his breath hitching into a jagged, uneven rhythm. The air, tasting of pulverized stone and parched resin, began to tighten in his chest like a closing fist, the fine desert dust acting as an abrasive against his throat. It was a familiar, suffocating sensation, one that usually arrived whenever the weight of Mike's overprotectiveness closed in on him. He forced a slow, deliberate exhale, refusing to let the desert smother him the way his father's well-meaning worry always did.

Angela found the first container quickly enough to confirm the pattern.

An ammo can, partially buried beneath loose stone.

She pried it open, already expecting what she would find, and sighed when it proved empty.

"A decoy," she said, setting it aside.

Not far from her, Sam uncovered a smaller container—a film canister tucked into a shallow depression between rocks. He opened it with more caution than hope, then shook his head when it revealed nothing.

Tom's eyes sharpened as he straightened.

"Do you think they know something we don't?" he called up toward the climbers.

Suzette stopped, her head snapped around. "Keep an eye on them," she said. "We're coming down."

The climb ended.

Within minutes, Quinn and Suzette were back on the ground, and the others spread out along the base, their presence shifting the atmosphere until the open ground was watched and the methodical search grew contested. Even the space itself tightened, as though every patch of ground carried the pressure of too many eyes at once.

Suzette moved toward Angela, stalking closer until the tension between them became unavoidable.

"Walk away, Angela," she said, her voice level and controlled. "You're out here for the narrative. I'm out here for the recovery. If you stay in my path, I will treat you like the problem you're becoming."

Angela stilled, the words landing less as a plea than as a measured assessment of the stakes. As she shifted, her pack gaped open, revealing the weathered leather of a pilot's log, the name Maria embossed in fading gold.

Suzette's gaze snagged on it, her calculated expression faltering. Her eyes moved from the log to Angela's face. Between them stood the weight of a ghost, something heavier than rivalry.

For a heartbeat, the ruthless edge in her eyes softened into a tired, shared recognition, the look of someone else living inside a predecessor's shadow, trapped by a legacy they hadn't yet escaped.

Then, as if punishing herself for the flicker of empathy, Suzette shoved her.

The moment broke.

Angela shoved back, the reaction immediate and physical, their contact sharp before they separated again, both breathing harder as the tension between them surfaced fully.

Beyond them, Sam had moved farther out, pulled away from the confrontation by something quieter.

He slowed as he scanned the ground, letting the pattern settle into something more readable.

Most of the stones lay irregularly, their placement shaped by time and weather.

One did not.

It sat slightly apart, its surface smoother, its placement just precise enough to resist blending in.

He crouched and rapped the stone.

The sound was hollow.

His pulse quickened with recognition.

He shifted his grip and lifted the rock.

Beneath it, tucked into the shallow space it concealed, was a small Altoids tin.

For a moment, he simply looked at it.

Then everything accelerated.

"Angela!" he called. "Over here—quick!"

Movement erupted around him.

Tom and Quinn broke first, closing the distance.

Sam did not wait. He grabbed the tin and ran, the desert air scouring his lungs with every desperate pull as red dust rose in small, suffocating clouds around his ankles.

Angela broke away from Suzette without hesitation; the victory was already audible.

"The car!" she called.

They ran together, the heat pressing against them as the distance collapsed into urgency. Behind them, the others gained ground, their movement direct now that the objective was clear.

Angela reached the car first, yanked the door open, and slid inside as Sam followed, pulling the door shut and locking it.

Tom reached them a second too late, his hand slamming the window, rattling the glass.

"Did you get it?" he demanded.

Sam ignored him, his chest laboring with a dry, whistling sound. He fumbled his inhaler from his pocket and pressed it to his lips, taking a sharp, desperate draw before handing Angela the tin, a flash of triumph breaking through the respiratory strain.

"This is yours."

Angela flipped the lid open, her hands steady despite the adrenaline still moving through her.

Inside was a single golden travel bug.

It caught the light as she lifted it, reflecting it with an almost deliberate intensity as she turned it to read the engraving.

"Meet me in Sydney," she said.

For a moment, everything else fell away, the pressure loosening as her hands stilled, replaced by a lightness that was almost as dangerous as the tension had been.

She laughed.

Sam joined her, the sound breaking through the strain as he grabbed his phone and snapped a photo.

"Take one close up," she said.

He did, then glanced at the empty signal bar. "We should send it to Dad as soon as we're back in range."

"The moment we hit a tower," Angela said.

But the moment did not hold.

Outside, the energy shifted again.

Suzette stepped in front of the car, planting herself there with a certainty that made it clear she was not bluffing, while Tom and Quinn flanked the sides, their hands hammering the vehicle, sending dull vibrations through the frame.

"You're not leaving," Suzette said.

The world snapped back into place.

Then something cut through it.

A shout—sharp and wrong—redirected everyone.

Angela looked up.

The rope above snapped taut.

Gia had slipped.

She hung against the rock face, her body twisted at an unstable angle, her feet searching for purchase that was not there. Below, Etienne struggled to hold the line, the strain visible in every movement as the situation began to unravel.

Suzette pivoted. "We need to help her."

Angela did not argue.

Distrust remained, but it no longer mattered.

She turned to Sam. "Stay in the car. Whatever happens, do not get out."

He nodded, tension still visible.

Angela ran.

By the time she reached the rope, Etienne's grip slipped in small increments he could no longer hide. His shoulders locked, his jaw clenched, and the line jerked in his hands with each impact of Gia's body on the rock.

"She's slipping," he said.

"I can see that."

Angela took hold of the rope, the rough fibers burning into her palms as the weight transferred into her grip. The force shocked her with its raw intensity. It wasn't controlled, only improvised, unstable, and heavy.

Quinn joined a moment later, followed by Tom, who hesitated before grabbing on.

For a moment, they were aligned by necessity.

"Gia," Suzette called. "Look at me. Don't fight the rope. Get your feet under you."

Gia tried, her movements uneven, the line shaking as her boots scraped against the rock.

"She can't find footing," Quinn said.

Angela scanned the surface. A small ledge sat to the left, invisible from Gia's position.

"There," she called. "Left side. Small ledge. Drop your heel and push."

Gia found it on the second attempt, her body stabilizing for the strain to shift from chaotic to controlled.

"Again," Angela said. "Use it."

Gia pushed upward. It wasn't enough, but it was something.

Suzette moved closer, her voice lower now. "You're fine. Keep moving. Don't look down."

Gia's breathing carried down to them, ragged but responsive. She found another foothold, then another, and with each adjustment the group below gained control.

The rope cut into Angela's hands, sweat blurring her vision as her shoulders burned, but they held.

"Now," Quinn said. "Pull with her."

They did.

The motion required coordination and instinct, lifting, bracing, taking up slack. Inch by inch, Gia rose until she reached a flatter section where park staff leaned down and pulled her the rest of the way.

When she collapsed onto the ledge, the release of tension jerked them off balance. Angela let go of the rope and stepped back, her hands shaking as the air seemed to expand again.

Suzette looked up first, confirming Gia was safe, then turned.

No one spoke at first. The silence held a sharp edge as the shared effort began to separate back into distance.

Tom brushed the fine, iron-rich grit from his palms, his movements edged with irritation. Quinn ignored him. Etienne bent forward, catching his breath.

Gia was guided away.

Angela turned back toward the car where Sam waited. Suzette did the same.

Their eyes met.

Recognition passed between them, less gratitude than acknowledgment.

"Leave," Suzette said.

Angela let out a breath that almost became a laugh. "That's generous."

"It's practical," Suzette replied. "You have what you came for."

Tom whirled. "What?"

Suzette did not look at him. "We lost this one."

Tom stepped forward. "Since when do we let them go?"

"Since Gia almost died," Suzette said, and the force in her voice stopped him.

Angela held her gaze for a moment longer, then turned and walked back to the car.

Sam unlocked the door as she approached.

"What happened?" he asked.

Angela sat for a second before answering. "Everything." Then she searched his face. "Are you okay?"

He nodded, his chest still rising and falling in a jagged rhythm. "I stayed in the car," he said, his voice thin and careful. "Didn't want to give Mike a reason to say I can't handle the outside world."

"Good."

A small shift of relief passed between them.

"I'm very obedient under extreme conditions," he added.

She laughed and started the engine.

As they pulled out, the mirror showed Suzette's team near the base of the rock, already dispersing. Beyond them, Uluru remained unchanged, vast and indifferent.

Sam held up his phone. "Photo's still there."

Angela nodded. "Keep it ready."

He rested it in his lap. "Do you think Dad's following this?"

Angela kept her eyes on the road. "Yeah. I think he is."

The thought settled between them as the road carried them back out into the wider landscape.

After a moment, Sam said, "Sydney seems less impossible than Paris did."

Angela's mouth curved. "That's not reassuring."

"It wasn't supposed to be."

She drove on, the ocher expanse stretching outward, the land beginning to exhale the day's heat with the faint, metallic ping of cooling stone as the light softened.

The bug rested in her pocket, warm from her hand.

Meet me in Sydney.

It no longer felt like a clue.

It felt like a summons.

As the highway reappeared ahead of them, the adrenaline faded, leaving space for the reality of the day to settle in. They had found the clue. They had held off the others. They had nearly lost Sam. They had helped save someone who might still have taken the bug from them.

The game was no longer just difficult. It had become dangerous.

Angela's grip tightened on the wheel.

Sam glanced at her. "You're doing that thing."

"What thing?"

"The one where you look calm but you're thinking in six directions."

Angela exhaled. "I think this is bigger than I expected."

Sam looked out the window. "It was already bigger when we left the Sierra Nevada."

She nodded. "And it's only going to get tighter once the trail turns back toward the finish in Arizona."

"But we're still ahead," he added.

That didn't make it easier, but it gave them direction.

Angela nodded once. "Yeah," she said. "We are."

For now, that was enough.

She kept driving.

Chapter 24: The Alice Springs Intercept

Sam Santiago adjusted the bridge of his glasses, his skin tightening as he stepped into the physical confrontation of the Alice Springs heat. He scanned the shimmering horizon for the man Rex St. James had promised, the scent of ozone sharp against the wavering air. As he moved past the terminal, the smell of sun-bleached asphalt and hydraulic fluid followed him, the silence broken by the erratic ticking of heat-stressed metal—a sharper, more aggressive weight than the Arizona hangar that turned every breath into a struggle.

Angela was already walking toward a corrugated metal shed at the edge of the apron. She moved with a strange, predatory grace that Sam had seen growing in her since San Francisco. Her posture was no longer defensive. She looked like someone who had stopped waiting for the world to break and had started looking for the seams where she could break it herself. Behind them, the wind hissed through the dry mulga scrub, kicking up a fine, ochre grit that settled into the creases of their boots like a permanent record of their arrival.

A man leaned against the shade of the overhang, his skin the color and texture of an old flight jacket. He was nursing a tin cup of tea, the steam rising into a radiant sky that was already boiling. This was "Dusty" Miller. He didn't look like a guardian of legacies. He looked like a man who had spent forty years trying to outrun the sun and had finally decided to let it win. His eyes, however, remained a startling, crystalline blue, clear enough to see through the wavering haze of the runway.

"You have her eyes," Dusty said. His voice was a low rasp, the sound of gravel shifting under a tire. He didn't stand up. He didn't offer a hand. He simply looked at Angela with a measuring intensity that made Sam's breath hitch. "Maria always said the sky was a conversation. Most people just shout at it. She knew how to whisper."

Angela stopped three feet away. "We aren't here for a eulogy, Dusty. We're here for the gear. Rex St. James said you had the final piece."

Dusty let out a dry, hacking laugh that ended in a cough. He looked at Sam, then back to Angela. "Rex is a boy playing with his father's checkbook. He thinks history is something you can buy in an auction house. But Maria's secrets weren't for sale. They were for the people who could find them." He reached into a weathered canvas bag beside him and pulled out a wooden box. It was mahogany, the edges rounded by decades of handling. Inside, nestled in velvet that had faded to the color of a bruised plum, sat a brass sextant.

A copper spike of adrenaline sharpened the back of Sam's throat as he felt a jolt of recognition. It wasn't the sleek, digital precision of the GPS units they had been using. This was an instrument of math and light. It was a tool for a world that didn't have satellites to lean on. Sam reached out, his fingers hovering over the polished arc of the brass. He could see his own distorted reflection in the metal, a pale, wide-eyed ghost set against the backdrop of the Australian desert.

"I don't just give this away," Dusty said, snapping the lid shut. The sound was as final as a gunshot. "Maria and I mapped things out here that the official charts still don't show. If you want the Silver Sky, you have to prove you can see it. There's a ghost town thirty miles east. Arltunga. I buried a cache there back when your mother was still learning how to read a thermal. Find it using only the sun and that brass. Then we'll talk about frequencies."

The drive to the ruins was a lesson in silence. Angela gripped the wheel of the rented ute, her knuckles white on the black plastic. Sam held the mahogany box on his lap like it was a live coal. He could feel the weight of it, a physical link to a mother who was becoming more of a legend than a memory with every mile they traveled. His breathing was shallow, the cab heavy with the scent of sun-baked resin and the sharp, medicinal bite of crushed eucalyptus. He reached for his inhaler but stopped. He wanted to prove he could master his own breath, even in a landscape that seemed determined to stifle it.

Sam stepped out of the truck and felt the world tilt, his boots crunching on quartz-strewn ground that sent heat vibrating upward in glimmering pools of false water. He followed Angela toward the stone skeletons of the mining town, the ruins bleached white by the sun until they looked more like a graveyard than a settlement. They navigated the maze of collapsed chimneys, finding no shade in the flat, concussive light that brought a weightless float to Sam's stomach.

"Noon sight," Sam muttered, his voice sounding brittle beneath the immense, static-charged drone of the scrub. He opened the box and lifted the sextant, the brass warm enough to sting his palms. He glanced at the chronometer in the truck, already visualizing the arc of the sun. There was no need to voice the math; they both knew the margin for error in this heat was razor-thin.

Angela stood behind him, her hand resting lightly on his shoulder. It wasn't a gesture of restraint; it was an anchor. "Take your time, Sam. The wind has dropped. Don't fight the light. Let it come to you."

Sam looked through the telescope of the sextant. He adjusted the index arm, moving the mirror until the blinding disc of the sun dropped toward the horizon. It was a delicate dance of reflections. The shimmering heat made the horizon line ripple, a blurred boundary that refused to stay still. He felt a bead of sweat crawl down his temple. His hands shook. The numbers on the arc were tiny, a language of minutes and seconds that felt impossible to read under the glare.

"It's moving," Sam whispered, frustration bubbling up in his chest. "The heat is bending the light. I can't get a clean lock."

"Stop looking at the sun," Angela said. Her voice was low, rhythmic, the same tone she used when she was teaching him how to feel the trim of a glider. "Look at the gap between the sun and the earth. That's where the truth is. The shimmer is just the desert taking a breath. Wait for the exhale."

Sam closed his eyes for a second, forcing his heart rate down. He waited. He listened to the wind whistling through the dry spinifex grass. The desert finally exhaled, a subsonic shudder Sam felt in the roots of his teeth, the heat reaching a crescendo before settling into a momentary, breathless pause. He opened his eyes and snapped the arm into place. The sun touched the horizon. He locked the screw.

The math was a slow, grinding process. Sam knelt on the scorched clay, scribbling figures into the sun-hardened crust with a shard of white quartz. He worked through the corrections for the shimmering air, his brow furrowed as he wrestled the variables into a single, pinpoint location. When he was done, he pointed toward a low ridge near the remains of the old police station. A single, gnarled ghost gum tree stood there, its white bark peeling in long, papery strips.

Angela knelt by a flat slab of ironstone near the remains of the old police station, her fingers digging into the scorched earth until she snagged the rusted edge of a tin. It wasn't a high-tech container, just an old ammunition box sealed with heavy wax. Angela pried it open with a pocketknife, the sound of the metal groaning like a long-held breath being released. Inside was a stack of hand-drawn maps and a single, black flight log. The handwriting was unmistakable. It was Maria's, but it was different from the logs at home. These were filled with sketches of light patterns and notes on the way the moon reflected off the salt flats.

"She wasn't just flying," Angela whispered, her thumb tracing a diagram of a heliograph. "She was building a network. A way to talk across the distance without using a radio that anyone could track."

Sam looked at the last page. There was a sequence of numbers circled in red. It wasn't a coordinate. It was a frequency. 123.45. The Silver Sky. It was a channel reserved for test pilots and ghosts, a quiet corner of the spectrum where the sky belonged to the few who knew how to navigate its silences.

When they returned to the airfield, Dusty Miller was standing by their truck. He didn't ask if they found it. He saw the ammo tin in Angela's hand and the way Sam held the sextant, no longer as a stranger, but as a keeper. He nodded once, a sharp, decisive movement that seemed to bridge the gap between their mother's generation and their own.

"She called it the Silver Sky because it was the only place where the noise stopped," Dusty said. He reached out and took the sextant back, his touch surprisingly gentle. "She knew Rex's father was trying to buy up the land under the school. She knew the corporate world would eventually try to ground her. So she mapped a route that didn't rely on their towers or their satellites."

Dusty stepped closer to Angela, his eyes searching hers. "The frequency you found? It's not just for Australia. It's a bridge. If you can reach the fire lookout in the Sierras, you can use the light to find the way home. But you have to be the one to start the conversation."

Angela looked toward the north, toward the looming shadow of Uluru that waited for them. The hunt had started as a way to save a building, a collection of steel and fabric in the Arizona desert. But here, in the ancient, iron-veined heart of a different world, it felt like something larger. It was a reclamation of a language they had almost forgotten.

"We're going to finish it, Dusty," Angela said. There was no hesitation in her voice. It was a statement of physics, as certain as gravity.

"I know you are," the old pilot replied. He turned and began to walk back toward the shade of his shed. "Just remember what she taught you. The wind doesn't care who you are. It only cares how you listen."

Sam climbed into the truck, his lungs feeling clearer than they had all day. The weight of those secret numbers sat in his pocket, a small, invisible treasure that was worth more than all the gold coins Rex St. James could ever mint. He looked at Angela as she started the engine. She looked like her mother, yes, but there was something else there now. A hardness. A clarity. They weren't just the Santiago children anymore. They were the pilots of a legacy that was finally beginning to climb.

A cloud of disturbed silt trailed them as they left the airfield, a rust-colored curtain that momentarily blurred the world. Sam watched the horizon through the rearview mirror. The shimmer was still there, but it didn't look like an illusion anymore. It looked like a path.

Chapter 25: The Hidden Frequency

A razor-thin cold gripped the Sierra Nevada, biting at the cockpit seals while the instrument panel rattled with a steady, metallic tremor. Below them, the peaks rose in jagged granite spurs, their shadows stretching long across the snowfields even in the midday light. Angela kept her eyes on the horizon, her hands resting lightly on the yoke as the steady rhythm of the engine filled the cabin, a mechanical pulse holding back the vast silence pressing in from every direction.

Mike sat in the co-pilot's seat, looking hollowed out, bracing for a blow that had already landed. His frame was rigid, his eyes fixed on the encroaching granite with a raw, unshielded dread. He didn't touch the navigation charts; his hands were clamped to his knees to keep them from shaking. The approach to the coast occupied the cabin like a low-pressure system, and Mike's voice was a strained whisper beneath the engine's hum. "We need to find a clearing, Angela. Turn it around. The pass is too high—we aren't going to make the ridge." Angela's gaze went rigid in the glare of the peaks, her silence the only answer to his mounting panic. In the back, Sam worked within a tangle of cables and equipment, the faint glow of his screens reflecting in the worn interior. The cabin carried the scent of old upholstery and ozone, a small, humming box of heat set against the immense and unyielding granite outside.

The engine's failure did not announce itself all at once. It began as a subtle break in rhythm, a disturbance that arrived before the sound, then resolved into a harsh, uneven vibration that spread through the frame. The next moment brought a tearing cough, wet and violent, followed by a drop in RPM so abrupt it struck like a physical blow. The propeller slowed, its blur collapsing into visible blades that cut through the air without resistance.

Then came the silence.

It expanded instantly, absolute and disorienting, as though the world itself had stepped back.

The drop returned as a presence, a cold compression tightening through her chest as the aircraft lost lift. Her hands held the yoke, but her focus threatened to fracture, pulled between instinct and the overwhelming proximity of the terrain rising beneath them.

Mike's hands were clamped onto his set of controls, but they weren't guiding; they were shaking, a visible, rhythmic tremor that telegraphed the frantic, shallow cadence of his breath. He stared at the dead propeller, his breath hitching in the sudden, heavy silence. "Angela," he whispered, his voice thin and trembling as he watched the ridge rise to meet them. "We're not going to make it. We're going to hit."

She couldn't answer, her gaze locked instead on the altimeter as the needle unwound, marking their descent with quiet indifference. The aircraft groaned, wind forcing its way through the structure with a strained, high-pitched whine, while the downdraft pulled them toward the ridge.

"Nose down!" Mike suddenly shouted, the impending impact finally shattering his paralysis into a jagged, desperate lucidity. It wasn't a return to form, but a frantic, white-knuckled focus—an efficiency born of absolute terror. "Angela, look at the air, not the ground! Trade the altitude for speed. Do it now!"

From the back, Sam's voice cut in, quick and precise. "Shear from the north-northwest. If we bank left, ten degrees, we might catch lift off the plateau. Descent is steep. We have maybe ninety seconds."

The numbers steadied her.

Angela drew in a controlled breath and shifted her focus from the ground to the aircraft itself, where the yoke grew slack in her hands, the loss of lift telegraphing through the controls as the thin altitude failed to support the wings. She eased the nose down, trading altitude for airspeed, accepting the movement rather than resisting it.

Ahead, the ridge resolved into a narrow strip of stone edged by scattered pine, too short and too exposed to inspire confidence, yet it was the only option available. Angela adjusted the flaps, the aircraft responding with a shudder as it pushed against the turbulence.

"Steady," Mike said, his voice strained and thin. "Just like home."

The landing came hard, the wheels striking stone with enough force to jolt through her entire frame. The aircraft bounced once, threatening to lift again, before settling into a rough, sliding contact. Angela held the brakes, the tires screaming against the granite as they skidded forward. The edge came too close, the nose dipping toward open space before the momentum finally gave out and the plane shuddered to a stop.

Silence returned, broken only by the ticking of cooling metal.

Angela remained where she was, her hands still curved around the yoke, her breathing uneven but controlled. The drop had come, and she had stayed with it.

"Nice landing," Sam said from the back, his voice cracking as he forced a brittle, paper-thin laugh as he released his harness.

Mike leaned forward, his hands braced against his knees, his breathing jagged as he struggled to steady it. When he looked up, his face was ashen, the skin pulled taut over his cheekbones as he swallowed against a dry throat. "That's it," he said. "We're done. I'm not risking this again."

Angela didn't respond immediately. She reached for Maria's flight log, opening it carefully and holding it out to him. "Read it," she said. "The horizon isn't a boundary. It's a heartbeat. You think stopping keeps us safe, but it just traps us somewhere smaller."

Mike looked down at the page, his thumb tracing the faded ink. The tremor in his fingers didn't stop, but he met her eyes with a slow, heavy blink, his features finally settling into a grim mask. After a moment, he reached out and took her hand, the gesture quiet but decisive.

They stepped out into the cold.

The wind met them immediately, sharp and relentless, carrying the scent of pine and snow. Angela turned, taking in the ridge, expecting isolation, and instead caught the glint of metal.

Another aircraft stood nearby, its lines clean and modern against the rough terrain.

Two figures waited beside it.

Suzette and Quinn.

"You followed us," Angela said.

Suzette approached with a stiff, deliberate gait, her hands held perfectly still at her sides despite the screaming wind. "Your route wasn't hidden," she said. "Neither were the coordinates. This ridge isn't the end; it's a filter."

Mike stepped forward. "This is restricted ground. Whatever you're doing, it stops here. Our engine is out."

"Then we all have a problem," Quinn said, gesturing toward the horizon where a wall of storm clouds gathered, dark and fast-moving.

The light shifted, flattening into a metallic gray.

"In less than an hour," Quinn continued, "this ridge becomes a wind tunnel. None of us are flying out."

Suzette stopped a few feet from Angela, her gaze flickering to the open flight log still gripped in Angela's hand. For a second, the rigid set of Suzette's jaw gave way, her eyes tracing Maria's frantic handwriting in the margins—notes on the crushing thinness of the altitude and the way the lungs seemed to seize when the horizon stopped moving. When Suzette looked up, the hard, defensive line of her shoulders dipped, her mouth losing its bitter curve. "I know that handwriting," she said, her voice losing its serrated edge. "Not the name, but the tone. My father wrote the same way when the debts started piling up. He used to say the sky was the only place he wasn't being hunted, until the fuel ran low." She straightened, her posture regaining its steel, though the sharp, predatory glint in her eyes had gone dim. "The prize in Sydney is conditional. If I don't finish this, I go back to a life that already ended. I'm not going back to nothing." Angela met her gaze; they were running from the same shadows.

"The bug is here," she said. "But the next step isn't solved."

Sam stepped forward slightly, tablet in hand. "There's a fire lookout two miles from here, aligned with old aviation beacons. It fits the signal pattern. We need to reach it before visibility drops."

The wind hit harder, colder.

Angela looked between them, then at the rising storm.

"We don't make it separately," she said. "We move together or we don't make it."

Suzette didn't answer immediately. She studied the ridge, the approaching weather, then Angela. "A truce," she said finally. "Only until we reach the lookout."

"That's all we need," Angela replied.

The climb tested them immediately.

The terrain shifted from broken stone to narrow ledges and steep inclines, the wind cutting through gaps with a force that made balance uncertain. Angela moved first, focusing on placement and rhythm, keeping her attention grounded in movement rather than distance.

Behind her, Suzette matched the pace with efficient precision, while Mike took the rear. He moved with a stiff, over-deliberate care, his boots scraping the granite as he forced each step. His efficiency was a brittle thing, a mechanical struggle against the panic that threatened to unmoor him with every gust of wind. Quinn secured lines when the path narrowed, tethering them together in a necessity that left no room for pride.

Sam struggled as the elevation increased, his breathing tightening until he paused, reaching for his inhaler with shaking hands.

Suzette paused for a brief moment, then stepped forward and braced herself against the rock, creating a foothold with her own body. "Use it," she said.

Sam hesitated only a second before stepping up.

One by one, they moved through the obstacle.

At the summit, the lookout stood weathered and silent, its structure worn but intact, a remnant of another time.

Snow began to fall.

Sam moved toward the door, scanning his equipment. "The signal peaks here," he said. "It's more than a location. It's a transmission point."

Angela turned briefly; back on the ridge, the planes sat as small, distant shapes against the vast landscape. The scale of everything shifted again, the race narrowing into something more immediate and physical.

They stepped inside.

The interior held a preserved stillness, smelling of dry wood and age. Angela rested her hand briefly against the Golden Bug in her pocket, its weight settling differently now.

The hunt had shifted again.

Outside, the storm gathered strength while inside they prepared for whatever came next.

The descent that followed was slow and punishing, the strain of the climb settling into their bodies as they worked their way back down through shifting terrain and rising wind. By the time they reached lower ground, a humid weight settled over the cabin, warmth replacing the sharp cold of the ridge as the landscape transitioned gradually from mountain to the foothills guarding the coast.

They stopped briefly at a remote station, refueling and regrouping in silence, the hum of neon cutting through the quiet as heat radiated from the ground.

As the Sierra peaks faded into the distance, the world shifted again. The Pacific lay ahead, vast and demanding, the sky lowering toward dusk.

The horizon shifted as they moved, marking a transition in both landscape and intent.

They kept moving, and the final confrontation in Sydney was closer now than it had ever been.

Chapter 26: Uneasy Alliances

The stairs leading to the fire lookout rose in a skeletal spiral of rusted iron and weathered cedar, each step ringing faintly under Sam's weight as he climbed with his head down, counting to steady his breathing. At this altitude, the cold scraped at the back of his throat, a brittle hollowness that refused to settle fully in his lungs. Behind him, he could hear the heavier rhythm of his father's steps and the lighter, uneven cadence of Quinn and Suzette, while above them Angela had already reached the top, her silhouette fixed against the darkening edge of the storm.

Inside, the lookout opened into a circular room of glass and aging wood, its windows dulled by decades of grit but still offering a sweeping view that made the ground seem distant and unstable. The Sierra peaks surrounded them in every direction, jagged and imposing, their arrangement less like a landscape and more like a trap closing in from all sides. In the center of the room stood a brass map mounted on a pedestal, its surface worn to a muted sheen, while the rest of the space held the quiet stillness of a place built for observation rather than habitation.

Angela stood near a built-in desk, a leather-bound book open in her hands. The cover was cracked and darkened with age, its pages swollen from decades of absorbing the mountain mist. Sam crossed the room toward her, the boards shifting faintly under his steps.

"What is it?" he asked.

Angela did not look up immediately, her fingers tracing a line of slanted script. "It's a flight log," she said. "Mom's. From before either of us."

The words settled into the room with unexpected weight.

Quinn moved past them with practical urgency, his attention already shifting to the mechanisms around them. "Then look at the margins," he said. "Those aren't GPS coordinates. They're bearings." He gestured toward a set of antique signal mirrors positioned near the south-facing windows, their mounts marked with degree increments. "Heliographs. Sun signaling."

Sam followed his line of sight, stepping closer to the mirrors. The brass fittings were heavy, the reflective surfaces imperfect where time had worn away the backing, leaving constellations of dark spots across the glass. He glanced between the instruments and the logbook, the connection forming quickly.

"It's a cipher," he said, reaching instinctively for his inhaler before continuing. "She wasn't just logging flights. She was mapping light."

Angela turned another page, her focus sharpening. "And air," she added. "Look at the thermal notes. She's describing lift patterns like routes."

Suzette, standing near the doorway, kept one eye on the sky. "The light is dropping," she said. "We don't have much time."

Mike took the book from Angela, his thumb settling into a familiar worn groove in the spine. Tucked into the back binding was a loose scrap of vellum, the ink faded but the hand unmistakable. The valley is a beautiful cage, Maria had written, but the silence here is a slow death. I would rather break against the sky than rust in the garden. He looked at Sam, who was steadying his breathing, and then at Angela. For years, Mike had played the anchor, thinking he was saving them from the wind. He realized now he was only ensuring they drowned in the calm.

"Then we use what she left us," Mike said, his voice carrying a new, hard-edged clarity. "Sam, align the mirrors. Angela, guide him. We're not staying on the ground anymore."

The work that followed compressed into urgency.

Sam and Quinn adjusted the mirror mounts together, their movements precise despite the stiffness of the old mechanisms. The metal resisted at first, then yielded in reluctant increments. Sam called out angles from the logbook, checking and rechecking against the markings, while Angela watched the sky, focusing less on the peaks themselves and more on the way the clouds shifted around them, tracing the invisible currents described in the pages.

"Wait," Angela said. She didn't look at the log now; she looked at the way the light pooled on the floor. "The hawk's turn. It's not a fixed point. It's a correction for the updraft." She stepped to the mirror herself, overriding the notches on the dial. "Sam, ignore the increments. Hold the base steady. I have to feel the tension in the glass."

He made the correction.

The sun broke through a narrow gap in the storm, a sharp beam of light cutting across the room and striking the first mirror. The reflection jumped to the second, then carried outward through the window in a focused line that seemed almost solid.

Quinn leaned toward the opening. "We need the exterior angle," he said. "The mounts won't hold in this wind."

Angela moved without hesitation, taking the smallest mirror and heading for the door, Suzette close behind her.

From inside, Sam watched as the wind hit them the moment they stepped onto the catwalk, the force of it visible in the way it pushed at their bodies. Angela struggled to hold the mirror steady, the flat surface catching the wind and pulling at her balance.

"She's going to lose it," Sam said, his hand pressed to the glass.

Angela's footing slipped, the beam scattering across the valley.

Then Suzette reached her, catching the back of her jacket and anchoring her to the railing. For a moment they held there, balanced between control and collapse.

"Hold it steady," Suzette shouted.

Angela adjusted, finding her footing again, and realigned the mirror. The beam steadied, extending across the valley until it struck a distant reflective surface.

A response came back, less a signal than a revelation of landscape. As the beam struck the distant peak, the shadow it cast across the valley floor stretched into a distinct, sharp-edged silhouette.

"It's not Morse," Angela said, her voice breathless. "Look at the shadow. That's the harbor entrance. Sydney. He didn't leave a message; he left a picture written in the geography."

The sun disappeared behind the clouds, the light collapsing into shadow as the signal ended. Angela and Suzette stepped back inside, both breathing hard, the strain of the moment still visible in their movements. Neither spoke, but something between them had shifted, no longer just rivalry but recognition shaped by necessity.

A panel on the desk clicked open, revealing a concealed laptop. The screen flickered, then resolved into an image.

Rex St. James appeared, the recording grainy, his expression stripped of the polish seen in public.

"Well," he said, his voice stripped of its usual razor-edged charm, sounding brittle and weary. "I wondered if anyone still had the hands for it. You didn't just follow the coordinates, did you, Angela? You felt the flaw I left in the alignment. I loved her, and I failed her, and I've spent twenty years building this labyrinth just to see if you could survive the world that took her from me."

He looked older than the magazine covers, a restless, cynical energy vibrating beneath his fatigue. He spoke of his father's obsession with the 'unbroken'—those rare few who could read the marrow of the world instead of just following a pilot's manual. He spoke of Maria with a jagged, private reverence, revealing a history rooted in a shared cockpit and a fatal misjudgment. He wasn't just a benefactor; he was the man who had cleared her for her final flight, and the hunt was less of a challenge than it was a penance—a way to see if he could find her ghost in her daughter.

Angela stepped closer, the words settling into something deeper than explanation. The hunt shifted in her mind, no longer spectacle but something closer to an altar, a final, desperate reckoning with the woman he had lost.

"The circus is over," Rex continued, leaning back until he was nearly a shadow in the frame. "The cameras are off. If you're seeing this, it means you've already figured out where the light was pointing. You saw the harbor in the shadow. The race doesn't end in the dust. It ends where the tide meets the sky. I'll see you where the dawn hits the steel first."

The screen went dark.

For a moment, no one moved.

Then Sam looked down at his GPS as the coordinates recalculated, the numbers resolving into something immediately familiar.

"He's confirming it," Sam said, looking from the darkened screen to Angela. "Sydney. You saw it in the shadow before he even spoke."

Thunder rolled across the ridge, the storm closing in fully now, the wind striking the structure with increasing force.

"We move now," Mike said.

Angela closed the logbook and secured it against her chest. The decision had already taken hold.

"Let's go."

They stepped back into the storm, the descent immediate and unforgiving as the trail shifted beneath wind and snow. Visibility narrowed, the world reduced to movement and balance, each step requiring attention.

Sam gripped the railing as they descended, no longer counting steps but measuring distance in a different way.

Not how far they had come.

But how close they were to the end.

Lightning split the sky, illuminating the ridge in sharp, fleeting detail before darkness closed again.

They kept moving.

The race had turned.

The race had turned, but the Sierra peaks were only a waypoint. The Cessna was a creature of the high desert, fit for the mountain passes but not the vast, salt-slicked distance of the Pacific. They brought it down at a private strip outside Reno, the wheels kissing the tarmac just as the rain turned to a steady, freezing curtain. Mike didn't park in the usual stalls; he taxied toward a hangar where a white-hulled long-range jet sat idling, its engines a low, predatory hum against the mountain wind. Rex's invitation had provided more than coordinates; it had opened a corridor through the sky. Mike's connections, rooted in a dozen quiet hangars and forgotten airfields, did the rest. They traded the cramped, vibrating cabin of the Cessna for the pressurized silence of a cabin built for the deep blue. As they banked west, the Sierra peaks faded into the storm, leaving the mountains behind for the long, dark arc toward the Australian coast.

Chapter 27: The Signal Fire

The wind was a physical weight, a shoulder pressed against the glass that groaned under the intrusion. Inside the fire lookout, the air tasted of ancient dust and the sharp, metallic tang of an approaching electrical surge. The heavy iron bolt of the trapdoor slid home with a finality that made Sam reach for his pocket. He took a single, deep pull from his inhaler, a quiet anchor against the rising dust before the familiar tightness could take hold. It wasn't the ghost of his mother that had locked them in. It was the house itself, a relic of a paranoid era, triggered by the same signal they had just sent into the dark.

"Electronic fail-safe," Quinn muttered, his fingers trailing over the keypad near the floor. The screen was a dead eye, dark and unresponsive. "The mirrors triggered a surge in the old legacy system. It thinks we're an unauthorized entry during a red-flag warning."

Mike threw his weight against the wood, but the trapdoor didn't even shiver. Out the windows, the storm was erasing the peaks one by one. The granite world was disappearing into a wash of gray and violet. They were suspended in a glass box, three thousand feet above the valley floor, with the lightning looking for a way in.

"The glass won't hold," Angela said. The shutters sang with a harmonic frequency that Angela felt as a prickling tension across her skin. "If one pane goes, the pressure will blow the rest. We'll be standing in a wind tunnel."

Suzette moved without waiting for a command or a consensus. She grabbed the heavy wooden handle of the primary shutter and pulled. The wind fought her, a wild, invisible animal trying to keep the house open. Angela stepped in beside her, their shoulders overlapping, two different kinds of strength pinned against the same frame. Suzette was all wire-taut tension and levered bone. Angela moved with the gust, timing her pull for the momentary lull between the pulses of the storm.

"Sam, look at the fire-finder," Angela shouted over the roar. Her face was pressed near the glass, her eyes fixed on the horizon, now lost to the storm. "There's a manual bypass. There has to be."

Sam turned to the center of the room. The Osborne Fire Finder sat on its pedestal like a bronze altar, a circular map of the Sierras etched into its surface. It was a mechanical computer, designed to triangulate smoke, but as Sam leaned over it, modifications appeared. There were extra gears beneath the sighting arm, their teeth fine and sharp, coated in a layer of preserved grease that smelled of clove oil. (His mother's scent. Always.)

He touched the brass rail. His hands were shaking, a fine tremor that hammered against the roof's percussive chatter. Don't think about the air, he told himself. Think about the math.

The fire-finder required three points of alignment. On the outer ring, the degrees weren't marked by standard compass headings. Instead, they were marked by the names of peaks: Cathedral, Banner, Ritter. Beneath each name was a small, recessed window revealing a numerical gear. It was a physical combination lock disguised as a surveyor's tool.

"I need the coordinates," Sam said, his voice small against the thunder. "Not the map coordinates. The flight ones."

Mike's face was pale in the flickering light of the storm. He reached for the brass sighting arm, his fingers twitching, but he pulled back as if the metal were white-hot. "The logbook, Sam," he managed, his voice a dry rasp. "Your mother's notes... you have to do it. I can't touch it."

Sam flipped through the weathered pages of the flight log they had found moments before. The ink was faded, a blue ghost of a script that spoke of lift and drag. The numbers Maria had scribbled in the margins stood out. They weren't just observations. They were the constants of her favorite sailplane, the math that kept a thousand pounds of fiberglass and hope suspended in a void.

The wind hammered the lookout, a sudden, violent gust that forced a groan from the timber. Angela and Suzette were forced back-to-back now, their boots sliding on the grit-covered floor as they fought to keep the shutters from swinging outward. The rivalry that had defined the last month was gone, replaced by the simple, brutal geometry of survival. They were two pillars holding up a falling sky.

"Sam, hurry," Angela gasped. The effort was turning her knuckles white. "The hinges are pulling."

Sam ignored the panic. He focused on the numbers. Wing-loading. That was the key. The ratio of the aircraft's weight to the area of its wings. For the K-21, fully loaded with two pilots, it was a specific value. In the hangar, she had tapped the fuselage and told him that every bird had a number it belonged to. If you knew the number, you knew the soul of the machine.

Thirty-four point two. Newtons per square meter.

He began to rotate the sighting arm. He aligned the sight with Cathedral Peak and dialed the first gear to three. The gear notched into the pedestal with a heavy, mechanical bite. He swung the arm toward Banner Peak and dialed the four. A low resonance climbed out of the floorboards, a soundless pressure that he felt as a hollow float in the pit of his stomach.

"One more," Sam whispered. "The decimal."

He moved the arm to Ritter. He dialed the two. For a heartbeat, nothing happened. The storm seemed to hold its breath, the wind dropping into a deceptive, hollow silence. Then, the fire-finder didn't just click. It began to turn.

The entire pedestal rotated, driven by a hidden clockwork mechanism that gnawed at the silence. As the gears aligned, a small radio speaker tucked into the rafters crackled to life. It was a sound from another decade, thick with static and the hiss of magnetic tape. It was the Silver Sky frequency, awakened after years of silence.

"Alpha-Sierra-Two-One, initiating final glide," a voice said.

The room went still. Mike froze, his hands still gripped around the frame of the trapdoor. The voice was clear, despite the distortion. It was Maria. It wasn't the voice of a mother calling them for dinner; it was the voice of a pilot in her element, calm and precise, reading the air as if it were a poem she had written herself.

"The lift is holding at six knots," the recording continued. "The peaks are aligned. If you're hearing this, Mike, you've stopped looking at the ground. You've finally looked up."

Mike recoiled from the pedestal, his face contorted. "Turn it off," he rasped. "It's a haunting, Sam. The air didn't talk to her; it broke her." As the western shutter reached a terminal pitch, he lunged toward Angela. "Get away from it!" he screamed, his hands locking onto her shoulders to haul her back into the center of the room. It was the same suffocating grip he'd used for years—the one that kept her grounded. But his weight threw her off balance just as the hinges snapped. Because Mike had anchored her, she couldn't pivot; the timber scythed inward like a guillotine, missing her temple by an inch only because she shoved Sam aside and wrenched herself from her father's grasp. Mike stumbled, nearly dragging them both into the path of the shattering glass; a low-frequency hum rattled his bones —his terror was the most dangerous thing in the room. From the floor, she was a study in leverage as she braced her boot against the fire-finder and caught the swinging shutter, using the very gust that sought to destroy them to wedge the timber against the frame. She wasn't a child to be shielded; she was flying the room with a terrifying, familiar lucidity.

"The air isn't an enemy, Mike," the voice said, fading into a wash of white noise. "It's a conversation. You just have to be quiet enough to hear the answer."

The recording cut out with a sharp, electronic pop, and the heavy iron bolt on the trapdoor snapped back. The exit was open.

"Move!" Quinn shouted, breaking the spell. He grabbed the handle and hauled the door upward, revealing the dark, narrow stairs leading down to the lower level.

A massive crack, like the sound of a bone snapping, shook the entire structure. Outside, a towering pine, its roots loosened by the deluge, surrendered to the gravity of the slope. It fell in slow motion, a dark jagged shadow against the lightning. A heavy limb struck the exterior catwalk, the impact tearing through the wood and sending a shudder through the glass walls.

"Down! Now!" Angela yelled, shoving Sam toward the hole in the floor.

Suzette followed him, her movements precise even in the chaos. Quinn vanished next. Angela reached for her father, who was still staring at the fire-finder as if he could coax the voice back out of the brass.

"Dad, we have to go," she said, her voice firm, the same tone she used when the altimeter dropped too fast. "She's not in the box, Dad. She's in the air. And the air is coming inside."

Mike turned to her, his face a pale map of exhaustion and old ghosts. The haunted look wasn't gone; it had merely been hammered into a desperate, wide-eyed focus. Angela reached out and grabbed his arm, forcing the logbook into his chest and shoving him toward the opening. He didn't move with a pilot's grace; he scrambled into the hatch, his boots catching on the rim.

Angela was the last one out. As she lowered her head beneath the floorboards, the western window gave way. The glass shattered into a thousand diamonds of light, and the storm rushed in, claiming the room with a roar of triumph. The fire-finder whirled in the gale, its gears screaming, a silent signal fire burning itself out in the dark.

They scrambled down the stairs, the wood groaning beneath them as the lookout settled into its new, broken geometry. They reached the ground level just as the secondary limb took out the stairs they had just descended. The world was a mess of mud and needles, but the air, though cold and violent, felt honest. They were out of the glass box. They were back in the movement of the world.

The Cessna waited at the forest strip, a fragile shell of aluminum in the wake of the storm. At a regional hub, Mike sat paralyzed at the controls until Angela reached across the console, her hand covering his to force the throttle forward. He steered toward the private hangar with a jerky, hesitant rhythm, every movement of the plane a visible struggle against his own white-knuckled grip. Rex's invitation had cleared a path, providing a bridge of pressurized steel that the smaller craft could never hope to cross. By the time the Sierra peaks had faded into the indigo blur of the horizon, the Pacific lay ahead—a vast and lightless expanse that brought the final confrontation in Sydney into a sharp, cold focus.

Chapter 28: The Long Way Down

The storm was breaking, but only in the rearview mirror. The transition had begun high above the Pacific, where the silent power of the long-range jet Rex's invitation had secured felt a world away from the rattling Cessna they had left at a regional airport. It was a long suspension between hemispheres that finally deposited them back on western soil. Now, it unfolded as a slow, aching shift in color and temperature, the mountains dissolving behind them mile by mile as the Jeep descended through long grades and thinning air. At a gas station near the border, a place suspended between movement and pause, Angela watched the last of the coastal salt and road grime drip from the wheel wells onto the cracked asphalt, the final trace of the hunt disappearing into dust. By the time the red rocks rose along the horizon, the humidity of the Sydney harbor and the cold of the peaks felt equally distant, as though they belonged to a different version of the journey.

The desert did not welcome them back. It remained what it had always been—vast, steady, and indifferent to their return. As the Jeep crested the final rise toward the valley, the sun settled low between the ridgelines, its light thick and amber, stretching the shadows of the sagauros across the ground in long, reaching lines. Angela held the wheel with steady hands, though her pulse carried a quiet urgency beneath the surface, a rhythm that had followed her across continents and now settled again in the place where it had begun.

Sam sat beside her in silence. The GPS rested unused in his lap, its screen dim, his attention fixed instead on the familiar outline of the hangar. The building stood against the horizon like something anchored against time, its corrugated surface catching the fading light. To anyone else it might have passed unnoticed, but to them it held a gravity that drew everything inward.

In the back seat, Mike watched the landscape through the side window, his hands resting loose in his lap. He was still processing the ghost of the Sierra storm—not the wind, but the moment his own panic had nearly ended them. High on the mountain pass, blinded by sleet, he had reached for the steering wheel in a fit of protective instinct, certain that Angela was driving them to their deaths. He had tried to force the Jeep toward the shoulder, toward a ditch he couldn't see, his 'protection' a blind, suffocating weight that had almost sent them spinning into a ravine.

Angela hadn't screamed or fought him with anger. She had simply held the line, her hands stronger and more certain than his, guiding the vehicle through the white-out while his interference became the very obstacle they had to survive. In the terrifying silence that followed their descent, Mike had realized the truth he'd been hiding from for years: he had spent a lifetime trying to ground her to keep her safe, never seeing that his grip was the hazard. By trying to keep her from the air, he had been the one making the journey dangerous.

The tension that once shaped every word hadn't vanished; it had gone brittle. He followed the movement of the wind through the brush, his gaze flickering between a desperate longing for the hangar and a deep, reflexive tremor. He was trying to let go of the control he'd wielded like a shield, but the shadow of the building still felt like an oncoming storm.

Angela pulled the Jeep to a stop several yards from the hangar. Another vehicle was already there, a black SUV cutting a stark line against the pale ground. Suzette and Quinn stood beside it, their posture guarded, the long arc of the hunt visible in the way they held themselves. Suzette's composure remained, but it no longer carried the same sharp edge. When she looked at Angela, the rivalry that had once defined their encounters seemed quieter, shaped now by everything they had crossed to reach this point.

The hangar door stood partially open, a narrow break in the metal revealing a line of shadow within. Angela stepped forward first, the gravel shifting beneath her boots as she crossed the distance. Inside, the air held the scent of oil and warm metal, familiar in a way that settled deeper than thought. The stripped sailplane wing caught the last of the light, its frame pale and skeletal against the darker interior. At the center of the space, a single work light cast a circle across the bench where her mother had once kept her flight logs.

Angela moved toward it.

A leather portfolio lay open on the surface, held in place by two brass geocaching coins. Sam reached toward one, then stopped, his attention shifting instead to the note placed between them. Angela picked it up, her eyes moving steadily across the page as the meaning settled.

"The hunt was a filter," she said quietly. "It was never about the prize."

She turned the page, revealing two sets of documents.

Suzette stepped closer, the restraint in her posture giving way to urgency. "What is it?"

Angela looked at the pages again, the weight of them becoming clear as she spoke. "Two options. The first is a buyout. Carlisle Industries takes the school and your family's center. They turn everything into a corporate operation. The money... it's total, Dad. It clears the mortgage, the liens, everything. You'd never have to look at a balance sheet again."

She paused, the weight of the numbers anchoring her to the floor. "The second is a grant. It's a fraction. It covers the back taxes and the roof repairs, but the debt remains. We keep the school, but we'd still be underwater. No backing. No guarantees."

Sam stepped beside her, his voice quiet but certain. "We can make it work."

Suzette moved closer, her composure tightening. "Angela, think about what this means. We could both walk away from this. We don't have to keep fighting."

Angela met her gaze, seeing both determination and exhaustion, the kind that came from pushing forward without pause.

She turned then, looking toward her father.

Mike remained outside, his boots anchored to the gravel as if the hangar threshold were a physical cliff. He looked at the structure—the place where his life had fractured—and his hands curled into tight, white-knuckled fists. "It's your choice," he said, his voice straining against the thin air. "But the grant is just a stay of execution, Angie. It doesn't solve the debt. It just keeps the bank from locking the gates tomorrow."

The words settled into the space between them.

Angela looked back at the documents. The buyout was an exit—lavish, absolute, and kind. It offered her father a life without the crushing weight of the school's failures. The grant was merely an invitation to a long, uncertain fight.

She lifted her gaze to the wing.

It remained unfinished, stripped back to its frame, but it held the shape of something that could still take flight.

Her mother's voice echoed in memory, steady and clear.

Listen to the air.

Angela exhaled slowly.

"I don't want to be safe," she said.

The decision settled fully as she reached for the pen and signed the grant.

The moment passed without spectacle, but something shifted within it, a lightness that felt less like relief and more like alignment.

Rex St. James stepped into the doorway as the pen left the page, his presence quiet but deliberate. He took in the scene without interruption, then moved forward and closed the portfolio, setting aside the unsigned contract without comment.

"The board will hate this," he said, his tone carrying more fatigue than frustration. "But they were never the point."

He looked around the hangar, then back at Angela. "My father believed everyone had a price. This was his way of proving it. Your mother never agreed."

The words lingered, not as explanation but as confirmation.

Rex gave a small nod, then turned toward the door. "Fix the place," he added. "It deserves it."

When he left, the quiet returned.

Sam moved closer, resting lightly against Angela's side. Angela reached back, her fingers finding Mike's wrist where he still lingered in the shadow of the doorway. She didn't ask; she simply pulled, a steady, uncompromising tug that forced him to take the final step onto the concrete floor. His breath hitched, a jagged sound in the quiet, but he didn't pull away. He stood there, his hand finally settling against the metal frame, not to block the way but to steady his own shaking.

The desert stretched outward beyond them, unchanged.

Angela looked up as the first stars appeared, the sky opening the way it always had, wide and uncontained.

Nothing had been resolved. The school was still unfinished, the future still uncertain, but the path felt clear.

"The roof first," Sam said.

Angela smiled, the tension easing. "The roof first," she agreed.

She rested her hand against the metal of the hangar, feeling its solidity beneath her palm.

The sky no longer felt distant. It felt possible.

For the first time, that was enough.

Chapter 29: Runway 19

The airstrip was a scarred ribbon of asphalt, a forgotten intent carved into the side of a granite ridge. After the salt-spray of Sydney and the grueling hours of the Pacific crossing, the thin, high-altitude chill bit at the lungs with a dangerous purity. It smelled of sagebrush and the sharp, metallic tang of ancient rain. Runway 19. The numbers were faded, nearly reclaimed by the encroaching scrub, but they still pointed south, toward the warmth they had almost forgotten. The Cessna sat at the edge of the tarmac, its nose tilted slightly down like a bird with a clipped wing. The silence of the Sierras was different from the silence of Arizona. Here, the sheer mass of the surrounding peaks seemed to exert a physical pressure that squeezed the breath from the lungs.

Mike stood by the cowling, his hands deep in the guts of the engine. Quinn was beside him, holding a flashlight even though the sun was beginning to burn through the high-altitude haze. They didn't speak. They moved with the synchronized economy of men who understood that a machine didn't care about their rivalry. A ruptured fuel line was a mathematical problem, a failure of physics that required a physical solution. Mike used a piece of safety wire to bridge a gap that shouldn't have existed, his fingers steady despite the cold that had turned his knuckles into knots of red and white.

"Hold that tension," Mike said. His voice was a low rasp, stripped of its earlier panic. The mountain had taken his fear and replaced it with a grim, functional competence. Quinn nodded, his jaw set in a hard line. He wasn't a competitor here. He was a second set of hands in a survival situation, a role he inhabited with a surprising, quiet grace.

Angela watched them for a moment, her own hands tucked into her pockets. She could feel the vibration of the climb still humming in her bones. The plane had held, but the margin had been thin. She turned away from the mechanical struggle and looked toward the far end of the strip, where a skeletal structure rose from the weeds. It was a wind-tee, a vintage navigation aid that had once told pilots which way the world was moving. Its wooden frame was bleached to the color of bone, and the fabric that had once covered it was gone, leaving only the ribs exposed to the sky.

"Sam, look at the orientation," Angela said. She gestured toward the tee. It was pointing toward a notch in the peaks that didn't align with the prevailing gusts. It was fighting the currents, a deliberate contradiction in a world governed by flow.

Sam adjusted his inhaler, his breathing a rhythmic, wheezing accompaniment to the wind. He pulled the GPS unit from his bag, but the screen was a dead smear of gray. The mountains were still blocking the satellites, or perhaps the hunt had simply moved beyond the reach of silicon and signals. He walked toward the wind-tee, his boots crunching on the brittle glass of a discarded bottle. "It's weighted," he muttered. "The tail isn't swinging. Something is holding it in place."

They reached the base of the structure. A small, weather-beaten box was bolted to the center pivot, hidden beneath a layer of rusted iron. It wasn't an ammo can or a plastic tupperware. It was a brass canister, the kind used for pneumatic tubes in old department stores. Angela reached out and touched the metal. It was cold, but there was a resonance to it, a vibration that seemed to pull at the scars on her palms. She unscrewed the cap and pulled out a single sheet of heavy, cream-colored stationery.

The handwriting was precise, a series of elegant, loops and sharp descents that mirrored the flight paths of a high-performance glider. It was addressed to the one who follows the wind.

"It's from Rex," Angela whispered. She felt Sam lean in, his presence a warm anchor at her side. She began to read, her internal voice taking on the cool, detached cadence of the man who had orchestrated their ordeal.

I spent three years in the Mojave trying to learn the language you were born speaking, the letter began. *I had the math, the airframes, and the finest instructors, but I never heard the music. Your mother was the only person I ever saw who didn't fight the atmosphere; she belonged to the sky. If you are reading this at Runway 19, you have found the line she once drew through the blue. Follow it.*

Angela paused, the paper fluttering in a sudden gust. She looked at the Cessna, where Mike was tightening a bolt with a sharp, decisive twist. She thought of Rex St. James in his glass tower, not as a puppet master, but as a man haunted by a grace he couldn't replicate. The Apex Hunt wasn't just a marketing stunt; it was an excavation. He had turned their flight into a prism, hoping to catch a glimpse of Maria Santiago's light one last time.

"He's still looking for her," Sam said. His voice was small, filtered through the realization that their tormentor was chasing a shadow. "He's using us to find a part of her he couldn't keep."

"He's obsessed, Sam. He didn't know her, he only wanted what she had." Angela folded the paper, the sharp creases catching the light. "He's testing us to see if the ghost is still in the machine."

A low, resonant sound drifted up from the valley floor, the heavy, guttural thrum of a truck rather than the smooth whine of a turbine.

Angela looked toward the access road, a narrow dirt track winding through the pines. A plume of dust rose behind it, a pale yellow veil moving with a steady, purposeful advance.

"Mike!" Angela shouted. She didn't have to explain. The urgency in her tone cut through the hangar's oily, stagnant heat. "We have company."

Mike emerged from the cowling, his face smeared with grease and hydraulic fluid. He looked toward the road, his eyes narrowing. A white SUV with a gold star on the door was visible now, navigating the ruts with a practiced, aggressive speed. A sheriff's patrol. An unauthorized landing in a closed mining district was a legal entanglement they couldn't afford, not with the finish line so close.

"Quinn, get the chocks!" Mike yelled. He vaulted into the cockpit, his movements fluid and certain. The hesitation that had paralyzed him over the peaks was gone, replaced by the muscle memory of a man who had spent his life navigating the boundaries of the law and the wild.

Angela and Sam sprinted toward the plane. A static charge seemed to crackle against their skin, the scent of ozone returning as the Cessna's engine coughed, sputtered, and then roared into a jagged, uneven life. The fuel line was holding, but the sound was raw, a mechanical protest against the hurried repair. Quinn scrambled into the back, his face pale, his competitive drive finally yielding to the simple necessity of escape.

"Get in!" Mike leaned over the seat, his hand firm on the throttle. Angela pulled Sam into the cabin and slammed the door, the latch clicking home just as the patrol car swung onto the tarmac, its light bar erupting into a frantic, rhythmic dance of red and blue.

The runway was short, a narrow corridor of decaying asphalt that ended in a sheer drop off the ridge. Mike didn't wait for the engine to warm. He jammed the throttle forward, and the Cessna surged, its tires screaming against the grit. The patrol car was closing the distance, the siren a high-pitched wail that was lost beneath the roar of the prop.

"The fence," Sam yelled. He was gripped the edge of his seat, his knuckles white. At the end of the strip, a chain-link fence stood as a final, silver barrier, its top wire glinting in the sun.

Angela watched the airspeed indicator. The needle was crawling upward, forty knots, fifty, fifty-five. The end of the asphalt was rushing toward them, a gray blur that ended in nothingness. She could see the individual links of the fence now, the rusted mesh that looked like a wall. She felt the tail lift, the plane seeking the heights, but the weight was too much, the runway too short.

"Pull," Angela whispered. It wasn't a command; it was a prayer. She reached out and placed her hand over Mike's on the yoke. She didn't take control. She simply added her intent to his, the two of them seeking the same sliver of lift. The plane felt the shift. It responded to the combined pressure, the wings flexing as they caught the rising thermal coming off the sun-warmed granite.

The Cessna jumped. It was a violent, ungraceful rupture from the earth. The landing gear cleared the top of the fence by inches, the sound of the wind whistling through the struts like a sharp, sudden intake of breath. For a second, they were suspended in the void, the ground falling away into a green and gray abyss. Then the lift took them, a solid hand of air that pushed the nose toward the horizon.

Below them, the patrol car came to a stop at the edge of the cliff. The deputy climbed out, a small, dark figure against the vastness of the mountains. He looked up, his hand shielding his eyes as the Cessna climbed away from the ridge, a white speck against the deepening blue of the afternoon.

Mike exhaled, a long, shaky sound that seemed to empty his entire chest. He didn't look back. He kept his eyes on the horizon, his hands relaxed on the yoke for the first time in weeks. The engine settled into a steady, vibrating hum, a domestic rhythm that made the cabin feel like a room instead of a cage.

"We're clear," Mike said. He looked at Angela, his eyes searching hers for a moment. He saw the brass canister in her lap, the letter tucked inside. He didn't ask what was in it. He knew the look on her face, the one that meant the sky had finally started to answer her again.

Angela leaned her head against the cool glass of the window. The Sierras were behind them now, their jagged peaks softening into the hazy distance. Ahead, the sky was wide and open, a pale, shimmering curtain that led toward the red dust of Arizona. She thought of Rex, standing in his office, watching the fog swallow the city. She thought of her mother, whose voice was no longer a ghost but a resonance in the frame of the plane.

The sky was waiting, and for the first time, Angela didn't have to wonder if she was ready. She was already there.

Chapter 30: The Silver Sky Cipher

The summit had been a fever dream of gold and glass, a momentary suspension of gravity. Now, the mountain was taking it all back. The storm did not arrive with a thunderclap; it arrived as a deletion. The sky simply ceased to be blue, replaced by a dense, suffocating wool that smelled of wet stone and static. The fire lookout, once a beacon of their mother's hidden language, vanished behind a curtain of sleet within minutes of their departure. They were no longer investigators of a grand mystery. They were just small, shivering things trying to stay upright on a slope that wanted them gone.

Angela led the way. Her boots found the rhythm of the descent, a jarring, repetitive impact that vibrated through her shins. She didn't look at the map. The GPS was a useless glow in Sam's pocket, its signal drowned out by the granite and the electricity in the clouds. She relied on the mountain logic Maria had whispered into her ears during a dozen childhood hikes. Look for the way the water moves, her mother had said. The water always knows the shortest path, even if it's the hardest one. Angela watched the silver ribbons of runoff as they sliced through the mud, using them as a compass through the gray.

Behind her, she heard the heavy, rhythmic rasp of Sam's breathing. It was a weight on his chest. Every few yards, he would pause, his hand reaching out to steady himself against the freezing rock. Angela didn't stop to offer comfort. She knew that if they stopped for too long, the cold would settle into their joints and stay there. She just adjusted her pace, keeping her footfalls loud enough for him to follow in the gloom.

Mike took the rear. He moved with a quiet, practiced efficiency that Angela hadn't seen in years. The fatigue that usually slumped his shoulders was gone, replaced by the professional alertness of a man who had spent his life managing the dangers of the wilderness. He wasn't just a grieving father anymore. He was a Parks and Rec veteran who understood exactly how fast a granite slope could turn into a slide. His eyes moved constantly, scanning the ridgeline for the telltale shift of loose shale or the sudden snap of a burdened branch.

The truce with Suzette and Quinn was a fragile, silent thing. They moved with the Santiagos, their high-tech gear plastered with mud, their faces masks of grim concentration. The rivalry that had propelled them across multiple continents was momentarily suspended by the mountain. Here, at nine thousand feet, there was no prize. There was only the next step. Quinn's breathing was a jagged echo of Sam's, his heavy frame ill-suited for the technicality of the descent.

The trail narrowed at the Devil's Rib, a thin spine of rock that dropped away into a white void on either side. The wind hit them here with the force of an actual blow, carrying the sharp scent of cedar and ice. It was a bottleneck, a place where gravity felt personal. Angela pressed her back against the rock, her fingers searching for purchase in the frozen cracks. She could feel the vibration of the wind in the stone itself, a low, tectonic hum that made her teeth ache.

A sharp, discordant chime—the sound of tempered steel on stone—echoed through the pass. Angela turned just in time to see Quinn's strap snag on a heavy, iron piton driven into the cedar's trunk. The metal was fresh and cold, an obstacle placed precisely where a desperate man would stumble. The impact threw him off balance. His heavy pack, weighted with tech and gear, acted as a pendulum, pulling him toward the edge of the slick granite. He didn't scream. He just made a small, choked sound of surprise as his boots lost their grip on the wet stone.

Before Angela could move, Mike was there. He didn't hesitate. He lunged forward, his hand catching the handle of Quinn's pack with a violent, grounding force. He planted his heels into a narrow fissure in the rock, his muscles straining against the weight of a grown man and sixty pounds of equipment. For a heartbeat, they were a frozen sculpture of tension, suspended between the rock and the fall. Then, with a grunt of effort that sounded like a physical rupture, Mike hauled Quinn back toward the center of the path.

Quinn collapsed against the stone, his chest heaving, his face the color of the sleet. Mike didn't say a word. He didn't wait for a thank you. He just checked the integrity of the cedar branch and then looked at Angela, his expression unreadable behind his fogged glasses. It was a gesture of instinctive grace, a remnant of the man who used to believe that safety was something he could provide through sheer will. He was still the protector, even if the things he was protecting them from were no longer just gravity and wind.

"Keep moving," Mike said, his voice low and steady. "The light is failing."

They found a shallow alcove an hour later, a curve in the rock that offered a momentary reprieve from the rain. They huddle together, five people bound by a shared exhaustion. Sam sat between Mike's knees, his inhaler clicking rhythmically as he fought back the panic that comes when the world vanishes into white. Angela watched the fog move past the opening of the alcove, a silent, ghostly procession of vapor. It felt as if they were the only things left in a world that had been erased.

Suzette leaned against the opposite wall. Her expensive technical jacket was shredded at the elbow, and a thin line of blood ran down her temple, but her eyes were still sharp, still calculating. She looked at Angela, and for the first time, the predatory edge was gone. There was only a cold, shared recognition of the distance they had covered.

"You're not what I expected," Suzette said. Her voice was thin, stripped of its corporate polish. "I looked at the data. I saw a girl who crashed a plane and a family that was falling apart. I thought you were just noise."

Angela tightened the laces of her boots. "We are falling apart. That's why we're here."

Suzette looked at Quinn, who was staring at his shaking hands. "My father wants a trophy. He wants a quarterly report that says I'm the best. He doesn't care about the mountain. He doesn't even care about the money. He just wants the win." She paused, a small, bitter smile touching her lips. "I envy you, Angela. You have a legacy worth fighting for. Something that isn't just a line on a balance sheet. You're fighting for a ghost. That's a lot harder to beat than a billionaire."

Angela didn't answer. She thought of the hangar in Arizona, the smell of oil and the way the sun hit the red rocks at dusk. She thought of the Silver Sky Cipher and the way her mother's handwriting had looked on the old vellum. She felt the Santiago name grounding her, an anchor in the storm. The hunt was no longer just about the prize; it was about the map Maria had left behind, a map that was still leading them into the unknown. She realized then that the descent hadn't been the end at all, but a clarification of what still remained to be found.

"The wind is shifting," Sam whispered. He was looking at his watch, the blue light reflecting in his wide eyes. "The pressure is dropping. We have to go now or we won't make the trailhead before the temperature hits freezing."

He was right. The air was sharpening, turning from a wet chill to a biting, crystalline cold. They stood up in unison, a single unit once more. The descent became a blur of motion and shadow. They moved through the lower switchbacks, where the granite gave way to mud and the gnarled roots of ancient pines. Angela's legs felt like lead, her knees screaming with every step, but she didn't slow down. She could smell the pine needles now, a heavy, resinous scent that meant they were getting closer to the earth.

Visibility dropped to nearly zero as they entered the treeline. The trees were silhouettes that shifted in the wind, their branches reaching out like skeletal fingers. Sam stumbled, his breath hitching in a way that signaled the start of a panic attack. Angela stopped and grabbed his shoulders, forcing him to look at her. His face was wet with rain and tears, his pupils blown wide with terror.

"Sam, look at me," she said, her voice a pilot's calm, steady and immutable. "Don't look at the trees. Look at my heels. Just my heels. One step. Then another. We are on a glide slope, Sam. We just have to follow the path down."

She held his gaze until the frantic rhythm of his heart slowed. He nodded once, a small, jerky movement, and tucked his chin into his collar. They kept moving. The forest was a cathedral of shadows, the wind howling through the canopy with a sound like a jet engine. But they were no longer afraid of the noise. They were moving with it, a part of the mountain's own frantic energy.

The trailhead appeared suddenly, a patch of gravel and the dull reflection of wet metal. Two vehicles sat in the small parking area, looking like toys abandoned in the mud. The relief was so sharp it felt like a physical impact. Angela stepped onto the flat ground, her boots crunching on the gravel, and for a moment, the world tilted. The horizontal line returned. The ceiling lifted. She was no longer a body in space; she was a girl standing in the rain.

Suzette and Quinn didn't linger. They moved toward their sleek, black SUV without a word. The alliance was over, dissolved by the presence of the road and the promise of a heater. Before she climbed into the passenger seat, Suzette turned back. She looked at Angela, then at Mike and Sam, who were leaning against the Jeep. She didn't wave. She just nodded, a brief, professional acknowledgement of the peak they had conquered, before turning her focus back to the pursuit. The taillights vanished into the fog like two red eyes.

Angela stayed by the Jeep, the rain soaking through her layers. She looked back up at the mountain, but the peak was gone, swallowed by the belly of the storm. High above, she thought she saw a flash of light, a flicker of something white and fast moving through the mist. It might have been a bird. It might have been a reflection. Or perhaps it was merely the architect's shadow, stretching across the ridgeline. On the dashboard of the Jeep, pinned by a single heavy stone, was a card of vellum that hadn't been there when they left. It bore no text, only a hand-drawn coastline that existed on no aeronautical chart Angela had ever seen.

"We're off the ridge," Mike said. He was standing by the door, his hand resting on the frame. He looked older than he had on the summit, the adrenaline having drained away to leave only the exhaustion. But there was something else in his eyes now. A clarity. A recognition of his children that hadn't been there when they left Arizona.

"Not yet," Angela said. She reached into her pocket and felt the weight of the Golden Bug, its secret frequency pulsing with a new, restless urgency. "The frequency has changed its mind, Mike. It isn't looking for a home anymore. It's found a new pulse, something cold and deep, and it's pulling us toward the empty blue of the horizon."

She climbed into the driver's seat. Her hands were steady on the wheel, her grip light but absolute. She didn't look at the mirrors. She just watched the road ahead as it wound down through the pines and toward the valley floor. The mountain had finished with them, but the true descent—the long, silent pull toward the deep water—was only just beginning.

Chapter 31: The Desert's Truth

A week after the frantic salt-spray of Sydney, the desert had settled, the heat a breathless, unmoving pressure against the skin. Back in Arizona, the morning light had changed.

It no longer carried the flat, oppressive weight of summer, but instead arrived with a lean, precise clarity that sharpened every edge of the landscape. The mountains stood cut clean against the sky, their ridgelines defined in a way that made them feel closer, more present, as though the atmosphere itself had thinned and sharpened overnight. Angela stood at the threshold of the hangar, her boots resting on the line where sunlight met the cool, oil-scented concrete. The transition between the two felt deliberate, a boundary she had crossed countless times before but never quite like this.

The "CLOSED" sign was gone.

In its place, a fresh board hung slightly uneven on its hooks, the wood still new enough to carry the scent of pine and varnish. Mike had sanded it himself; she could see it in the care of the edges, in the way the grain had been left visible instead of painted over. The lettering was steady but not ornamental.

Santiago Soaring School.

Open.

Inside, the hangar no longer held silence.

Sound moved through it in steady layers—the scrape of metal against metal, the measured hiss of the air compressor, the low murmur of a radio playing something old and acoustic. The heavy, stagnant silence that had once anchored the space had been replaced by motion, by purpose, by the kind of noise that belonged to work being done rather than something being preserved.

Mike stood bent over the fuselage of the K-21 sailplane, his hands steady, stained with grease in a way that spoke of hours rather than minutes. He wasn't wearing the park ranger uniform anymore. The flight suit had returned, faded at the shoulders where years of sun had worn it down, the fabric carrying its own memory of use.

Sam stood beside him, holding a torque wrench with focused intensity, his glasses slipping slightly down his nose as he worked. He wasn't in his school uniform either. The work pants and t-shirt he wore were already marked with smudges of carbon and grease, and for once he didn't seem to notice.

He glanced up as Angela stepped in.

"The tension on the control cables is within three millimeters of spec," Sam said, and there was pride in it, quiet but unmistakable. The nervous edge that had once lived in his voice had softened into something more grounded. "Dad says we can air-test the stabilizers by noon."

Mike straightened slowly, his back giving a soft, audible pop as he wiped his hands on a rag. He studied the aircraft the way he always had, with a professional attention that didn't miss anything, but the exhaustion that used to define him had shifted. It was still there, written faintly into the lines around his eyes, but it had changed shape. It was no longer the weight of holding something together. It was the weight of building it.

"Noon might be optimistic," he said, though the corners of his mouth lifted slightly. He looked at Angela, and the look was different now. Not calculation. Not concern held too tightly. Recognition. "But the wind is holding steady from the west. If we get the wings pinned, she's yours for the first tow."

"I'll help with the pins," Angela said, stepping fully into the space. A certain buoyancy met her, though the heavy scents of oil and dust remained unchanged. "Sam, grab the grease. We're going to do this right."

They worked for hours.

Not in silence, but in something close to it, a shared rhythm that didn't need explanation. Tools passed between hands without being asked for. Adjustments were made and checked without commentary. The work itself became the language, each tightened bolt and aligned surface carrying meaning without needing to be spoken aloud.

They weren't repairing the plane. They were clearing something else away.

The last year had left its mark in ways that couldn't be named directly, but here, in the repetition of motion and the certainty of process, those marks began to loosen. The hangar no longer felt like a place where something had ended. It felt like something had resumed.

By mid-morning, a long shadow stretched across the open bay.

Angela looked up, lifting a hand against the brightness.

Suzette stood just outside the threshold, where the light broke against the interior. She didn't step in. She remained at the edge, her posture as composed as it had always been, but without the sharpness that used to define it. She wore a simple linen shirt and jeans, her hair pulled back in a way that suggested function over presentation.

"I heard the compressor from the road," she said. Her gaze moved across the sailplane, following the line of the wings now fully assembled. "She looks different with the wings on."

Angela stepped toward her, stopping just short of the doorway. "She's ready to fly. We're finishing the checks."

Suzette nodded once. There was no tension in it, no challenge.

"Rex sent the confirmation," she said. "The sponsorship's finalized. My family's gym stays open. We're calling it the Saunders Center for Excellence. It's a bit much, but my father likes it."

"It's a good name," Angela said. "The grant came through yesterday too. We're keeping the school independent."

Suzette's gaze shifted slightly. "He wanted you to take the buyout."

"I know."

"He was testing you."

Angela glanced back toward Mike and Sam, who were now in the middle of a quiet disagreement about fluid grades that neither of them was actually losing. "It wasn't about pride," she said. "It was about who gets to decide what happens next."

Suzette studied her a moment longer, then reached into her pocket and pulled out a laminated card.

"The last of the Sydney clues," she said, holding it out. "I didn't think it belonged in the harbor after the race. I figured you'd want it for the collection."

Angela took it, the edge of the plastic firm against her fingers. "I'll put it next to the bug," she said. "A reminder."

"Of what?" Suzette asked.

Angela met her gaze. "Of how close you actually came."

Suzette didn't smile.

But she nodded.

"I'll come back in the spring," she said. "I want to see if you can teach as well as you can fly."

"I'll charge extra," Angela said. "Rival rate."

This time, something almost like a smile touched Suzette's expression.

She turned and walked back toward her car, her stride steady, unchanged in its confidence.

When Angela turned back, Mike stood near the office, holding something.

"Found this in storage," he said, stepping aside.

The desk was Maria's.

Angela crossed the space slowly, her hand brushing the surface as she reached it. The wood carried the small marks of years—scratches, worn edges, places where tools had rested too long. It smelled faintly of cedar and paper.

She opened the middle drawer.

At the back, tucked behind old charts, sat an ammo can, identical.

Her breath caught, not sharply, but in a slow, steady shift.

She pulled it forward and opened it.

Inside was a folded sheet of parchment, and the original deed.

She unfolded the paper.

The handwriting was Mike's, but the meaning belonged to all of them.

You didn't just save the school.

You saved us.

It's yours now, Ang. All of it.

She looked up.

Mike stood across the hangar, watching, not waiting for a reaction, just present. He gave a single nod, then turned back to help Sam.

The weight of it settled not as pressure, but as foundation.

By early afternoon, the sailplane rested at the edge of the runway. The desert stretched outward, heat shimmering faintly above the ground, the scent of creosote rising with the promise of lift.

Angela climbed into the cockpit, the familiar interior closing around her in a way that felt both known and newly claimed.

She checked the instruments. The variometer needle held steady. The stick hummed against her palm, translating air into something she could read.

No fear came.

The memory of the peaks remained, but it had lost its hold. It no longer dictated what came next.

"Radio check," Mike's voice came through.

"Loud and clear," Angela said.

The tow plane surged forward, the line pulling taut as the sailplane followed, lifting as the ground dropped away in a motion that felt inevitable rather than forced.

At two thousand feet, she released.

The line fell away, and silence followed, not empty but full.

The wind pressed against the wings, steady and insistent. Angela adjusted, listening for the lift in the shifting pressure of the controls, finding it along the edge of the ridge where invisible currents surged upward, unmistakable in their pull.

She turned into it.

The glider climbed higher, past the point where memory used to take over.

Today, nothing broke. The lift held true.

She looked out across the horizon, the land unfolding in every direction, no longer distance to cross but space to read.

The sky didn't feel empty. It felt unfinished.

She leaned into the turn, following the next thermal she sensed before she could see.

The movement felt natural, continuous, certain.

For the first time, Angela Santiago wasn't trying to leave or prove anything.

She was exactly where she needed to be, and she knew how to stay there.

Chapter 32: The Wind's Command

Sunday, 03:14 AEST --- Eight Hours Remaining

The Sydney Opera House stood out against the black water, its white shells sharp against the dark skyline. From the harbor front, the sound of the victory gala drifted across the quay in muffled bursts of brass and forced laughter, while inside Rex St. James was likely raising a glass of expensive champagne to Suzette Saunders and her team, crowning them the victors of the hunt as the world watched across a dozen different live streams. To the spectators, the race was over: the Golden Bug had been found at Uluru, the final cache had been logged, and the Santiago family had been reduced to a footnote in a billionaire's game.

Angela sat in the deep shadow of a concrete pier, her back against a rusted pylon. The air along the quay carried the scent of diesel and wet timber, a utilitarian honesty that stood in contrast to the perfume-soaked air of the gala. She held the Golden Bug in her palm. Its unexpected weight—a dense knot of gold and circuitry shaped like a mechanical scarab—settled into her hand with the insistence of something that refused to be dismissed. Suzette had the trophy, the one handed to her beneath the lights and cameras. Angela watched a single white gull pick at a discarded oyster shell on the edge of the pier, oblivious to the music across the water. Her fingers loosened. The artifact tipped toward the oily dark, hanging for a second over the void. If they had already lost, there was no reason to carry the artifact forward, no reason to keep holding onto something that seemed to belong to a version of the outcome that no longer existed.

She turned it over instead, her thumb tracing the intricate carvings along its wings, and as she did the surface resisted her expectations. It was not polished in the way a prize should be; it was functional, constructed with purpose rather than display. Maria had once said that the most important parts of a plane were the ones you could not see from the ground, and the memory settled into place with a clarity that cut through her exhaustion. Angela tilted the bug toward the distant streetlights, forcing her eyes to focus despite the dull ache of sleeplessness that blurred the edges of the world. Along the inner edge of the left wing, hidden beneath a nearly invisible layer of resin, a series of microscopic etchings registered at first as texture before resolving into something more deliberate.

"Sam, the GPS." She didn't look up.

Sam moved beside her, his school tie loosened and his movements edged with fatigue as he handed over the device. His fingers shook before he pulled his inhaler from his pocket and took a sharp, controlled breath, the sterile hiss cutting through the quiet of the pier. "We're on a clock." He didn't look at her, his voice tight. "Eight hours until the window closes."

Angela steadied the GPS in her hands, forcing her focus into something precise as she activated the macro lens and brought the wing into view. The screen flickered, then sharpened, revealing two distinct lines of text: the first a set of coordinates pointing to a remote stretch of the Great Dividing Range, the second a radio frequency—122.85.

"It's a UNICOM frequency." Sam's eyes brightened as the numbers clicked into place. "Non-towered airports. It's where pilots talk to each other when no one else is listening."

Angela looked back at the Opera House, seeing the gala lights less as a finish line and more as a bright, distracting lure. Rex hadn't been searching for speed or spectacle; he had been testing persistence, looking for the person who would continue past the moment that felt like an ending.

"Do you have the handheld?" she asked.

Sam reached into his backpack and pulled out the portable aviation radio they had carried since Tucson, dialing the frequency with a practiced rhythm. At first there was only static, a wide, hollow hiss that filled the space between them, but then the sound shifted, resolving into a sequence of sharp, rhythmic chirps—a discrete data burst that cut through the static like a digital heartbeat. "It's a burst transmission." Sam hunched over the device, isolating the playback. "It's carrying an audio file and an encrypted header." He tapped the screen to isolate the playback, and a voice emerged from the grit, distant and intimate at the same time.

"Watch the horizon, Ang. Don't chase the needles. Feel the air under the wing. If it wants to lift, let it. If it wants to drop, you find the floor."

Angela's thumb searched for a throttle that wasn't there. The pier seemed to dissolve, replaced for a heartbeat by the vibration of a seat against her thighs and the smell of high-altitude ozone. It wasn't a ghost, but it carried enough of one to tighten her chest, her mother's voice guiding her through air she had not yet learned to trust.

"The header is locked with a Vigenère cipher," Sam said, his eyes fixed on the tablet's scrolling data. "I need a key."

"The key is Maria." A voice spoke from the shadows behind them.

Angela jerked toward the voice, the Golden Bug shifting in her grip as Mike stepped into the light. He looked as though he'd been folded into a small space for too long, his shoulders hunched and his face mapped with new, deep lines around his mouth. He didn't meet her eyes; he was staring at the Golden Bug, his jaw working in a hard, rhythmic clench. His jacket hung loosely, creased from long hours in cramped seats, and his eyes were bloodshot, fixed on the dark horizon where the water met the sky.

"Dad?" Angela's grip on the Golden Bug tightened.

Mike crossed the short distance between them and sat on a nearby crate, his gaze moving first to the bug, then to the Opera House beyond it. "I found her auxiliary logbook, Ang. The one she hid in the rafters of the hangar." Mike's voice broke, the sound barely audible over the lapping water. "I spent a year trying to scrub her memory out of the house because I thought the silence was the only way to survive. But she'd written a note on the flyleaf. She said that a pilot who stays on the ground out of fear isn't safe—they're just a ghost who hasn't stopped breathing yet. I realized then that Rex wasn't just chasing a ghost; he was testing the person who would inherit her courage, not just her license." His hand hovered near the radio without touching it. "The key isn't just her name. It's her license number. N-four-two-five-five-Zulu."

Sam's fingers blurred across his tablet. "The packet is clearing… it's a set of coordinates and an altitude. Thirty-seven south, one hundred forty-seven east. Six thousand feet."

"The Victorian Alps," Mike said, his hands tightening into fists. "It's like the Minarets, but the weather turns in heartbeats. That's a graveyard. There's an old high-country strip up there, narrow and exposed, out of service for years. I came here to stop you, to drag you to the embassy and force us onto a flight home because I thought I could save you from her fate by keeping you in a quiet room."

Angela looked at him, noticing the way he gripped the edges of the crate until his knuckles turned white. "Dad, listen to her," she said, pressing the radio into his hand so he could feel the vibration of the recording. "Listen to the rhythm. She's not telling us to stay grounded. You think you've been keeping us safe, but we've just been stuck in something else. The hangar, the silence—that wasn't safety. This is the only way forward."

She gestured toward the coordinates. "Safety isn't the ground. It's having enough air to recover. If we stop now, we never pull out."

Mike held the radio for a long moment, the tension in him shifting rather than breaking, settling into something heavier but more stable. He reached into his jacket and pulled out a worn envelope filled with manifest slips. "I called in what was left of her contacts," he said. "I was going to use them to get us home quietly, to end this without anyone noticing, but Maria never knew how to stay down once the engines were running, and neither do you."

"He's helping us?" Sam looked between them, his fatigue momentarily forgotten.

"He's trusting you." Mike pulled a worn envelope from his jacket. "I found a freight carrier heading south for the mountains. It's not comfortable, and it's not forgiving, but it will get you close. The landing is still yours, Angela. If you do this, you're flying into a ghost strip in mountain air that doesn't give second chances. Can you handle it?"

Angela felt the phantom stall in her gut, that sudden lightness of a plane losing its grip on the sky. She didn't flinch. She tightened her laces and waited for the sensation to pass. Her mother's voice had not been a warning. It had been an invitation.

"I can." Angela met his gaze, the lightness in her gut finally settling into a steady center. They left the harbor behind as the city receded into something distant and irrelevant. By the time they reached the cargo terminal, the sky had begun to shift toward morning, the first pale light spreading across the water. The plane waiting for them was worn and functional, its surface marked by years of use, its engines already rumbling with a steady, grounded power that carried none of the spectacle of the gala.

Angela climbed aboard, the interior narrow and utilitarian, the air thick with the scent of fuel and metal. She settled into the jump seat, the vibration of the airframe running through her as she wrote the frequency across the back of her hand.

"Ready?" Mike asked, adjusting her collar with a familiar, careful motion that held both hesitation and acceptance.

"Ready." Angela didn't look back.

The engines surged, and the plane began its slow roll, the skyline of Sydney receding behind them until it collapsed into a distant line of light against the horizon. The flight was a grueling race against the clock, the steady vibration of the airframe measuring out the shrinking hours until the jagged line of the Great Dividing Range finally rose to meet them.

By the time they reached the staging field near the base of the peaks, the light had shifted again, the mountains casting long shadows across the valley. The larger plane could go no farther, and waiting for them near the edge of the field was a smaller aircraft, its frame built for the kind of terrain that demanded precision rather than endurance.

Angela stepped into the cockpit, her hands listening for the pressure of the air through the controls as the familiar tension returned, less as fear than as awareness.

The clock was running.

The jagged spires of the high country rose ahead, the final hurdle before the journey would come full circle, back to the red dust of Arizona.

And the final approach had begun.

Chapter 33: The Night Before the Blue

The hangar was no longer a tomb of stasis. It had become a lung, holding a deep, pressurized breath before the release of morning. The smell of old grease and floor sweepings remained, but it was layered now with the sharp, clinical scent of carbon fiber and the clean smell of polished resin. In the center of the floor, the EOS prototype sat, its high-aspect-ratio airframe finally made manifest—the physical, shimmering conclusion to the 'Project EOS' development project Sam had first flagged in Maria's bank records and the record-breaking high-altitude specs they'd spent months hunting through the margins of her flight logs. It was no longer a ghost of theoretical physics, but a thing of carbon fiber and consequence. Its wings were long and impossibly thin, designed to flex with the invisible architecture of the atmosphere, catching the light from the overhead sodium lamps in a way that made the aircraft seem to vibrate even while it was tethered to the concrete.

Angela moved along the leading edge of the port wing. She didn't use a flashlight. She didn't need one. Her fingers traced the seam where the skin met the spar, searching for the slightest irregularity, the microscopic burr that might whistle at a hundred knots. She let her fingers read the structural marrow of the wing as if it were the air itself, letting the machine's hidden vibrations speak through the marrow of her hands. The aircraft felt different than the 1-26 or the K-21. It felt hungry. It was a machine built for a geography that didn't exist on any standard sectional chart, a craft intended to live in the Silver Sky, that thin, high-altitude frontier of stratospheric waves her mother had mapped in secret long before 'Project EOS' had become more than a cryptic notation in a ledger.

Mike was at the tail, his shadow stretching long and thin across the floor. He wasn't the man with the white knuckles and the mask of fatigue anymore. He moved with a quiet, functional grace, his hands familiar with the tension of the control cables. He reached out and plucked the rudder cable. The note it returned was high and clear, a perfect middle C that resonated through the hollow structure of the fuselage. He looked up, his eyes meeting Angela's across the silver span of the prototype. There was no fear in his expression. There was only a grave, steady acknowledgement of what was coming.

"Tension is true," Mike said. His voice was low, barely carrying over the hum of the cooling fans on the diagnostic bench. "She's ready to climb, Ang."

Angela nodded, her hand resting on the cockpit sill. "The center of gravity is right where the manual said it should be. Even with the specialized oxygen system and the high-altitude avionics suite."

The silence that followed wasn't the heavy, indifferent quiet of the months after the crash. It was a shared space, a communal wait. Angela thought of the drop, the way the world had once seemed to fall away into a void of grief and debt. She remembered the way the lost engineering drafts had felt like a fever dream in the Paris archives, and the way the complex barometric data had pulsed against the red indifference of Uluru, defying every standard meter. It had seemed like madness then, a disparate collection of difficult clues, but standing here, she saw the architecture of the payoff. All of it had been a descent, a long dive into the dark so she could learn how to pull back up. The Hunt hadn't just been about saving the school. It had been about finding the air again.

Mike walked toward her, his boots making a soft, rhythmic sound on the concrete. He reached into the pocket of his canvas work coat and pulled out a small, heavy object wrapped in a piece of faded chamois cloth. He didn't hand it to her right away. He held it in his palm, looking down at it as if he were weighing the years it represented.

"I took this out of the flight bag after the accident," he said. He unwrapped the cloth to reveal a brass magnetic compass. The housing was battered, the glass scratched from years of vibration, but the needle was steady. "She used it during the record run in the Alps. She told me once that when the electronics failed over the Matterhorn, this was the only thing that knew which way was home."

He pressed it into Angela's hand. The metal was cold, but it warmed quickly against her skin. It was a small, physical anchor, a piece of Maria's history that wasn't a legend or a ghost. It was a tool. By giving it to her, Mike was finally finishing the work he had started with the new sign on the hangar door. He was no longer trying to keep her on the ground. He was equipping her for the ascent.

"Keep it on the dash," Mike said. "Next to the digital stuff. Just in case the sky gets crowded."

Angela closed her fingers over the compass. "I'll keep it centered, Dad."

Across the hangar, Sam was hunched over a ruggedized tablet, his face illuminated by the cool blue glow of the screen. He wore a hoodie with the sleeves pushed up, his forearms smeared with a thin film of hydraulic fluid. He wasn't the fragile boy who needed an inhaler as a talisman. He was the navigator, the mind that had unraveled the global puzzle of Maria's research and found the atmospheric resonance buried in her old flight computer—the same soaring conditions Maria had tracked from the archives in Venice to the edge of the stratosphere. He tapped a final command into the interface, and a soft, rhythmic pulse began to beep from the EOS's avionics stack.

"Telemetry is locked," Sam called out. He didn't look up, his fingers still dancing across the glass. "The Silver Sky sensor array is holding—the same wave-pattern they'd first caught in the records in Venice. It's a live signal, Ang. It's waiting for the climb."

Angela walked over to him, looking down at the data streams. "How far out is the lift?"

"Hard to tell from the ground," Sam said, finally looking up. His eyes were bright, filled with the intellectual fire that had carried them across three continents. "The wave is peaking in the upper atmosphere. It's high. Higher than anything we've ever flown. But the EOS has the glide ratio to get there if we catch the morning wave off the mesa."

He reached for his inhaler, took a measured breath, and tucked it back into his pocket without a hint of the old desperation. He looked at the prototype, then at Angela, then at their father. They were no longer three people living in a house of silence. They were a flight crew. The realization settled into Angela's chest with more weight than the brass compass. They had survived the drop by refusing to let go of the controls.

The side door of the hangar was propped open with a brick, allowing the desert night to bleed inside. The air was cool and smelled of sagebrush and the distant, metallic scent of a storm that had passed hours ago. There was no wind yet, just the profound, unmoving pressure of the Arizona night. Somewhere out in the dark, a coyote barked, a lonely, jagged sound that was swallowed almost instantly by the vastness of the basin.

Angela stepped toward the door, looking out at the silhouette of the mountains against the star-crowded sky. The peaks were jagged teeth, black against the deep purple of the horizon. Tomorrow, those peaks would provide the lift. They would be the engine that pushed the EOS into the thin, cold air where the secrets lived. A fine vibration hummed in her teeth, a resonant shift in the marrow that mirrored the thrum of a plane before it leaves the runway.

"We should get some sleep," Mike said, though he didn't move toward the door. He stayed near the tail of the plane, his hand resting on the rudder as if he were afraid it might drift away if he let go.

"In a minute," Angela replied. "I just want to listen to the air for a second."

She closed her eyes and let her awareness drift beyond the hangar walls. She didn't listen for the sound of the wind, but for the change in pressure, the subtle shift that signaled the arrival of the morning thermals. It was there, a low-level hum in the structure of the world. The atmosphere was preparing itself. The sky was opening a door, and for the first time in years, Angela wasn't afraid to walk through it.

Sam joined her at the door, leaning his shoulder against the corrugated metal frame. He looked small against the backdrop of the desert, but there was a new solidity to him, a competence that had been forged in the damp limestone of Paris and the salt spray of Venice. He held the tablet like a shield.

"Do you think she knew?" Sam asked quietly. "About the EOS? About what she was really building?"

Angela thought of the flight logs, the maps of light and air that Maria had left behind, and the recovered Project EOS blueprints—the ones that had transformed from a suspicious line item in a bank ledger into the schematics for an experimental high-altitude glider they'd finally reconstructed. The complex atmospheric data they'd tracked across the desert finally had a physical heart. She thought of the way the flight recorder had felt in her hand, a piece of engineering that had turned out to be the master key to this mountain. "I think she knew the sky had more to give, Sam. She was the one who designed the bridge. I think she was just waiting for us to be ready to cross it."

Mike walked up behind them, placing a hand on each of their shoulders. The gesture was simple, lacking the suffocating grip of his previous protectiveness. It was a steadying weight, a reminder that they were grounded in each other even as they prepared to leave the earth. The three of them stood there in the opening of the hangar, a small pocket of order and purpose in the middle of the indifferent desert.

The lights of the hangar flickered once, a surge in the local grid, and for a moment the EOS seemed to vanish into the shadows, leaving only the silver outline of its wings. It looked like a ghost, or perhaps a precursor. It was the bridge between the grief of the past and the blue of the morning. Angela felt the brass compass in her pocket, a small, circular weight that pointed toward a future she finally had the courage to claim.

"Five o'clock," Mike said, his voice firm. "We pre-flight at dawn."

"I'll have the telemetry ready," Sam said.

Angela didn't say anything. She just looked at the stars, counting the seconds between the breaths of the wind. She was no longer the pilot who feared the drop. She was the one who knew how to use the fall to find the lift. The night was cold and the desert was vast, but the hangar was full of light, and the morning was only a few hours away. She turned back toward the EOS, her boots striking the concrete with a finality that bypassed thought. She was ready for the blue.

Chapter 34: The Silver Sky Flight

A bruised violet dawn bled into pale, translucent gold at the edges of the Arizona horizon. After the salt-heavy winds of Sydney and the long haul back across the Pacific, at four thousand feet, the air grew thin and cold, the scent of ozone biting at the back of her throat. The stick shivered against her palm. She felt the air's harmonic tension through the control surfaces, a sharp frequency that mirrored the quickening of her own pulse.

Sam sat in the front seat, his head bent over the GPS unit. The device was rigged to a backup battery pack, its screen a steady glow in the dim cockpit. He wasn't looking at the map. He was watching the numbers, the raw coordinates they'd decrypted from the stolen St. James logs—the same 'EOS' designation Sam had flagged in the bank records weeks ago, the one that had first appeared as a ghost in her mother's earliest flight logs. They were miles beyond the charted flight paths of the Santiago Soaring School, drifting over a section of the high desert where the maps simply gave up and turned to a flat, featureless beige. It was the same 'quiet pocket' Maria had circled in her final reports—a place where her mother's theories on high-altitude endurance and specialized wing geometry finally met the earth. It was a thermal stability point where the lift signatures were remarkably consistent, as if the very heat of the desert was being channeled by the stone. They had seen the same signatures in the Sydney archives, a pattern of air movement that pointed to this exact ridge.

"Three miles," Sam said. His voice was clear, lacking the ragged edge of the asthma that had haunted their trek through the Outback. "The heading is steady.

If the math holds, the thermal should be right where the shadow hits the base of the mesa."

Below, the salt flats were a shimmering mirror, reflecting the sky so perfectly that for a moment the glider was suspended in a vast, bright void. The horizon had vanished, leaving only the glare of the sun reflected in the salt. She eased the rudder, bringing the nose around. The K-21 responded with a grace that felt like a secret shared between friends. Behind them, miles away and invisible in the haze, her father was waiting at the radio. Mike hadn't tried to stop them this time. He had simply checked the tire pressure and squeezed Angela's shoulder, a silent acknowledgement that some flights had to be taken alone.

The mesa rose out of the salt like a jagged tooth. It was a fortress of red rock and ancient silence, its top leveled by eons of wind. As they drew closer, the line where the sun met the stone sharpened. A hawk spiraled there, a dark speck against the rising heat. She followed the bird, banking the glider into the invisible column of rising air. The variometer began to chirp, a frantic, happy sound that signaled a climb. They rose with the heat, the world shrinking beneath them until the salt flats were nothing more than a silver thumbprint on the earth.

"There," Sam whispered, pointing toward a shadow. But Angela was already adjusting her bank. She wasn't looking for visual cues; she was listening to the air. There was a specific, hollow whistle echoing off the mesa—a precision intake integrated into a wind-sculpted vent. She steered not for the rock, but for the frequency.

A narrow, recessed shelf of rock appeared, hidden from the world by a fold in the mesa's skin. She felt it before she saw it: a sudden drop in resistance that signaled a hollow in the rock. It was a landing strip that shouldn't have existed. There was no room for error. If she overshot, they would vanish into the canyon on the far side. If she came in too short, the K-21 would be toothpicks against the cliff face. The old phantom weight of the crash settled in her stomach, the memory of the ground rising up to claim her. She didn't fight the fear. She let it sit beside her, a passenger that had earned its place.

She pulled the blue handle, deploying the spoilers. The glider began its long, controlled fall. The wind rose from a whistle to a roar, its force a mounting pressure that she felt in the tightening of her skin. Angela kept her eyes on the notch. She wasn't flying by the instruments anymore. She was flying by the pressure in the seat of her pants, by the tension in the cables, by the thinning pressure of the air against the wings. The rock rushed toward them, red and unforgiving. At the last second, she flared the nose, the main wheel catching the dirt with a soft, dusty thud.

The glider rolled to a stop inside the shadow of the overhang. A heavy silence settled over the cockpit, pressing against their ears. Angela sat for a moment, her hands still curled around the stick. Heat radiated off the rock, carrying the scent of parched earth and ancient dust. They were here.

Angela didn't wait for the mesa to offer up its secrets. She climbed out of the cockpit, her boots crunching on the dry silt, and walked toward the deepest part of the shadow. She wasn't looking for a door; she was feeling for the resonance. She pressed her palm against the stone, moving slowly until the hollow whistle she'd heard from the air became a vibrant tension that stirred the fine hairs on her arms. Behind a weathered fold of sandstone, she found a recessed latch, its metal cold and real. She didn't just find it; she recognized the placement—the same ergonomic logic her mother had used to design the K-21's emergency releases. She braced her weight and pulled.

A section of the rock wall groaned. It was a mechanical sound, the protest of heavy hydraulics. A seam appeared in the stone, a jagged vertical line that widened as a massive door slid backward into the heart of the mesa. Soft, recessed lighting flooded the interior, revealing a hangar that looked more like a cathedral. There was no welcoming committee, no billionaire waiting in the shadows. Only the smell of machine oil and old cedar, and the vast, echoing silence of a secret finally uncovered.

"He didn't open it for us," Sam whispered, stepping into the cool air of the interior. "You broke the seal."

"The Hunt wasn't an invitation, Sam. It was a test of whether we could find the back door," Angela said. She walked toward the center of the room. There, resting on a specialized cradle, sat the resolution to every missing blueprint and whispered rumor they had followed from the Outback to the Seine. It was the culmination of the aeronautical research that had been the school's true heart. It was a sailplane, the ultimate expression of the high-performance aeronautics Sam had found mentioned in the Chapter 6 archives—a lightweight composite Maria had once only dared to describe in her private journals. There was no propeller, no visible engine, only the lean, graceful lines of a craft designed to navigate the world's highest currents and find lift in the freezing, thin reaches of the atmosphere where the school's older fleet could never reach.

Angela walked toward it, her fingers reaching out to touch the leading edge. The surface was cool, polished to a mirror finish. Markings on the tail fin stood out—not a corporate logo. It was a small, hand-painted hawk, the same one that had joined her in the sky over Arizona. This was Project EOS. She didn't need a recording to explain it. The evidence was right there in the cockpit: her mother's flight logs, the original telemetry from the Paris test flights, and a stack of legal deeds to the Santiago valley that Rex St. James had never quite had the courage to sign over—until now.

She picked up a tablet resting on a nearby console. It wasn't playing a message; it was a digital archive of the research. Rex hadn't been a mentor; he had been a witness to his own family's greed, leaving a trail of crumbs he hoped she was fast enough to follow. The schematics were rendered in her mother's unmistakable handwriting. It was a map of a future where the Santiago Soaring School wasn't a relic of the past, but the epicenter of something new. They wouldn't just be teaching people how to fall gracefully. They would be the owners of the very air they occupied.

"Rex didn't give this to us," Angela realized, her voice echoing in the vast space. "He left the door unlocked because he knew he couldn't fly it. He needed a pilot who understood that the air isn't something you conquer—it's something you join. He spent ten years waiting for someone to prove Maria wasn't the last of her kind."

Sam stepped up beside her, his hand resting on the fuselage. "We can build more of these," he said, his voice small but certain. "The hangar in Arizona has the space. We can retrofit the old gliders. We can change everything."

Sam wasn't a fragile child anymore. He was a partner. The grief that had smothered them for so long had finally thinned, replaced by the sharp, clear light of a new morning. They were no longer a family in a state of preserved loss. They were a family in motion.

Outside, the sun finally cleared the rim of the mesa. The light flooded into the hangar, striking the wings of the EOS and turning the polished composite into a blinding, liquid gold. The machine breathed, a low-frequency hum that Angela felt in the small of her back. It was the same melodic resonance that had lived in the K-21, the same ghostly echo of her mother's arms. She felt the air's pressure through the stick, a steady, physical rhythm.

The choice was hers. She didn't need a hologram to tell her what came next.

The cockpit of the glider was small and intimate, designed for a single pilot who knew how to trust the sky. She thought of her father, waiting by the radio in the valley below. She thought of the "CLOSED" sign she had painted over. She thought of the hawk that had guided her here.

"I've been ready for a long time," she said.

She climbed into the seat. The canopy closed with a faint, airtight hiss, sealing her into a world of quietude. The instrument panel came to life, a soft blue glow that mirrored the dawn. There were no dials, no needles, only an elegant, streamlined interface that spoke to the instincts she had honed in the Arizona thermals. A surge of lift rippled through the wings, a sudden, weightless float in her stomach.

The hangar door opened fully, revealing the long, red stretch of the mesa top. The air on the mesa top was perfectly still. Angela eased the glider forward. There was no roar of an engine, only the clean, sharp whistle of the wind as it began to move over the wings. The EOS moved, its long wings dipping slightly as it gathered speed. The ground blurred, the red rock becoming a smear of color beneath the wheels.

Then, the lift took hold.

The transition was seamless. One moment she was bound to the earth, the next she was part of the sky, the sheer power of the lift finally singing in her very teeth. She banked the glider, the wings catching the full force of the morning sun.

The hangar and the lingering silence of the valley fell away. Ahead lay the vast, violet expanse of the Arizona desert. Below, the salt flats shimmered, the same mirror that had guided her home.

She reached for the radio. "Arizona Base, this is Santiago One. Do you copy?"

There was a moment of static, a sharp, electronic rasp that tore through the quiet of the cockpit. Then, her father's voice came through. It was thick with emotion, but steady. "I copy you, Santiago One. We see you on the scope. You're high, Angela. You're really high."

"I'm where I'm supposed to be, Dad," she said. The altimeter ticked upward, past the point where the memory used to take over. Today, nothing broke. The lift held.

The sun rose, the sudden warmth pulling the glider into a steady climb. The glider climbed as Angela leaned into the turn, finding the core of the thermal. She wasn't flying in her mother's shadow anymore. She was flying alongside it, two hawks caught in the same eternal thermal. The world below was small, a collection of points and coordinates that no longer felt like a prison. She was eighteen years old, and the heights were finally hers.

The glider climbed. Higher. Past the point where the old machines would have stalled, finding lift in the cold, thin air. The sky was clear, the horizon finally opening before her.

The wind hissed against the canopy, steady and cold.

About the Author

Alejandro Alexander writes character-driven adventure fiction that explores risk, memory, and the limits of control. *The Apex Hunt* is his debut novel. He is currently at work on his next novel.

Stay Connected

For updates on new releases and future projects, visit:

www.alejandroalexander.com

www.ingramcontent.com/pod-product-compliance
Lightning Source LLC
LaVergne TN
LVHW091124080826
845145LV00008B/2036
9781956146790